May you always
follow your compass.

David Smith

the Dark Eagles

first flight

by David R. Smith

www.thedarkeagles.com

Fundautum ✦ *Publishing*

www.thedarkeagles.com

Fundautum Publishing and associated logos
are trademarks of Fundautum Publishing

ISBN 978-0-615-57132-4
Printed in the U.S.A.
Second edition August 2012

To my lovely wife Jenelle and three amazing sons,

Joshua, Tate, and Porter for your patience,

inspiration and always believing.

Thank you for going on this adventure with me.

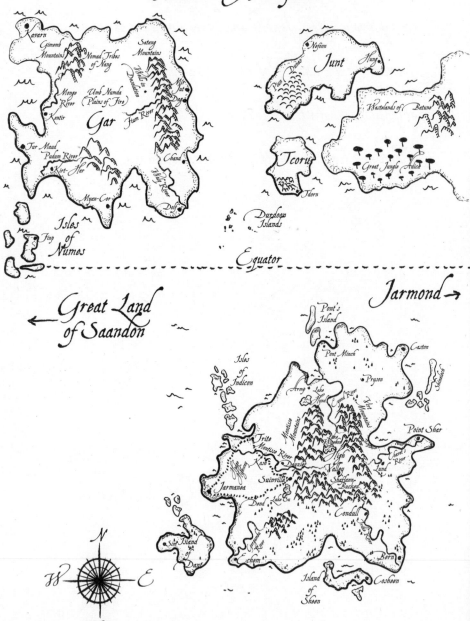

World of Fundautum
Western Hemisphere

Kavarn
Gimomb
Mountains
Nomad Tribes
of Nang
Satang
Mountains
Wall in Desolation
Monge
River
Umb Numda
Plains of Fire
Wit
Jut
Dag
Kentir
Gar
Flum River
Tur Maud
Pudum River
Kirt Har
Chand
Myan-Cor
Holy River
Dolf
Isles
of
Numes
Finp

Nefoon
Plum Dunes
Junt
Hung
Tcoru
Wastelands of Batune
Tdorn
Great Jungle Adice
Durdoqu
Islands

- - - - - - - - - Equator - - - - - - - - -

← Great Land
of Saandon

Jarmond →

Pont's
Island
Pont Minch
Caston
Pryson
Isles
of
Indicon
Armyn
Lake
Hynd
Equal River
Hit
Mountains
Montisu
Mountains
Trite
Montisu River
Rush
Lake
Minshon
High
Valley
Point Shar
Mifdend
Dauzier
Shaffann-
Bucken
Charst
River
Land
Suinville
Jarmanoa
Dend
Lake
Su
Condull
Oggmund
River
Born
Sint Island
of Dayit
echem
Cosheen
Island
of
Sheen

N
NW NE
W   E
SW SE
S

Confederation of Holpe's Island

Shaflann Bucken

Fundautum Time

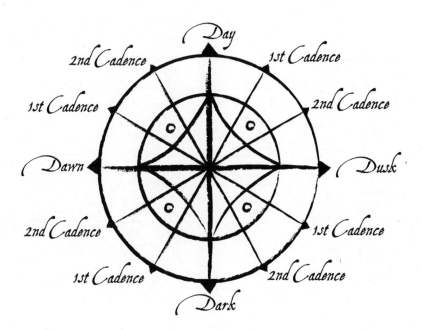

1 cadence equals 2.1 hours
1 stroke equals 1.26 minutes

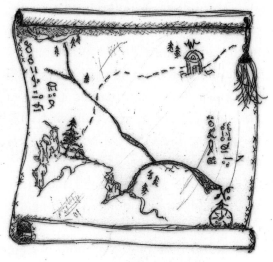

the Birthday Present

"So—your dead grandfather left you a map for your birthday, huh?" Tarc said leading Daz out of the stall, the early morning sun shining through the open barn door. "What kind of a present is that?"

"Depends on where it leads," Kief grinned as he pulled his saddle off the wood-planked wall.

Tarc grabbed a brush from the dusty shelf and stroked Daz's back, "He's been dead for years, why'd your grandma wait until now to give it to you?"

"She said he didn't want me to have it until I was ready to leave for academy," Kief threw the saddle onto his horse Natch. His sorrel coat was thickening with the changing seasons. "Good boy," he said rubbing the white blaze down Natch's forehead.

"Anything else with it?" Tarc was hoping for something big as this was Kief's last birthday before leaving home.

"Nope, just the map," Kief smiled to himself as he reached under Natch for the girth strap.

Tarc never received much on his birthdays. His father was killed in a mining accident when he was a boy, so Kief shared everything with him. He always rode one of Kief's horses when they went out exploring and even the coat he was wearing was a hand-me-down from Kief's father.

Tarc grabbed his saddle with one hand and easily tossed it up on Daz's back. "It's a bit strange don't you think... the map?" he said.

"You know the stories I've told you about my grandpa."

Kief had told Tarc all about the amazing things his grandpa had in his study; the telescope, maps of the moons and stars, tidal charts, an altimant and brass compass for navigation... Kief remembered staying up late into the evenings listening to his grandpa's tales of adventure as a young sailor. It was his grandfather that first instilled in him a love for the sea. It was more of an awakening than anything else. He remembered like it was yesterday, his grandpa helping him hold the altimant to his eye teaching him how to take a sight. His hands were worn and leathery but gentle. When his grandpa worked, studying and writing, Kief would get lost in play, charting his imaginary course through monster-filled waters to lands never seen by man.

Tarc finished saddling Daz and turned to Kief hitching his thumbs in his pockets, "Well, let's have a look."

Kief pulled the map out of the satchel that he always carried slung over his shoulder. The heavy paper curled stubbornly as he unrolled it.

He held it up like a trophy, smiling ear to ear, "Something huh?"

The paper's texture was just like his grandpa's old maps. Leather was stitched around all four edges with a long leather tassel tied to the top right corner. Strange worn characters and symbols covered the page.

"Now if it were only written in a language we could understand," Tarc ran his thick fingers through his curly blond hair.

"I don't know what this weird writing is but the map is on the back," Kief turned it over. They both stared. Kief pointed to a symbol at the start of a path that wandered down the page, "That looks like a lantern there, so I packed one, just in case."

"It better not take until dark to find it. I'm not traipsing around the forest all day with you."

"It shouldn't take that long. Look—see this. The path leads from the West Fire Tower through the forest to the southern cliffs," Kief tapped the paper with his finger.

"Yeah, that's easy enough, but it ends at this tree," Tarc pointed. "There are hundreds of trees up there, how do we know which one?"

"It's next to these two stacked things, I think they're rocks," Kief tilted his head.

Tarc looked closer, "Could be, but then what?"

"I don't know," Kief shrugged his shoulders, "Guess we'll see when we get there."

"Whatever's up there, why didn't the crazy old hoot just give it to you?" Tarc said.

"Hey, that's my grandpa you're talking about," Kief punched Tarc's burly arm. Tarc just grinned. He loved ruffling Kief's feathers to get a scuffle out of him. But this morning Kief was too occupied with his map for Tarc to get much of a rise.

"Well, we'd better get going before we have to use that lantern," Tarc turned for the door.

They rode up the cobble stone roads winding through their mountain village of Shaflann Bucken. The clopping of their horses' hooves was the only sound in the early morning stillness. The scent of dewy pines and smoke streaming from the myriad of rooftops swirled in the air. It was the middle of Harvest Rhythm and the red and brown leaves had already begun to drop. Kief turned up the collar of his sheep skin coat. Harvest Rhythm was his favorite season. And there was no place he'd rather be than on his horse, Natch, in the forest.

Kief gazed up at the West Fire Tower as they approached. Its oil soaked beams were weathered gray with age. The oil helped protect the beams from rot in the heavy rainfall and harsh seasons of the mountains. The tower was constructed when Shaflann Bucken was established thirty years earlier. The first settlers built three of them to help warn the village of forest fires. Kief had climbed to the top of all of them—the views were spectacular. He could even see beyond his own little town to the city of High Valley, far below.

Passing the tower they crossed over a stream and entered the thick pine forest. Kief chuckled to himself when he thought of his grandfather putting together this little adventure for him. A couple of years ago he and Tarc would have felt like they were going on a real expedition. But maybe his grandpa left him something useful for academy—after all, he didn't want him to have it until he went away. Perhaps his own altimant or a compass, or a new spectascope, one with enough power to see the craters on the moons. An atlas of Fundautum would be good to take with him.

He and Tarc usually didn't talk much when they went out riding. It almost seemed wrong to interrupt the solitude. Only the soft thud of their horses' hooves on the forest floor was heard as they worked their way up the mountain. Under the trees, a rich smell rose from the moist soil and decaying leaves. A crow, perched on the limb of a dead tree, cawed as the cool air whistled through the branches. Giant pines swayed gently like giant swings, back and forth, back and forth. The distinct chill the forest had before the snows would fly blew on Kief's face. He shivered at the thought—it wouldn't be long now.

Emerging from the forest, they reached the cliffs, the gray granite extending straight up so high they couldn't see the top. Small patches of tall brown grass growing in spots on the rock face fluttered in the wind. Strong currents blew up from the valley below and at times created marvelous thunderstorms. Kief had been to the top of the cliffs many times. To reach the peak, it was a long ride up the canyons, and Kief had explored all of them. On top, the updrafts were so strong that Kief felt if he jumped off, he would shoot right back up again.

They followed along the base looking for a lone tree and stacked rocks like the drawings on the map.

Tarc sighed, "Why couldn't he be more specific? There are rocks and trees everywhere."

"We'll find it," Kief replied.

They searched throughout the morning, Tarc letting out an occasional grumble.

"I've had enough," he finally said when they couldn't find anything.

"Come on, my grandpa put a lot into this. We can't just quit."

"He's dead, he's not gonna care," Tarc threw his hands in the air.

"Like you have anything better to do anyway."

"The fish are jumping on Lake Shandon, that's better..."

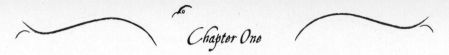

"They'll be there tomorrow," Kief kept riding.

Tarc followed Kief but stopped looking. He'd resigned himself to enjoying the ride while Kief searched for clues. He examined what Tarc said was "every rock along the way" and occasionally pulled out his map to study it. Tarc joked asking him if the strange characters were beginning to make sense the more he looked at them.

Around Day, Kief spotted a stack of rocks. "Is that it?" he exclaimed as if it were the treasure.

"Well, have we found another mound of rocks anywhere? Of course that's it," Tarc replied indifferently.

"You're all grown up and boring now," Kief swung down off his horse.

"Hey, a real treasure hunt would be great," Tarc climbed down slowly and stretched his back.

"Aw, where's your imagination?"

Standing next to the rocks, Kief unrolled his map. His eyes became small as he concentrated.

"Now what," Tarc peered over his shoulder, his breath sounding in Kief's ear.

"I think that's the tree there," Kief pointed at a tall lone pine in front of them.

"Okay, but we need more clues than that," Tarc said.

Studying the map, a flash of shadow passed over it. And then again. Swoosh! It dove at them nearly taking Kief's head off; and then the map was gone. Ripped from his hands, the leather tassel was caught in the beak of a huge black raptor, the map fluttering behind him.

"Wha…!" Tarc cried.

They watched in astonishment as the eagle carried away the map.

"After him!" Kief shouted.

Jumping on their horses they chased the eagle leaping over old fallen trees and dodging boulders. It flew along the tree line and then banked and disappeared into the cliffs.

"Where'd it go?" Kief said in a panic.

"I saw it, I saw... " Tarc blathered, pointing. "It went behind those rocks there!"

Following the eagle, they were surprised to find a narrow pass in the cliff they'd never seen before. They rode up the small canyon in single file, their heads whirling back and forth as they searched the walls and sky. Kief broke a branch off a tree for something to throw at the bird when it showed itself. Then the canyon suddenly ended.

Kief turned Natch around to face Tarc, "What do we do?"

"I don't know but that bird seems to be as crazy about treasure as you. I'd get rid of that stick. You might wanna keep him."

"Haha, real funny. We've gotta find him."

The cry of the eagle pierced their ears. Spinning around they looked up and saw it on a ledge above them as if taunting them.

"Come on," Kief jumped off Natch and scrambled up the cliff.

The climb was steep but there were good hand holds in the jagged rocks. Reaching the ledge, he stood still, staring, and Tarc came huffing up behind him. Kief was tall and lean and could outpace Tarc every time.

"Whoa, a cave," Tarc's voice echoed through the canyon. The cave had been completely hidden from below. The map lay on the ground in front of the entrance, but the eagle was gone.

"What was all that?" Tarc laughed, dismayed.

"That bird was huge! I think it grazed my head," Kief checked for blood.

Tarc picked up the map and handed it to Kief, "Do you think your grandpa knew about this?"

"I didn't see anything on the map that looked like a cave—did you?" Kief wiped his perspiring brow and unbuttoned his coat.

Tarc had completely removed his and had it wadded under his arm.

"Nope, I might have been a little more excited if I had. But it looks like we're gonna need that lantern," Tarc grinned looking into the blackness.

"I'll get it," Kief climbed back down the rocky ledge to fetch it.

"What do you think is in there?" Tarc asked as Kief returned and lit the lantern.

"Who knows, let's have a look," Kief smiled as he stepped into the cave.

The tunnel was a little taller than their heads and about as wide. They walked tentatively into the darkness, straining their eyes to see beyond the reach of the lantern light. The walls were smooth and damp and it smelled like an underground food cellar. There were a few loose stones along the path but it was mostly clear. The light from the entrance slowly faded.

"Keep a watch out for that eagle, and a tight grip on your map," Tarc chuckled.

"Yeah—uh, eagles don't fly in caves Tarc," Kief replied.

"And they don't take people's maps either," Tarc came back.

The path gradually sloped downward for about fifty paces and then suddenly opened up into a spectacular cavern.

"WOW!" Tarc shouted out as Kief held up the lantern.

Magnificent formations hung from the ceiling and shot up from the floor glistening in the light of the lantern. Milky crystals covered the roof of the cave. Mounds like hardened mud dotted the ground. They walked under what looked like a petrified sea creature with hundreds of tentacles reaching down to entangle them.

"This is amazing! Too bad we didn't find this when we were younger, what a great hideout!"

"Oh yeah," Kief spun slowly taking it all in. He took mental notes of the cave to record in his explorer's journal, the place where he'd documented all his expeditions. Most of them were insignificant, a new canyon or fresh spring, but writing them down made Kief feel like he was a real explorer. This discovery surpassed them all a hundred times over. The cavern was roughly triple his height and about seventy paces long by thirty paces wide. At a low spot in one of the corners they found a small opening leading to another passageway. Tarc agreed they should return with more equipment to explore it.

Coming around a stalagmite toward the rear of the cavern, Kief tripped.

"What's this?" he crouched down, setting the lantern on the ground. There was a small wooden chest with iron bands and two iron latches. There was no lock.

"There really is a treasure chest!" Tarc slapped Kief excitedly.

Kief ran his fingers over the chest; the wood was smooth with a worn oil finish.

"This can't be my grandpa's treasure. The map said nothing about a treasure in a cave," Kief's heart was pounding.

At that Tarc laughed, "As far as I can read, that map hasn't said anything that I can understand."

"Yeah, well, you don't read so good, do ya," Kief poked.

"Aren't you gonna open it?" Tarc nudged, anxious to see what was inside.

He handed the lantern to Tarc. Their heavy breathing sounded in the silent cave. Kief unlatched the lid. The iron was cold and damp. The hinges creaked and sputtered as he opened it. Peering inside, the chest was empty except for a small leather pouch sitting in the center. Kief reached inside. He could feel that it held something thick and solid. It wasn't an altimant, a compass, or a spectascope. It must have been some old treasure they'd stumbled upon, Kief supposed. Tarc fidgeted eager to see what it was. Loosening the draw string and upturning the bag, Kief dumped the contents into his hand. Out slipped a single polished white stone about the size of his palm. It was an oval flat shape, smooth and white, the whitest stone Kief had ever seen. He tilted his head as he turned it over in his hand a few times.

"Huh," he muttered, bewildered at the treasure.

"A rock. Some treasure that is," Tarc gave a disappointed sigh.

"It must be something important. Else why would it have been hidden here?"

"Sure, I guess it's about the best skipping stone I've ever seen. Or maybe a good paper weight," Tarc shook his head.

"I like it," Kief said staring at the treasure.

"Well, I'm starved," Tarc plopped down on the floor pulling his lunch out of his satchel, his disappointment about the treasure overshadowing the excitement he'd had about discovering the cave.

Kief joined him. The lamplight cast long black shadows on the walls. Kief set the stone down and pulled out his lunch. It almost glowed in the dark it was so white.

"Let me see that thing," Tarc finally reached out. "Hmph, I guess it's kind of a clever little rock."

"I think it is," Kief snatched it from him and slipped it back in the pouch. As he did he noticed something else inside. It was a folded note. "Hey, this is my grandfather's insignia," he pointed at a symbol on the outside.

"How do you know that?"

"He had it on everything. He stamped all his books and maps with it,"

"Well what does it say?"

Kief unfolded the small note, "Keep the oath."

"That's it? What's that supposed to mean?" Tarc asked, a mouth full of beef sandwich.

"I don't know," Kief replied staring at the rock. "I think he wants me to keep it secret." He looked at Tarc and shook a finger at him, "You can't tell anyone about this, got it."

"Right, what am I gonna say?" his mouth still full of food. "Kief's grandpa hid a little white rock in a cave. Who's gonna care," Tarc took another bite bigger than he could hold.

"My grandfather knew about the cave and hid it here. But there is no cave on the map."

"Maybe those funny symbols say something about it," he wiped his mouth.

"Could be," Kief shrugged.

They finished eating and searched the rest of the cavern for more treasure, but didn't find anything. Tarc went on about bringing up more lanterns and fuel barrels and even stashes of food. Finally, Kief placed the pouch with the stone in his satchel and they walked back up the tunnel to the entrance.

Squinting, they stepped out into the sun. Kief scanned the sky for the eagle but there was no sign of it. All his time in the mountains exploring with Tarc, they'd never seen an eagle like it.

It was a clear, crisp day and they could just make out the time tower in the center of High Valley. The city had been settled fifty years earlier by farmers. The cool climate the mountains provided was perfect for growing chatra, a fruit used to make sugar. It had become such a bountiful business, that soon other trades had moved up to the valley building an industrious, lively city. When silver was discovered in the mountains above the budding city, a few settlers began to inhabit a little town and build a profitable industry mining silver. They called it Shaflann Bucken, after the two men who had found the first veins of silver when they were forced into a cave by a late New Rhythm snowstorm. It was the mines that had brought Kief's family there as well. His father was Chief of Operations at the Dunton Silver Mine.

Kief unrolled his map one last time to make sure he wasn't missing anything. Other than the strange writing, there was nothing.

"How many more times you gonna look at that thing," Tarc sighed as he climbed on his horse. "If we hurry, I might make it home for dinner."

"You just ate!" Kief replied stuffing his map in his satchel.

"That was just a morsel to hold me over."

"I'll give you a proper burial if you don't make it," Kief chuckled.

"You better hope I make it—you won't stand a chance against Flinch in that urt championship if I don't!"

"Oh, I can take Flinch all right," Kief replied tightening his jaw.

Flinch was Kief's rival. He was tough, and he knew it—always acting like he was above everyone else. Kief hated him. Losing the championship to Flinch's squad the year before was humiliating. This was Kief's last chance for payback. He could hardly wait.

Kief was exhausted, he'd gone over the move a hundred times and Tarc was still drilling him on it. But that was Tarc, and that was why he was captain of their squad—everything had to be perfect. While they came up with their moves together, Tarc did the coaching. He had pushed them to make it to the championship a second year in a row.

After long weeks of hard practice, Kief found himself looking forward to the weekends when he could return to the forest near the cave to search for the eagle. Sometimes Tarc would go with him and other times he'd go alone. When the snows began to fall he went less frequently. Then the week before the urt championship, he spotted the eagle again. He watched it a long while gliding near the cliffs. It must have been riding on the air currents coming up from High Valley because it never flapped its wings. And then, he saw it dive. Like an arrow from a bow it shot with such speed Kief didn't think it could pull up in time. It disappeared into the snow covered forest. When it swooped out again it was carrying a white rabbit in its great talons. Kief watched in awe, his fist spontaneously shooting in the air as he cheered the eagle flying over his head and vanishing into the high cliffs.

Kief decided to swing by the school library to see if he could learn more about the eagle. He found a large leather-bound book on birds and raptors and situated himself in one of the big leather chairs near the fire place. Nearly every page had a drawing of a different kind of bird. Some were simple ink sketches, others were detailed colored drawings.

"So many birds," Kief mumbled.

About a quarter of the way through the book, he turned the page—a dark eagle was staring him in the face. Kief stared back, nearly forgetting he was looking at a picture. Its feathers were as black as the dark sky with a bit of orange on the tips. A feathery crest came off the back of its head. It had golden yellow eyes that glared out over a black hooked beak. Knife-like claws were black as well.

Kief read, "Dark eagles are the rarest of the raptor class of birds. They prefer high altitudes and usually make their nests among the cliffs. They are mostly solitary creatures, although there have been a few unusual times when they have been seen gathering in large numbers, but the reasons are unknown." Kief looked into the crackling fire and tapped his finger on the page. The eyes of the eagle matched the gold of the flames. He continued reading, "The bones of dark eagles are black, the only animals ever known to have them. Ancient legends held that they were placed on Fundautum to defend freedom; their black bones shielding them from evil." It was a fitting myth for such a bird. It was the most majestic animal Kief had ever seen.

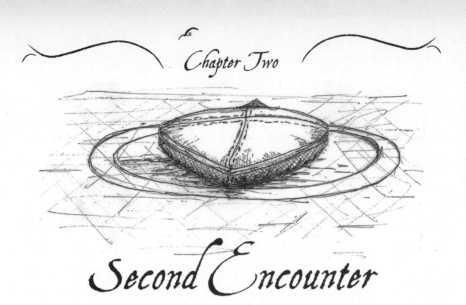

Second Encounter

Kief's lungs burned, as if fire were consuming his chest and throat. A steady stream of sweat stung his eyes and the cut on his cheek. The crowd roared all around him in a sea of swirling purple and gold banners. But Kief noticed them no more than he had the cliffs or clouds in the sky as he searched for the dark eagle that had snatched his map. His eyes were fixed on Flinch, gauging his every move. His bare toes gripped the leather mat as he prepared to spring. Halfway between him and the edge of the round mat the lead-bead bag lay unguarded. But Flinch stood in his way, an awesome figure in both size and appearance. His shimmering blond hair and engaging green eyes were as intimidating as his stature. Kief launched at the leady, driving through Flinch. He snatched it up, but Flinch was on his back in an instant. As he came down, Kief flung the leady to Tarc. The heavy red bag rolled slowly through the air, suspended momentarily before Tarc grabbed it out of its trajectory. Blindsided by his giant opponent, Tarc's entire body jolted knocking the leady loose from his grip. It landed with a thud near the edge. Smashing into the mat, Tarc's shoulder popped. His shriek of pain brought everything to a stand-still. Tarc lay motionless under the big mass, his cheek

squished flat against the mat.

"No!" Kief shouted slamming his fist into the mat. They were down by a point with only a few strokes of the last round remaining. If they didn't score now, it was over.

Flinch let go of Kief to protect the leady from being pushed over the edge. He knew Kief was hungry to even the score and wasn't about to let that happen. But Kief took Flinch completely off guard when he turned to help his squadmate Montos who was pinned down under his opponent. Flinch lunged back at Kief and Montos, but it was too late. Montos was free, and Kief caught Flinch in a lock-up. In a flash, Montos slipped past Flinch. Diving, he pushed the leady over the edge scoring a point just as the the judge blew an ear-piercing screech through his pipe ending the match.

A flurry of purple flags and cheers filled the arena. Flinch shoved into Kief gritting his teeth.

"That's enough boys!" the burly judge forced himself in between them, thrusting a hand into each of their chests. Kief threw a smirk at Flinch as they posted a point for his squad at the scorer's table. The judge wiped his wide brow. The few strands of black hair he had left pasted against his sweaty head. He blew into his pipe. "Breaker round!" he shouted and the cheering from the crowd intensified.

The boys staggered off the mat with their squadmates. Gasping for air, Kief grabbed a towel and wiped his face.

"I'm out," Tarc groaned holding his shoulder.

"Oh and I can see you're heartbroken about not being able to go up against that beast of a kid again," Kief jabbed.

Tarc grimaced, "You know I've been waiting all year to watch you and Flinch go at it!"

Montos plopped down in his chair at mat side. "This one's

all yours Kief."

"Well then, enjoy the show!" he smiled.

Tarc smacked his towel at Kief. "Don't do anything stupid."

Kief nodded guzzling his water.

"And whatever you do, don't tie up with him. He's the best thrower in the league. Do one of your leg shots," Tarc drilled.

The crowd hushed as they waited to see who would fight the tie-breaker round. The coalman added another shovel of fuel and banged the heavy door closed on the furnace that kept the arena warm from the bitter cold outside.

The judge approached Tarc's squad, "Who's it gonna be?"

Kief lifted his hand and the crowd erupted. He stepped up on the mat, revenge written in his glare as he met Flinch at the center.

"You ready for another beating?" Flinch bobbed his head proudly.

"We'll see who does the beating," Kief came back.

The judge thrust his arm through the air, his thick finger pointing at Flinch announcing to the crowd that he would be on offense first. Years of yelling had left him hoarse. His voice was barely audible above the din. It didn't matter though; his abrupt hand signals and contorted facial expressions said it all. He swiped his foot over part of the inner circle painted on the mat. "The leady has to be completely outside this to score a point," he declared, touting his clout in spite of the fact that everyone knew the rules of a tie-breaker. The whole town had been attending urt matches for years—it was the highlight of the season.

They took their positions. In their tight knee-length trousers, sleeveless shirts, and bare feet, they looked like two rogue sailors squaring off in a duel. Their legs were so weak and wobbly; they had to keep their knees locked to prevent them from buckling.

Slumped over at the waist as if their heads were made of lead, they raised their hands at the ready.

With the shrill blow of the small wooden pipe the tie-breaker began. Kief and Flinch circled in slow motion around the leady; it was a careful play of catching their breath without letting the opponent get too much rest. Flinch kept going for his deadly lock and throw, but Kief knew the move too well and wouldn't give it to him. Breaker rounds were short. Kief knew Flinch would soon try another throw from his collection of well-rehearsed moves. But suddenly he dropped to his knees for a low shot. It wasn't his strong point and certainly not something Kief had anticipated. He came up under Kief turning his back toward him. Flinch grabbed the leady with both hands. Catching Kief off guard, Flinch had a real chance of scoring, threatening to snatch victory from him once again! But before Flinch could crawl across the line, Kief came down hard on his back knocking him flat. He circled his arms around Flinch's ribs squeezing the air out of him. Flinch squirmed violently, clawing at the floor. Tarc's voice cut through the screaming fans counting down the last ten pulses of the round. In desperation, Flinch threw his elbow behind him catching Kief in the mouth. But Kief locked down even tighter burying his shoulder into Flinch's back, the taste of blood on his tongue. Flinch extended his arms pushing the leady as far as he could reach. But it wasn't enough. The pipe blew. Flinch slapped the mat and threw another elbow into Kief's ribs. Kief felt a twinge of satisfaction. He knew it irked Flinch that he was getting the better of him.

Without giving them time to catch their breaths, the judge called them to position. Tarc's warning not to tie up with Flinch still sounded in Kief's ears. But Kief wanted to beat Flinch at his own game.

At the pipe, Kief lunged forward and locked arms with Flinch.

"No, get away, get away!" Tarc hollered.

Montos screamed, "Shuck him off, don't stay there."

Flinch began pummeling to set up a throw. Kief countered. Back and forth their arms flailed, swimming around each other as they fought for inside control.

"There it is," Tarc yelled seeing Kief was fixed on throwing him.

Flinch moved into position for a throw. Kief's wasn't quite there yet. If he didn't make a move now, Flinch would pitch him and the match would be lost. But Kief's impatience had cost him matches in the past. This was too important. Restraining his urge to rush the throw, he waited.

"Now, Kief, now!" Tarc screamed as loud as he could.

Kief continued to work the move, waiting for Flinch to take the right step.

"He's going, he's going," Tarc yelled frantically as Flinch locked up to throw.

Quick as a flash of lightning, Kief struck first. Stepping into Flinch, he sucked him in and launched him. The throw was flawless. Flinch sailed through the air landing a good three paces outside the inner circle giving Kief just enough time to grab the leady and dive over the line. The judge rushed into the fray blowing his whistle again and again. In a dramatic display, he swooshed his arms giving the official declaration that the match was over. Kief lay motionless on the mat still clinging to the leady. Fans stomped and screamed, the oil lamps around the perimeter of the arena swaying in the commotion. Montos and Tarc rushed onto the mat piling on top of Kief. Pulling him to his feet, the crowd flooded the floor. Kief hoisted the leady above his head and then hurling it to the mat he shot his fist in the air with a roar of victory.

"You idiot, what were you thinking tying up with Flinch like that?" Tarc smacked him.

"But it was an impressive throw... wasn't it?" Kief laughed triumphantly.

"The best you've ever done," Tarc shouted in celebration.

Pushing past Tarc, the judge grabbed Kief's wrist and thrust it in the air. The crowd exploded simultaneously as Tarc and Montos shot their arms up as well. Pumping their fists above their heads they spun slowly around. Grins stretched across their tired faces as they cheered with the applauding throng. This was it—the sweet taste of victory. Kief caught a glimpse of Flinch out of the corner of his eye sitting in his seat at mat side; his head slumped down in his hands. Kief swelled with an indignant satisfaction to see him so humiliated. Flinch deserved it. He turned back to the crowd waving and shouting encouraging their cheers.

The School Director, Mr. Kir-Trad, squeezed his way up onto the mat for the presentation of the awards. He was all proper and amiable, always wearing the appropriate attire as if he were attending a statesman's dinner. He gave a short speech to the crowd that seemed to be more focused on him than the victors.

"Another shiny treasure," Kir-Trad said looking Kief straight in the eyes placing a medal around his neck.

Kief stared at Kir-Trad perplexed.

"This is superb!" Tarc thumped Kief and Kir-Trad broke away from Kief's stare placing medals around Tarc's and Montos' necks.

Eventually, Kief's dad worked his way through the crowd. Wrapping his big arms around his son he lifted him off the ground, "Congratulations, Kief. That was fantastic," he smiled proudly.

"Thanks dad."

"You sure are some lucky kid! If you ever learn to think things through before you just go for it... always pulling your crazy stunts. Tarc about had a heart attack when you tied up with Flinch. I was more worried about him than you."

"Yeah but it worked," Kief answered proudly.

"It sure did," he shook his head.

"You did it, you're the best!" Kief's little brother Balt charged into him.

"Yep, and you'll be here soon," Kief punched him.

"And I'll be better than you," Balt butted his head against Kief's chest.

Kief grunted. He pitied any boy that would have to face Balt.

"How's that arm Tarc?" Mr. Stadd asked as he shook Tarc's other hand. The swelling and stiffness had already started to set in and Tarc could hardly move it.

"I messed it up good. I'm just glad it didn't happen until the end of the season."

"So are we," Mr. Stadd smiled. He knew as well as the others that without Tarc's level-headed coaching and strength, they would have never made it to the championship.

In the dressing room, Tarc struggled to get dressed with his bad shoulder. Kief helped him put on his coat.

Tarc ribbed Kief, "Flinch was a little off this evening, maybe he was sick?"

"No, I don't think so," Kief flexed his arm grinning.

"Yeah, yeah," Tarc shoved him and grimaced from the pain. "I still can't believe you did that wild move."

"I told you to enjoy the show."

"What a way to end the season," Tarc shook his head.

Gathering their things, they walked back into the empty arena.

Moments before, it had been filled with screaming fans hailing their victory. Now it was deserted and silent save a few workers who were swishing their brooms and turning out the oil lamps. Kief looked up into the stands, the applauding of the crowd still echoing in his ears. He had defeated Flinch. Urt season was over. It had gone as fast as it had come. He and Tarc walked without a sound across the arena floor. A cold wind gusted in their faces as they stepped out into the snowy dark.

Tarc groaned as Kief helped him up into the saddle, the frigid air biting their cheeks. Kief climbed up in front of him and reined Natch toward Tarc's house, taking an easy pace. Natch's hooves crunched on the snow-packed road. They passed a couple bundled up close and talking and giggling in a horse-drawn sleigh. Reaching Tarc's place, his mother met them at the door. She helped him inside and Kief filled a bowl with snow for Tarc to put on his shoulder.

"I'll swing by in the morning," Kief said leaving him with his mom.

It was late. Kief was tired but not sleepy. The street lamps and double moons of Fundautum illuminated his path. The shadow of him sitting on Natch grew and then disappeared each time they passed a lamp post. The streets were empty. The wind had died down, no longer carrying away Kief's frosty breath. Natch snorted out what looked like clouds of smoke in the bitter cold. Kief was still warm from the match.

At a dark spot along the road between lampposts he pulled Natch to a sudden stop. Ahead in the forest, two glowing eyes were staring at him. His heart raced and then slowed when he realized they were too high in the tree to be a hill cat. But, he still jumped, nearly falling off the back of his horse, as the shadowy thing came at him. It was a dark eagle. Flying low, the eagle swooped directly over him and up through a clearing in the trees. Kief turned and galloped after him. Natch struggled, lifting his hooves high to clear the deep snow. But the eagle flew low and slow and Kief was able to keep up with it. He followed him a good distance into the forest before he lost him in the shadows of a thick grove of trees. He and Natch paused in the darkness, drawing in deep breaths of air and exhaling frosty puffs. He heard the fluttering of wings, and pine boughs rustled all around him. Then, as if someone turned on all the lamps in a room at once, Kief was surrounded by ten or so pairs of glowing eyes. He crouched, waiting for them to fly at him. But they didn't. After a moment, he relaxed and sat up straight in his saddle. Natch stood alert, his ears twitching backwards and forwards. Kief turned about slowly, looking at each pair of eyes. The eagles stared back not moving. And then one behind him let out a cry splitting the silence of the forest. Kief jerked his head toward the sound, ready to kick Natch into a run. Startled, Natch pulled at the bridle and stamped at the snow. But the eagles remained still. As soon as one ended its song, another would cry out. It continued until Kief was certain he'd heard every eagle. Though an eerie thing, eagles screaming at him in the dark forest, Kief felt calm. Then the eagles fell silent. After a moment they launched into the air each flying off in a different direction and Kief was left alone with Natch standing in the dark forest.

"Strange, don't you think boy," he leaned over and patted Natch's neck.

He hadn't realized how long he'd been out there but he was now feeling the cold. Natch followed the path he'd made back through the fluffy snow. Kief started to shiver, the adrenaline wearing off from his victory and the encounter with the eagles. He clicked Natch to pick up the pace.

The barn was dark. Kief didn't bother lighting a lantern. After dumping a bucket of oats into Natch's trough, giving him a little extra for warmth, Kief closed the door and went inside. As Kief slept, he dreamt of flying with the eagles.

For days after the urt championship, Kief felt as if he were a pair of wet leather boots that had been left to dry by the fire and gone stiff. Eventually the stiffness wore off.

Kief returned to the forest looking for the eagles. But he didn't find any except the one up by the cliffs. He wondered where the others had gone, there were so many of them that evening in the forest. He was fascinated with how they soared so effortlessly through the air.

One day he went to the library to do some research after school. The librarian looked at him funny when he asked where he could find books on flying. She showed him a few in the science section. He pulled a thin book from in between two big ones entitled "The Mechanics of Flight." Looking at the cover, it seemed rather unimpressive. But when Kief turned to the first page and started reading, he was hooked, "Flight is made possible by air just as swimming is made possible by water...." Kief looked around for a place to sit. He wanted one of the big comfortable leather chairs but they were both occupied. One was taken by Clemens, a rather annoying know-it-all boy a year younger than Kief; the other by a fat middle aged man looking through a pair of what looked like child-sized spectacles. Kief resigned himself to sitting on one of the hard wood chairs at a table. It turned out okay though, for he soon removed his journal from his satchel and was vigorously taking down notes as he read.

He poured through the pages, going so fast he had to follow the words with his finger to keep up. He would stop to scribble down a few notes and then continue reading. Before he knew it, he had filled ten pages and it was dark outside. He studied until the librarian started to turn out the lamps for the evening. Clemens and the pudgy man had long gone home but Kief hadn't taken one of their chairs; he was too occupied by what he was reading. He continued until she dowsed the final lamp in the study hall and had to ask him to leave. Returning the book to the shelf, he had what he needed to design his own flying apparatus.

Finding Wings

"So, you're really going to try this," Tarc asked as he came through the barn door. His shoulder had mostly healed by now and he was once again accompanying Kief on one of his escapades. He was always willing to go with Kief, even though most of the things Kief did he'd never even think of trying himself.

"Well yeah, I didn't make it for nothing," Kief replied leading Natch out of his stall.

Tarc opened Daz's gate, "Right, well I suppose it would be an awful waste of time to not kill yourself then after all that work."

"Exactly," Kief patted his horse's rump. A poof of dust rose, suspended in the morning rays. "But it'll work," he smiled confidently.

"You've spent enough time making it—I hope for your sake it does. But I guess if it doesn't, it'll make a nice big hammock for you, me, and half of Shaflann."

"It'll work," Kief insisted as he strapped on the saddlebags loaded with his scoop sail and gear.

The snows had finally melted and the naked trees were covered with tiny red buds. Kief and Tarc cut through the worn path to the road, the hooves of their horses sinking into the soft ground.

Kief ran through all the preparations in his mind. He saw himself as not only an explorer, but an inventor too. He'd come up with a number of crazy contraptions. He'd built a clocked mechanism that would dump Natch a bucket of oats in the morning. He'd gotten tired of using a ladder to clean the chimney so he designed a rope and basket chair he could sit in while he swept it out. He had even built an extension arm with a small oil lamp on it next to his bed for reading.

"I guess Dondor Bridge is next if you survive Tubin?" Tarc interrupted his thoughts.

Dondor Bridge was the highest bridge on Holpe's Island. It

was more than an island really, it was a continent. But the early explorers called it an island before they had realized how big it was and the name stuck. The land had been full of wild game of all kinds but it was uninhabited by people. Lowland plains and rolling hills along the coastlines rose up to majestic mountains inland. Most of the lowland plains around the entire continent were soon dotted with towns and cities, but it was quite some time before the inland mountains were established. Sheer cliffs and deep gorges had hindered development of the mountains until sweeping bridges were constructed. Kief's town was nestled between the Montisse and Virt Mountain ranges and Dondor Gorge was one of the deepest gorges where settlers had ventured to build a bridge.

"I'm not crazy enough to jump off Dondor Bridge," Kief replied.

Tarc shook his head, "Could have fooled me."

Kief was fearless; he got that from his mother, Sarna. He bore her same striking appearance as well, with deep blue eyes and black shaggy hair that curled down over his ears and at the nap of his neck. He was tall and lean from years of playing urt. Tarc was convinced that the survival mechanism in Kief's brain had broken when he took his first fall from a tree as a kid. Though tough as steel, Tarc was a sissy when it came to daring things, especially anything to do with heights. But not Kief, he was as calm as the morning.

The warm New Rhythm sun heated the air as they winded down Tubin Road to the bridge. Tubin Bridge was as old as the road, built when Shaflann was first settled. It spanned a small, but steep canyon. Large timbers in a criss-cross pattern formed a framework on both ends that tapered to an arch in the center and supported the narrow bridge. It was barely wide enough for a

horse and carriage to pass over.

"So you're gonna test this first, right?" Tarc looked down at the river.

"Yeah, my mom made me promise to test it before I jumped."

"Aw... she loves ya," Tarc pinched his cheek.

Kief swatted his hand away, "Everybody loves me." Opening his saddlebags, he pulled out two heavy canvas bags used for shipping oats and tossed one to Tarc, "Fill that up with a bunch of rocks."

"How many do you want in here?" Tarc asked as he began to pile rocks into it.

"Until it weighs about half of me," Kief replied.

"You know that's what we're gonna have if this doesn't work."

"It'll work I told you," Kief chucked a stick at him.

They attached the sail lines and lugged the two bags bulging with rocks out onto the bridge, the old planks creaking under their feet. Lifting the bags up on the railing, they placed the folded sail and coiled lines neatly on top. Kief's mother had helped him sew the sail from rolls of cotton fabric he'd bought at the mercantile. The shop keeper had thought he was crazy when Kief had asked for three rolls of the stuff. The ropes and harness he'd gotten from the mine where his dad worked.

Kief looked over the edge of the bridge; it was higher than he'd remembered. He'd been cliff-jumping into lakes before but never from that high.

Tarc gave him a nudge, "What do ya think?"

"No problem."

"Yeah, I see that look in your eye, this is mad!"

"Come on; let's send these rocks for a ride. One... two... three..." they pushed them off the edge.

Kief leaned over the railing begging the bags of rocks to fly.

They plummeted to the canyon below, the sail fluttering behind. Suddenly with a loud "POP!" the sail filled with air looking like a giant bowl that had been overturned. The bags jerked to a sudden stop swaying back and forth underneath it. The canyon winds carried the sail across the river. Like a small white cloud, it dropped along the bank, settling softly in the brush.

"Yahoo!" Kief shouted out slapping hands with Tarc. "Did you see that?"

"I can't believe it!" Tarc exclaimed.

They sprinted across the bridge and scrambled down the canyon wall. Coming through the brush and onto the riverbank, they ran to where the sail lay flapping in the breeze.

Kief inspected the sail and lines; it all looked good, no damage. He untied the bags and spilled the rocks over into the brush.

"Well, I guess it's time to test a live bag of rocks," Tarc jabbed.

"How about if I throw you off next—and without the sail," Kief came back.

They pulled their way to the top of the canyon, clinging to branches and tall grass. Huffing and puffing they flopped down onto the bridge.

"Urt season ends and you're worthless," Tarc joked.

"I was carrying the sail! And you're no better Mr. I-can-hardly-breath."

Tarc shook his head, "I can't believe you figured out how to make one of those from a book."

"It wasn't that hard," Kief replied.

"True, your mom did most of the work."

"Hey, I designed it. And if I'd known how to sew, I would have sewn it."

"Of course," Tarc stood and peered over the wall. "So when's

your dad coming?"

"Any moment now."

Just then Patin and Sefrana came around a bend in the road.

"Did we miss it?" Sefrana called out.

"Kief died, the river took him," Tarc wiped imaginary tears from his eyes.

"You're such a goof," Sefrana replied.

"We did a test flight. It works perfectly," Kief said. "Just waiting for my dad. My mom made me promise not to jump till he got here."

"At least your mom has some sense," Patin replied swinging down off his horse.

"Aw, come on. What's the worst that can happen?" Kief defended his craziness. "If it doesn't work I take a plunge in the river."

"You'd better hope not, that river is freezing cold," Sefrana shivered. "It doesn't warm up until the middle of Sun Rhythm."

"It's warmer than it was a few weeks ago," Tarc shrugged.

"'Cause it had ice on it a few weeks ago," she came back.

"So, have you made adjustments for the wind?" Patin asked lifting a wet finger.

"Do you feel any wind?" Tarc retorted at his always annoying know-it-all-ness.

"A little wind to you can be a big deal when you consider the size of the sail."

"Yeah, yeah, enough Patin," Tarc waved his hands, "Some things you just gotta do."

"Well jumping off a bridge isn't one of them," Patin replied.

"Ha! That coming from the man who's been giving me a hard time all morning long!" Kief laughed at Tarc.

"I'm glad your friends are giving you a hard time!" Kief's dad said as he rode up on his horse.

"Hey dad, the test flight worked perfectly," Kief called out as his dad tied up his horse next to Natch and Daz.

"That's good to hear," he replied walking over to where they were standing on the bridge. He looked over the side, "That's a long drop."

"But my scoop sail works so there are no worries."

"Let's hope. I can't believe your mom is letting you do this!"

Kief's mom understood his adventuresome spirit and often had to persuade his dad to give Kief room. He would go along reluctantly, but even she had to admit that this was the craziest of Kief's pursuits.

"I don't want to have to report to her that you broke your leg."

"His neck, more like it," Patin interjected.

"Right," Mr. Stadd grinned. "Just remember the harness quick release in case your sail gets hung up on something."

"I will."

"So where's the best place to get down to the river?" he asked.

"Right over there," Tarc pointed. "You can't miss the trail we made."

"Yeah, Tarc yanked out half the plants coming back up the canyon," Kief said.

"I'll go with you Mr. Stadd," Sefrana said following him.

"No reason to climb down," Patin crossed his legs leaning back against the railing. "View's as good from up here."

"Just don't get in the way," Tarc went to push him aside but Patin smacked his hand.

Tarc and Kief refolded the sail, making sure none of the lines were tangled. Then he helped Kief strap on the harness he'd

gotten from the mine and attach the sail lines. His father was the Chief of Operations at the Dunton Silver Mine. Kief had spent the last few Sun Rhythms working at the mine. From the very first week, Kief knew that mining was definitely not for him. It was slow and monotonous. He needed something thrilling and adventurous, not the same old thing day after day.

"It's a little different now that you're not just dumping a bunch of rocks off the bridge, huh?" Tarc bumped Kief with his elbow as he looked down at the river.

"I'm feeling good," Kief replied, jumping up and down like he was getting ready for an urt match.

"I hope you're feeling like a bird!" Tarc slapped his back.

"And not a chicklet," Patin snickered settling in for the show.

"I'm ready, it's a perfect day for flying," Kief took a deep breath and stepped up on the edge.

A few clouds drifted high above in a crystal blue sky. The sun shone brightly on the brilliantly colored buds bursting on the trees amongst the evergreens. Kief looked at the cold water below, he was going in whether the sail worked or not. He leaned his head and shoulders forward. He felt like the eagles that he'd watched as they launched off the cliffs. He'd been fascinated at how with the twitch of a wing's feather or the bend of their tail it would send them into banking turns and dives. But he didn't have wings. There was no way to steer his scoop sail. He'd be at the mercy of the wind. Grasping the bundle with his sweaty palms, Kief hollered down to his dad, "You ready?"

"Ready," his father's voice echoed up the canyon.

"Tarc?"

"Let's see you fly," Tarc gave him a thumbs up.

"Here we go," he said slowly bending his knees and leaping off the edge.

It was a strong jump, up and out, away from the bridge. As he dropped, he tossed the bundled sail above his head. He tumbled rapidly to the river below dragging the sail behind him like a comet's tail. Then, just as they'd tested, the sail popped open jerking Kief upward.

"Wahoo!" he shouted out finally able to take a breath, his voice echoing off the canyon walls. His legs flailed back and forth. He could hear Tarc screaming with excitement. Spreading his arms like an eagle, he soared through the air. He felt like he was born to fly! But the flight was short, too short. The breeze had nearly carried him across the river as he touched lightly upon the water like a duck, and then sank under. Shock filled his body in the freezing cold. The sail settled softly on the water's surface in front of him. Gasping for breath he swam quickly for the bank. His legs wobbled from chill and excitement as he stumbled out. His father gave him a hand to the nearest rock to sit down. The heat from the sun-baked surface flowed into Kief's legs.

"That was incredible!" He shivered.

"That was really something," his dad said gazing up at the bridge. "It actually worked!"

"Oh, that was the best thing ever; you can't imagine how it feels!" Kief sputtered as he dragged the sail to shore. He couldn't wait to do it again.

"It looked spectacular from down here," his dad said shaking his head.

Tarc rumbled down the canyon path. Whatever vegetation that had remained from their ascent was certain to be gone now.

"You did it! You did it!" he shouted as he burst through limbs and underbrush. "That was so great. I saw you were falling... and then the sail opened... you were completely covered by the sail... it was amazing!" Tarc puffed to catch his breath.

"Oh, it was fantastic!" Kief replied, "You've gotta give it a try."

"I'm good watching you," Tarc quickly refused. He was plenty fine being excited for Kief—on the ground.

Sefrana sat down on the rock next to Kief.

"At least you didn't break anything," she smiled putting a hand on his shoulder. Her eyes matched the blue of the sky, "You crazy boy! One of these days you're going to kill yourself."

Kief laughed, "Not today."

They scrambled back up the steep canyon wall to the bridge. He'd built a scoop sail and it had actually worked!

Patin had waited at the top. He took a few steps to meet them, "I was right, the wind did carry you across the river."

"Is that all you got to say," Tarc barked.

Patin ignored him, "That was impressive Kief."

"Thanks Patin," Kief dropped his sail on the bridge.

"That was spectacular Kief!" Mr. Stadd said. "Your mom would have loved to see you. I'm headed home to tell her you're all in one piece. I'm sure she's worried about you."

"Okay dad," Kief replied plopping down next to his sail. He knew his dad was probably more impressed with his makeshift engineering skills than his daring jump. But he took whatever praise he got nevertheless.

Patin walked back to his horse to get his canteen. Tarc and Sefrana sat down by Kief.

"I'm glad it's you and not me that's going away with him," Tarc rolled his eyes towards Patin. "The guy would drive me crazy."

"It's more school that would drive you crazy," Sefrana said.

"That's true," Tarc acknowledged. "But more school with Patin, now that would be torture."

They laughed as Patin strolled back.

"Not too many weeks now," Sefrana sighed.

"Yea, I can't wait to be done with school," Tarc replied.

"I mean not too many weeks until Patin and Kief leave for the academy."

"It's going to be great to finally have teachers that know more than me," Patin leaned on the rail.

"See what I mean?" Tarc looked at Kief who just grinned.

"Wish I was going with you guys," Sefrana sighed again. Her mother had abandoned her when she was young. Her father encouraged her to follow her dreams. But she couldn't leave him alone; she knew how much he relied on her at home and around the store. Kief couldn't imagine not being able to get away and was certain there was nothing that could hold him back.

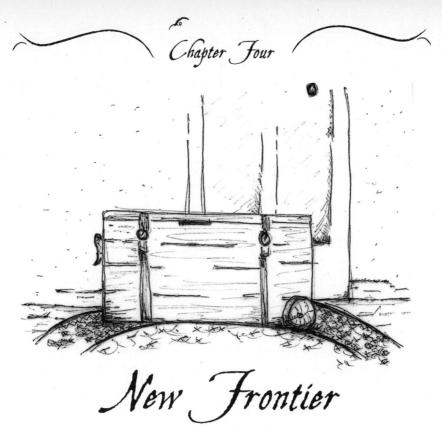

New Frontier

Kief lay on the moose rug in the family room in front of a flickering fire watching shadows dance on the ceiling and walls. He felt like he was back in the cave. He and Tarc had been several times since they'd found it. They'd taken up an assortment of supplies including buckets of fuel and lanterns, and dried meats and nuts. But only Patin and Sefrana knew about it and they made them promise not to tell anyone. Kief would be turning twenty-two soon and couldn't believe he was leaving in the morning. He'd dreamed of attending the Merchant Academy ever since he could remember. He'd be there three years, only coming home to visit during seasonal breaks. At graduation, he'd be promoted to the rank of Chief Sailor and have the opportunity to work for one of the five merchant shippers headquartered in Trite. It was the biggest port on Holpe's Island, and was haven to some of the most prosperous shipping companies on the island including Indicon Shipping; the largest and most prestigious shipper there was. The great grandson of the famous explorer Indicon was president of the vast enterprise. Most graduates vied to work there, but not Kief. At sea, the waves treated every sailor the same. They had no respect for class, rank, or money. Wits and tenacity were all that mattered. Kief didn't need an establishment to make him great. He would do that all on his own. From Chief Sailor, he planned to climb the ranks through Master Sailor, Second Mate, First Mate, and then Captain faster than anyone ever had. He'd captain his own ship by the time he was thirty years old. It was an ambitious goal. Only one other graduate of the academy had ever done it in that short of time, Captain Lui Stein. But his promotion was the result of unfortunate circumstances. Their ship was caught in a tempest. A rogue wave slammed into the ship hitting the helm deck sweeping off the captain, his first mate, and ten of the crew into the sea. They never found them in the blackness and the swirling waves. Stein piloted the ship through the storm saving the lives of the rest of the crew, not to mention the cargo of cloth and spices from Jarmond. For his heroics, he was promoted to Captain. It seemed fitting though, he proved himself an able leader in the event. He clearly had the grit to be a great captain. And that's how Kief saw himself. But he knew he wouldn't be satisfied with just the rank of Captain either. He wanted his own ship. Most captains were employed by the trading companies and they piloted one of the company ships. Very few had their own. Kief had already begun saving his money. He had enough to pay for the rudder; he knew he had a long way to go. But to sail where he pleased and not be under the thumb of an establishment was his ultimate dream.

As he lay on his back dreaming about the sea he hadn't noticed that the rest of his family had joined him in the room until his little sister Myri started pestering everyone. His older sister Atela sat reading some book about a romance in the chair next to the fire. Curchin and Balt plopped down on the rug with Kief. Balt was holding his stomach moaning that he'd eaten too much. Like that was anything new. Atela laughed at him, he always ate like a pig.

Curchin was Kief's younger brother by two years. He planned on studying law at the academy in Point Shar. It was near Council Hall, where the Confederate Council of Holpe's Island met. There were fifteen provinces on the island and each province was represented by an elected councilor. Each councilor had a legal advisory board. Curchin aspired to be a member of the board that served the Province of High Valley. That wasn't for Kief, he had to have adventure and danger. The Engineering or Law Academies would never do. Being a merchant captain was perfect; he could earn a good living while exploring the world. His father didn't agree and wished he'd pursue something less dangerous and closer to home. He didn't feel Kief could become a responsible young man while off chasing his childhood dreams.

On the other hand, Balt hated school altogether and couldn't imagine why his brothers would want to attend more. Myri bounced onto Balt's stomach.

"Agh!" Balt yelled, "get off of me!"

Myri just laughed, her blond hair and fair skin matched her personality perfectly—vivacious and bubbly but, like most little sisters, whiny when she didn't get her way. Balt shoved her off—just as Mr. Stadd walked into the room.

"What's going on, Balt?"

"Oh nothing... so what was it like when you went to academy, dad?" he said hoping to avoid getting in trouble—which was something he always seemed to be getting into.

It worked. Mr. Stadd started in on stories of his time at the Engineering Academy in Bern. His recounting of their class experiments with explosive powder captured even Balt's attention. Suddenly, academy didn't seem so bad.

"If I went, could I blow things up too?" he asked.

Kief's mom looked at his dad and shook her head with that what-are-we-going-to-do-with-him look she so often had.

"He's your son," his dad replied.

Kief's family often gathered around the fire to listen and tell stories and it always ended with Myri falling asleep on the rug. That was something he was definitely going to miss, he thought as he climbed the stairs with his brothers. He shared the large room on the top floor with them. Houses in Shaflann were circular, tall, and narrow, sometimes even five floors high built from large pines and mountain stone. The expensive ones used imported brick. Kief's had stone. He preferred it that way; it made him feel like he was a part of the rugged landscape. He'd never really been interested in wealth or prominence.

He sat on his bed and jotted down a few final details about his upcoming journey in his explorer's journal. It was a single book but he was certain that one day his adventures would fill volumes!

"Tomorrow is the beginning of my greatest adventure." He finished writing and then turned to the pages with the maps of the cave. He had paced out the dimensions of the tunnels and caverns and had used a compass to lay out everything in its proper direction. He made a few touch ups to his drawings, and then dowsed the lamp he'd built and pushed its arm back over his desk. He'd have to build himself a new one once he got to academy. It took him awhile to fall asleep as he thought about what school would be like, his professors, and his first day sailing.

It seemed he had just blinked and his mom was already calling up the stairs to get Kief and his brothers moving. He took his time dressing, made his bed, and put his things neatly away. He sat back down on his bed and looked around the room. Curchin and Balt had thrown on their clothes leaving blankets and pajamas in piles around the room and had run down stairs to fill their starving bellies. When he wasn't exploring this was where Kief had passed his time. He had spent many rainy days in the window seat reading exciting stories of great men and watching the storms outside. The huge rug in the middle of the room was almost worn through from countless urt matches with Curchin and Balt and Tarc.

"Kief!" his mother called up again. "You're going to miss the train!"

Kief collected the last of his things and walked down to the kitchen.

"Get yourself some milk," she said setting a plate on the table. Kief went into the pantry and opened the stream box in the floor. Like most houses in Shaflann, they had a small stream that ran under their house where they stored food to keep it cold. He pulled out the glass jug.

"Are you all ready?" his mom asked as he sat down.

"Yep, I've been ready for weeks," he replied digging into the flat cakes and jam his mom had made. She was a great cook. He hadn't thought about being away from her cooking, and all of a sudden he hoped the academy had good food.

"I'm going to pick up Patin," Kief's dad announced as he came into the kitchen. "So today's the day Kief's off to take on the big city," he said grabbing a flat cake from the stack on the table and breaking off an edge.

Kief looked up from his breakfast and smiled.

"My odds are on Kief," he placed his hand on his shoulder and gave him a reassuring nod. Kief had made his decision to become a Merchant Sailor and, at that point, Mr. Stadd would do all he could to support him. Though Kief felt like his father hoped he'd maybe change his mind after the first year. "Set your things out front," he said walking out the back door to the barn. "Patin and I will be right back."

Patin's father was a business man and he and Patin's mother were away on travels to Condull so he'd be going to the train station with Kief and his parents.

Kief passed Atela on his way to the front door, "Where are Curchin and Balt?"

"Do you think I know?" she replied with a smirk.

"Right," he shook his head as he unlatched his trunk. Kief piled a few last things inside including his explorer's journal and the map with all the strange writings. His stone he kept at his side in his satchel.

Curchin and Balt ran around to the front of the house as their dad returned with Patin. Tarc and Sefrana had also come to say goodbye. Kief's mom started to cry as soon as the hugging began.

"Oh, mom, I'll be back for Star Rhythm break before you know it," he laughed. "You won't be crying all the way to the station will you?"

"No, I'm fine," she smiled through her tears.

"I'll keep a lantern burning for you at the cave," Tarc nodded.

Kief wished Tarc was going with him but he'd never last at the academy. School wasn't his thing. He planned on working the mines until Kief reached Captain and then he'd join him on his ship as First Mate. Tarc could certainly rouse a group of unruly sailors to make sail. This Kief knew from years of Tarc yelling at him on the mat.

"See you all at Star Rhythm break," Kief waved as they rode down the path disappearing behind the trees.

Shaflann Bucken was built on the side of a mountain overlooking High Valley. A maze of stone-laid streets and paths winding through the forest connected the hundred or so homes to Main Street where all the shops and businesses were located. Though a rural town, the silver mining industry brought many educated and highly skilled people to Shaflann. There were businesses of all sorts from food merchants, weavers, artisans, and cobblers, to wood carvers, glass blowers, and metal craftsmen. There was even a theatre—Atela's favorite.

Located at the lower end of town was Mountain Station where Kief and Patin would board the train. Mr. Stadd went inside to buy their tickets while they unloaded their trunks. Kief walked to the front of the carriage and wrapped his arms around his horse. Natch nudged at him with his nose. He'd accompanied him on all his expeditions. This was the first time he wasn't going with Kief.

The pathway up to the station was lined with flowers and signs mourning the loss of the Winzert family. A few weeks previous, the last car of a steam train carrying lamp oil for the mine had caught fire and broken loose rolling all the way back down the mountain into High Valley. The Winzerts, a mom, dad and two children were crossing the tracks in their carriage when the flaming car hit them. It was a tragic accident that had left the townspeople of both High Valley and Shaflann Bucken stunned. As she read the signs, Kief's mom started to cry again. She hugged him tight, tears streaming down her cheeks.

"I'll be fine mom," he reassured her hoping that would make the tears stop.

"I know you will. You and Patin look after each other, you hear me?" she said firmly, wiping the tears from her face.

"We will," they promised.

"You'll both do great," she said and then covered her mouth with her hands holding back a new surge of tears.

"Keep your eyes open Kief, Trite isn't like Shaflann," his dad said as he gave him a big hug.

"I will, dad. I'll be back soon to tell you all about it."

"I look forward to that, my boy."

Kief and Patin picked up the end of their trunks by their handles and dragged them on their two wheels into the station. Kief turned and waved one last time before the station doors closed behind him. As they did, a rush of excitement filled his chest.

They quickly made their way to the loading platform as most of the passengers had already boarded. The line hand took their trunks and they bounded up the steps onto the train. Kief found an empty bench and sat down next to the window and Patin sat across from him. As the train began to chug forward, butterflies stirred in Kief's stomach. It wasn't long before Shaflann slipped out of view. Kief and Patin didn't say much for awhile, just looked out the window with big smiles drawn across their faces. They passed the maintenance platform where Patin had worked the previous Sun Rhythm. His father thought it would be good to get him out of the books and experience a real hands-on job so he set him up working with the line maintenance crew doing track repairs. Patin hated it, but he boasted about his big job with the crew like it was the best thing he'd ever done. Beyond the maintenance platform was Dondor Bridge. They stood to get a better view of the canyon and river far beneath them.

"That would make an amazing ride with the scoop sail!"

"It's the tallest bridge on Holpe, Kief. You don't want to jump," Patin looked at Kief with that same look he'd had every time Kief went off Tubin Bridge.

Since his first jump, he'd gone ten or more times. He never could convince any of his friends to try it—even though they'd watched him land safely after each jump.

"But it would be a great ride," Kief mumbled.

The rich smell of freshly turned soil streamed through the open windows as they reached the farmlands of High Valley. A few farmers were in their fields gathering their harvests; mostly snow wheat and early potatoes. Horses pulled heavy equipment, dragging dark tails of earth behind them across the landscape. Every once in a while they would catch the faint sweet scent of the chatra. Huge chatra orchards sat on the east side of High Valley. Large, brown, pear-like fruits hung on medium round trees. They didn't taste good but were loaded with sugar. One large boiler house stood in the center of the orchards and was the only facility for extracting the sugar which was shipped all over Holpe's Island. Just as silver was the backbone of Shaflann Bucken, sugar was the backbone of High Valley.

The train passed Town Center. A flock of red-winged gulls fluttered up from the massive stone-paved square retreating into the eaves of the time tower. It was the tallest building in High Valley and could be seen from almost anywhere, even Shaflann. The city streets were crowded with people, horses, and carriages. The work of skilled craftsmen was seen everywhere; from the lampposts lining the streets, to the stone paths, to the elaborate wood carvings on the doors and window frames. A few blocks past Town Center was the Travel Plaza. It was the central hub of all lines coming in and going out of town. Entering one of the towering archways, they came to a stop in the shadowy expanse of the station. Enormous timber pillars made up the main structure of the plaza. An intricate lattice-work of smaller beams formed an immense domed ceiling scattered with small windows. Vendors with wooden carts selling trinkets and scrumptious foods called out in a symphony of persuasion at passing travelers.

Kief and Patin bought their tickets for the train to Trite. It was a two-day journey down the vast Temblin Canyon and across the lowland plains to the ocean. Again, the line hand took their trunks and they found a spot across from each other next to a window. This time the train was much more crowded, but at least the long distance steam trains were more luxurious than the day trains like the one up to Shaflann. The benches were wider for sleeping with thick cushions and a space to store things under the seats. They couldn't resist bouncing up and down on the springy seats, like a couple of kids. The warm sun beamed through the windows. As the train entered the canyon, Kief couldn't keep his eyes open any longer and he drifted off.

He woke some time later to the wind on his face, someone had opened a window. Patin was reading a book. Kief stared out at the spectacular canyon. Towering granite mountains covered with pine trees surrounded them. A large bird soared through the air.

"A dark eagle," Kief whispered excitedly.

Patin glanced up from his book for a moment and then returned to his reading. Kief kept watching it as it glided effortlessly, never flapping its wings. It looked like it could go on like that forever. The eagle followed the train for some time and then banked and disappeared into the cliffs.

Through most of the canyon, the tracks followed the Montisse

River. A much less-used horse and carriage path ran alongside the tracks. In the days before the steam line had been built, the path was the only way to get to High Valley. Carriages laden with goods had taken almost an entire week to navigate the canyon. Construction of the steam line had completely changed the valley opening it up to many settlers.

The skies darkened and storm clouds gathered around the mountain peaks like rushing rivers in the sky. White streaks flashed across a deep blue backdrop. The river turned brown and swelled with the heavy run-off. Hundreds of tiny waterfalls cascaded down the cliffs splashing off ledges and outcroppings.

By the second day, they'd made it to the plains. The storm had passed and golden blades of wheat waved in an endless sea. They came to the first town since they'd left High Valley. It wasn't much of a town. But line towns were known to be small, making their living by supplying the steam trains that passed through them.

The conductor came over the loud pipe, "Dayzier! Approaching the town of Dayzier! Stopping for water and supplies. Passengers are free to exit the train but are to return promptly at the whistle."

Kief and Patin were anxious to stretch their legs and see the tiny place. Rushing past their fellow passengers, they bounded off the train. The old rickety platform squeaked as they landed on it. Walking up the only dirt road into town they passed a short row of shops. Store clerks attended to a few customers. There really wasn't much to the town.

"How would you keep from going crazy in such a small place?" Kief wondered.

"If they had a decent library I think they'd get along just fine.

Since they're a line town they could even trade books with some of the other line towns," Patin replied matter-of-factly.

"I was just wondering out loud, Patin—anyway that's a stupid idea."

An elderly man riding a stout little donkey popped out from one of the side streets between the shops.

"Hello gents," he greeted in a funny sort of an accent, nearly bumping into them.

"Hello," they replied back, at a loss for words.

"I suspect you're travelers from High Valley," he eyed them.

"Shaflann Bucken, actually," Patin answered.

"Oh," he said rubbing his prickly chin. "And given your age, I suspect you're headed to... an academy?"

"You guessed right," Patin smiled, happy that someone finally thought he looked his age. "We're both going to the Trite Merchant Academy."

"Oh, education is the key to success," he commended them. "I've had to make my living in a variety of ways—none of them too easy, mind you. But things have been good for me," he confessed to himself. "Yes, indeed they have," he continued to ramble; more to himself than to Kief or Patin. And then remembering that he'd been talking to the boys, "Shaflann eh... I've got a package coming in from Shaflann today."

"A package, what kind of a package would you have coming from Shaflann?" Kief wondered. Dayzier wasn't much of a manufacturing town.

He smiled at them with eyes that sparkled like those of a youth even though he was bent over with age.

"You two look like honest lads..." he leaned in close to the boys, "silver, a package of silver," he whispered though no one was around to hear him.

"Silver? From the Dunton Silver Mines?" Patin burst out.

"The very same," he continued to whisper putting a wrinkled, knobby old finger to his lips.

"Kief's dad is the Chief of Operations at that mine," Patin replied astonished at the coincidence.

"Is that a fact," the old man grinned showing a mouthful of little yellow teeth and gaping holes where some of his teeth used to be.

"Yep, I've spent a few Sun Rhythms working at the mine myself," Kief replied proudly.

"Well, then, come with me to my place," he invited them as if they were close family he hadn't seen in years.

"Is it nearby?" Patin asked not wanting to miss the train.

"Take a look around," he laughed, "everything is close in Dayzier."

Kief and Patin chuckled and followed the man back up the alleyway to a worn trail through the grass. It led to a white gate at the base of a small hill. The man dismounted his donkey and extended his hand.

"Mye Homer's the name."

"Kief and Patin from Shaflann," they replied shaking his hand.

They followed him up the stone path through a wildish garden to a modest home. They were met by a meticulously furnished entryway with items that looked like they'd been imported from all over the world.

"This way," he said opening the door to his studio.

His masterpieces lay on display shelves before them. Silver bracelets, gem set rings, time piece chains, women's hair pieces, beautiful works of art surrounded them. Kief studied the delicately colored gems and stopped when he came to a white one. It was the same color as his stone though the gem was more brilliant. Kief turned to the old man.

"I wonder if you wouldn't mind taking a look at something for me." He was hesitant, but he would never see this old man again, and it was obvious he knew a little about rocks.

Patin's head swiveled to look at Kief. His brow wrinkled with curiosity.

"Sure," Homer replied, whistling through the gaps in his teeth. He sat down at his work table and tilted a mirror to reflect sunlight in from the window. "Let's see what you have there," he lifted his hands like a beggar.

Kief pulled the leather pouch out of his satchel and dumped the stone into his hand.

"What's that?" Patin tried to touch it, but quick as a whip the old man snapped his fingers shut and pulled his hand away.

He placed the stone on a small stand and strapped on a headpiece with long tubular lenses, one for each eye. He made mumbling noises as he studied. Kief fidgeted and let out big sighs. Patin was leaning so far forward he almost fell onto the old man. After a long moment, Homer sat back in his chair and lifted the lenses up onto his speckled forehead. He looked at Kief and smacked his lips.

"Well...?" Kief said when there was no immediate explanation.

The man slowly pushed himself up and out of his chair and walked over to a hutch. He grabbed a fist-sized rock and set it on the table.

"Do you know what kind of stone that is?" he asked.

"It looks like marble, just like Kief's," Patin replied.

"Precisely," he threw up his hands excitedly.

"And...?" Kief didn't know where he was going.

"Do you know the difference between my marble and your marble?" he looked at Kief.

Kief turned to Patin and back to the old man, "No, that is why I asked you."

"There's no difference," he replied slapping the table with his hand.

Kief's enthusiasm sank, "What do you mean no difference, that's a special rock."

"Indeed it is," he agreed. "There is no difference except that your piece of marble is perfectly pure, no other particles. I've never seen anything like it. Even in white marble you can see a trace of impurities but yours is pure crystal. It's absolutely amazing."

"What's it worth?" Patin's eyes widened at the prospect hoping to share in Kief's riches.

"Hard to say. A lot, it's a one of a kind. I'd hang on to it though," he said handing it back to Kief.

"I intend to," he took the stone and put it back in its pouch.

Patin sighed disappointed; his dreams of early prosperity disintegrating as fast as they'd appeared.

"Now, to remember your visit, come on over here to this shelf and pick out anything you'd like. It's my gift to you."

"Oh, thank you but... " Kief didn't want to take from him.

"Really?" Patin didn't hesitate and started inspecting the items.

"I insist, go on," the man pushed Kief.

It didn't take long for Patin to find what he wanted, an intricate silver chain for his time piece. Kief searched more methodically, examining each one until he found something that caught his eye. He picked up a simple silver ring with a small sculpted eagle. It was perfect. The wings were tucked behind him, not flying and not perched, more like it was just launching.

"Thank you," Kief replied excited about his new treasure.

"Next time you see your dad tell him I'm much obliged for all the splendid silver."

"But it's your craft," Patin nodded lifting his chain in front of him, "that makes them so beautiful."

In the distance a sharp whistle blew.

"Oh, we have to go!" Kief said. He'd almost forgotten how he'd come upon Homer in the first place. "We don't want them leaving without us."

"It's a long walk to Trite," Homer chuckled.

They thanked him again running out the door for the train. As the train lunged forward, Patin started pestering Kief with questions about the stone.

"It's a little gift from my grandpa. Just don't go blabbing about it," he replied.

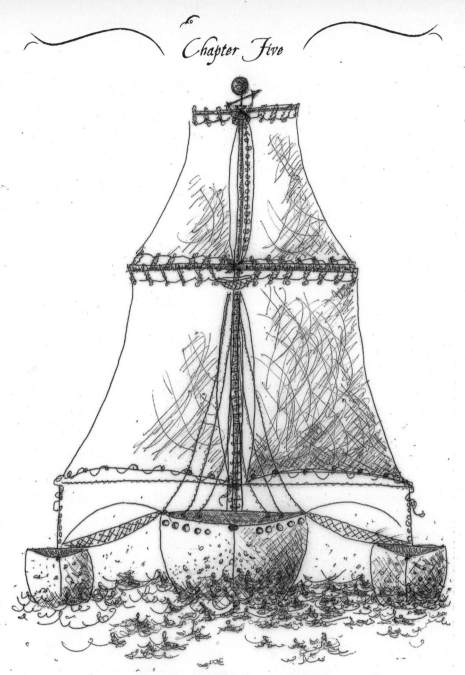

Northern Torch

"Do you see it? To the left of that little hill right there," Patin pointed.

Kief was perched on the edge of his seat, his eyes fixed on the horizon. Then he saw it. Rising up from the quiet prairie, the city grew out of the ground until it seemed as tall as the mountains they'd just left. Kief and Patin pressed their faces against the window. Towering buildings filled the sky everywhere. They hadn't even entered the city and Kief could already feel its pulsating energy. Everything that he'd always imagined about the city raced through his mind; the architecture, commotion, exotic people, it was all coming to life before him.

"Approaching Trite Station, prepare to disembark," the conductor called over the pipe.

Trite Station was ten times the size of High Valley Station. Kief strained to see the top of the domed ceiling as the train chugged through the entrance. It was so tall he couldn't see it until his eyes adjusted. Kief and Patin were on their feet before the train had stopped. Gathering their things they moved to the door anxiously waiting on the station hand to open it. Bounding off the train, Kief immersed himself in the moving crowd. Patin grabbed the back of Kief's shirt before he disappeared completely.

"Kief! We don't know where we're going yet."

The swarm of people and barking vendors made High Valley Station look like a quiet fruit stand in the countryside. Patin spotted the handlers where their trunks were being thrown onto the station floor.

"Boy they sure know how to ruin a new trunk fast," Patin grumbled as they wove their way through the crowds and peddlers to the carriage platforms.

Kief was awed by all the travelers and couldn't imagine where they all were going.

"Do you know where we're supposed to meet?" Kief asked Patin.

"Well, if you would slow down and look at your letter the commission sent, you would know," Patin sighed trying to gain a sense of direction and order.

"Why don't you just tell me, I know you know!" Kief huffed.

"Yes, but you need to start paying attention to these things yourself if you... "

"Ok, ok dad!" Kief waved a carefree hand at Patin. He pulled his acceptance letter from his satchel, "It says here at Post 32. There! How's that for responsibility, Patin?"

They searched the tall wooden posts with painted numbers. Sunlight from the big windows in the ceiling showered into the station.

"There's Post 25," Patin pointed, "32 must be further down this way."

"You must be Kief and Patin?" greeted a tall and thin young man wearing a leather brimmed hat as they reached Post 32.

"Yep, I'm Kief and this is Patin," Kief introduced them.

"The carriage master will take your trunks," he nodded toward a stout man in uniform. "Name's Luften. So, what do you think of the city?" he asked.

"It's our first time and it's amazing," Kief replied excitedly.

"Well, I guess it's good so far," Patin interjected, "My trunk isn't in the same condition it was when I left Shaflann but at least I haven't been robbed yet!"

"Been here two years and never been robbed, the city isn't what you might think it is."

"Well, I, uh...," Patin jabbered.

"Is the school far from here?" Kief asked.

"We'll be there soon enough, climb on board and we'll get

going."

They jumped up into the carriage next to Luften and had barely sat down before it darted out of the station. They cut in front of another carriage narrowly dodging a collision, both drivers shouting at each other.

"Guess everyone's in a hurry around here," Patin mumbled grabbing a hold of his seat.

They flew up a shadowy canyon of buildings. Kief hung his head out the window.

"Watch it; you'll get it taken off," Luften warned.

He pulled his head back in some but he couldn't resist. A merchant town, Trite was a crossroads of the southern hemisphere. The streets were filled with people of all nationalities coming and going in every direction. They were dressed in varying attire from tailored suits and dresses to bright tunics and ornamental clothing. He smelled foods he'd never smelled before. In the shops, jewelry, pottery, rugs, and things that he had no idea what their uses were, hung in their windows. He heard languages of all kinds as customers negotiated with the shopkeepers. While the city and its people were alluring, it certainly wasn't clean like High Valley and Shaflann. There was trash along the streets and rundown buildings mixed in with newer ones. And the people mirrored the buildings, some were rich, some were poor all mingled together.

The carriage turned so sharply that the outer wheels lifted from the ground as they now headed west. Nearing the ocean, the smell of fish permeated the air and Kief could taste the salt on his tongue. He could hardly wait to reach the shore. His anticipation spilled over when he caught his first glimpse of the great blue expanse on the horizon.

"There it is!" he shouted. He jumped up nearly falling out the window as he did so.

Luften grabbed him by the belt of his trousers pulling him back in, "First time?" he grinned.

"We lived near the ocean when I was little but I don't really remember it."

Kief's mother had told him stories about growing up in Bern where he was born while his father was going to the academy. She talked of how he would wander the beach all day playing and exploring in the rocks and caves and surf. When he was six, his father was hired for an engineering position at the salt mines in Suinville. She said he cried and cried when they left the ocean and that he was never very happy in Suinville. Of course, the whole family felt the same way. Suinville was a hot, rough, mining town. But Kief's dad, always practical, said it was fine pay and would benefit them in the long run. It seemed the only good thing that came out of Suinville was Natch. His father bought him from one of the miners for Kief's tenth birthday. They were inseparable. Kief would ride up to the mine every day after school and ride home with his father.

It turns out Kief's father was right, though. When he was twelve, they moved to Shaflann Bucken. Kief loved his new mountain home. He and Natch explored the endless forests and canyons. His mother said the sparkle in his eyes finally returned. When Kief was old enough, his father got him a job working at the mine. He grew tired of his meaningless meandering of the mountains saying that nothing productive really came from it.

"There's nothing like the ocean," Luften drew in a deep breath.

A fleet of docked merchant ships came into view. Kief was awestruck at the towering masts, the mazes of ropes, the painted hulls, and the bundled sails awaiting their next voyage.

"Hey, what's that?" Patin asked pointing at a large ship without sails.

"That's the newest addition to the Merchant Fleet," Luften said showing a bit of pride.

"But where are the sails?" Kief asked.

"It doesn't have sails," Luften replied.

"What do you mean no sails, it would take a thousand men to row a ship that size," Patin reasoned.

"It doesn't need oars or sails," Luften continued. "It has a combustion engine that drives a propeller aft."

"A combustion engine?" Kief asked.

Patin jumped in, "It uses fuel called petrol that burns and turns the engine. It's a new technology they developed in Jarmond."

"Anyway," Luften interrupted not wanting to be outdone by a younger know-it-all, "it can sail without the wind, in any direction."

"So, where do you get petrol, Patin?" Kief asked.

"They dig it out of the ground, similar to a water well. They have lots in the eastern part of Jarmond and in some other countries. Not much here though. I suspect they have to import it."

Luften looked out the window trying to ignore Patin. The combustion engine ship didn't have the same appeal to Kief as having the wind in his sails. Depending on the wind and the stars to get you where you were going seemed more authentic.

Then, the Merchant Academy came into view, a magnificent stone structure bordering the sea. Wide granite steps leading up to the main entrance were flanked by the statues of Chavet and Indicon, the two captains who had led the first exploratory expeditions of Holpe's Island.

The carriage came to an abrupt stop in front of the steps.

"Look at the size of this place!" Patin exclaimed.

The carriage master unloaded their trunks and sped off as if he were late for his next pickup. Kief and Patin heaved their trunks up the endless steps past the historic sentinels. They entered through the enormous wood doors onto a polished stone floor covered with elaborate woven rugs, tables, and ornate furniture. Large paintings of former Academy Directors and historical explorers and traders hung on the walls.

"One day my picture will be in this hall," Kief thought.

"You're the first ones to arrive, the others will be coming throughout the week," Luften said leading them to another set of stairs. "The dormitories are on the upper levels."

"What!" Patin grumbled. He was still huffing from the first set of stairs.

"You'll be fine," Luften sighed, "we have a lift for your trunks."

"Of course you have a lift," Patin replied not wanting to look stupid.

Luften stopped in front of a short door in the wall.

"Put your trunks in here and they'll be at the top when we get there."

"Oh these are great," Patin declared like he'd used them before. He struggled lifting his trunk and missed the boxed compartment banging the wall instead.

"Easy there," Luften said.

Kief loaded his trunk next to Patin's. He was curious to see how it worked. Luften closed the door and pulled down on a lever. Patin's eyes followed the knocking noise that slowly traveled up the wall.

"Come on Patin, it's not going to carry you up," Luften teased.

"Hey, that trunk is heavy," Patin defended himself. Luften just ignored him.

They followed Luften up four flights of granite stairs to their dormitory level, walking down a narrow hallway with brass numbers on the doors. They stopped at 5-42.

"Here we are," Luften pushed open the door.

"A little cramped, but not bad," Patin commented stepping inside.

"Let's go get your trunks," Luften continued down the hall not wanting to hear Patin's assessment of the room. "I'm in dorm 5-12 that way," he pointed. "Drop your trunks off and come on down and we'll go get some dinner."

Retrieving their trunks, Kief and Patin dragged them back to their room.

"Which bed do you want?" Kief asked.

"Well, it appears the room is perfectly symmetrical..."

"Fine, I'll take the one on the left," Kief cut off Patin's decision process.

They slid their trunks under their beds and hung their satchels on the bed posts.

"Acceptable view," Patin stared down into the courtyard.

"An ocean view would be better," Kief turned away.

"They probably save those for the older students," Patin figured.

"I'll get one next year," Kief assured Patin.

"But I don't think that's allowed... I don't think you'll get one until your last year..."

Kief walked out of the room and down the hallway to Luften's dorm. Patin followed behind still blabbering.

"Patin!" a girl's voice shouted down the hallway.

"Clarin!" Patin called out and ran ahead brushing past Kief.

"How was your journey?" she asked as she gave him a big hug.

"It was long."

"Well you made it. How are you Kief?" she turned and gave him a hug too. Kief felt his cheeks flush.

"I'm good Clarin—it's been awhile."

"Yes it has. Where are you boys headed?"

"To eat, we're starved. Our mentor, Luften, is taking us to the dining hall."

"Great, I'll join you."

Patin and Clarin kept talking as Kief tapped on door 5-12 that had been left slightly ajar.

"Yep," Luften called.

"So, wonderful place huh?" Clarin said still enthused after two years at the academy.

"Oh yeah," they both agreed.

"Hey Clarin," Luften said as he came to the door.

"Luften."

"I guess you know these guys, they're from Shaflann too."

"Yes, I know them. Patin's my brother."

"Oh... that's surprising," Luften wrinkled his brow trying to see the similarities. They were both short and thin with a few freckles but that was the extent of it. Clarin's dark hair and amusing personality were nothing like her dusty blond haired, overly analytical brother. And it was clear that Patin gave little thought to appearances; he dressed rather plainly. Clarin, on the other hand, looked fabulous. Wearing a ruffled short sleeved blouse in a subtle yellow-flowered pattern and tan cotton pants that ended tucked into her mid calf boots; the wide belt that sat on her hips complimenting her petite figure, she was the perfect combination of cute and flirtatious with just the right amount of rough around the edges.

"Well, are we going to eat or aren't we?"

"Uh, yeah," Luften stuttered, trying to ignore the fact that Patin was Clarin's brother.

The dining hall had enormous windows offering spectacular views of the ocean. After stacking their plates high with food, they sat at a table near the window. Waves gently rocked the boats tied at the docks along the shoreline. Seagulls glided above the water and combed the beaches, plucking small creatures out of the sand.

"Food's good," Patin remarked, his mouth full, not noticing the scenery beyond his plate.

"Yeah, our head cook, Skimmer, is the best. Sea captains fought over him for years until we were lucky enough that he retired to the academy," Luften said savoring the steak he was eating.

"So we'll be putting on a little weight I take it," Patin said stuffing his mouth with another spoonful of potato dumplings. Patin ate like a horse but it never showed. He burned everything he consumed. Kief said it was all the thinking he did.

"Uh, with early morning drills you'll get plenty of exercise. In fact, you may go home even skinnier than you are now," Luften poked.

After dinner, Luften showed them around the bath house, the main lecture hall, and a few of the class rooms. But he cut the evening short so they could get some rest; they were exhausted from the journey.

Kief leaned back on his bed to record the past couple of days' experiences in his journal, writing about the train ride, his sighting of the eagle, and their strange encounter with Homer and what he knew about his stone, his first impressions of Trite and how good it was to see the ocean and Clarin again. A crescent moon shone through the window that he'd left open. In the quiet of the evening he could hear the waves crashing on the shore. Kief could think of no better way to fall asleep.

The next morning, Luften stopped by late to wake them. At breakfast, Kief wondered where Clarin was but didn't ask. He assumed she had things to do in preparation for her last year at the academy. Patin piled on the food again like a bear coming out of hibernation. Kief loaded his plate with scrambled eggs and flat cakes, his favorite. Only the jam wasn't as good as his mom's. She made the best jam. Near Lake Shandon, above Shaflann, there were hundreds of wild berry bushes. Kief and his brothers always complained about having to pick the berries, but during the cold season they were glad they'd done it as they slathered her jam on their flat cakes.

"This morning we'll take a tour of the academy and the docks," Luften said. "But this afternoon you'll be free to get settled in and wander around on your own."

Eager to get the tour started, Kief ate quickly and wouldn't let Patin go back for seconds. He complained, but followed Luften and Kief out of the dining hall. On the main level, Luften showed them the lecture halls and the academic sections of the academy. The only two Kief cared about were the Mariner Section and the Medical Section, the section where Clarin would be spending most of her time. As they passed the Language Section, Kief remembered his map and wondered if the professors might know something about the strange writings. He decided he'd pay them a visit before dinner.

Through a large archway fitted with huge double doors, Luften took them outside to the exercise field. It was an enormous grass field marked off with stakes and ropes dividing up the different stations for jumping, climbing, running, lifting, carrying, and sports of all kinds. Kief and Patin tried part of the climbing station. Patin could barely pull himself over the first wall and fell

flat on his face.

"Guess he doesn't get out much," Luften said.

"You could say that," Kief said and they both chuckled.

Next they went to the docks, the place Kief had been dying to see all morning. Three long wooden piers jutted out like peninsulas into the sea. The weathered planks were as thick as Kief's leg, the pylons as big as trees. They were built to support the heavy loads and endless streams of goods toted to and from the ships. Sandy beaches off both sides of the wide boardwalk stretched all the way to the horizon. Thick braided ropes tethered the magnificent ships to the heavy posts of the docks. They walked up the first pier while Luften told them all about the ships. There were five great tri-hull freighters, including the combustion ship. They were used for carrying heavy loads across vast oceans and had a crew of at least 100 men. There were seven tri-hull haulers which had a smaller crew of around 40 to 60 men and were used for transporting lighter loads, but could easily handle long voyages. Then there were at least ten small bi-hull skits. The skits were for sailing from port to port around the continent and out to nearby islands. They could handle the open sea but didn't have the capacity to support a large crew. They usually had around 20 men.

Forger, Storm Runner, Sea Bull—Kief wanted to board one of them but Luften said they weren't allowed without the captain's permission. The tri-hull haulers were his favorite; big enough to carry a good sized crew and the spoils of their discoveries and small enough to be swift at sea. He could have stayed all afternoon watching them undulate up and down in the waves. But Patin bothered him so much that he eventually agreed to go back to the dorms.

Luften told them he'd return later for dinner and left to go about his own things. Patin was done touring for the day and hopped up on his bunk with a book. So, Kief grabbed the map from his trunk and headed for the Language Section. He wandered for awhile looking at the amazing architecture of the building. Some hallways were made of brick, others polished marble, and others fine woods. He liked the wood the most, it made him feel at home. When he finally reached the Language Section, he found the head master's office and knocked. He wasn't in, but his clerk directed Kief to Professor Elenda who specialized in ancient languages. He knocked on her door. There was no reply so he knocked again.

"Come in," called a woman's sharp voice.

Kief pushed open the door slowly and stepped in. A wooden sign with the name Professor Elenda hung on the wall behind her. Old-looking framed documents written in various languages covered the walls. The woman was sitting at her desk, magnifying glass in hand, hunched over a large piece of paper with an ink pen. Her fingertips on her writing hand were black and she was fixed on the symbols she was sketching.

"Professor Elenda," Kief said politely.

"That's me," she replied without looking up. "You know if someone doesn't answer when you knock—it probably means they're busy. What do you want?"

"Uh... I need help in reading a language," Kief said.

"Leave it and I'll take a look when I have a moment," she replied curtly, her head still down.

"I can't... I can't leave it with you so I'll come back another time," Kief turned to go out.

"Suit yourself," she said and then looked up revealing a rather unpretty face with bushy eyebrows and a small pointy nose. "Do you know what language it is?"

"I have no idea," Kief answered, staring.

"Oh, very well," she sighed heavily slapping down her pen. "Let's have a look," she reached out stiffly.

Kief handed her his map hesitantly, concerned he was bugging a professor in his first week at the academy, and maybe just a little bit concerned about bugging this professor in particular. She unrolled it and hunched back down over her desk as she had been when Kief walked in.

"Sit," she snapped.

Kief dropped in the chair in front of her desk. Professor Elenda spun around on her swivel chair and pulled a book off the shelf behind her. She became completely engrossed in what she was seeing.

"Do you know...?" Kief tried to say something.

"Shhhh," she hushed him.

He closed his lips. She turned the pages of her book. Kief leaned slightly forward to get a peek at her book. The pages were covered with exotic looking symbols though Kief didn't know if it was an ancient or modern language.

"This language is as ancient as Fundautum. Some of these characters are similar to Sactin, the oldest language we know. I can only interpret a few of the symbols... "

Kief walked behind the desk leaning over her shoulder. She was too involved to be bothered by him now.

"This is the symbol for four, this is the symbol for one," she pointed at a line of characters. "It says something about the one bearing a token of some sort." She followed along down a few lines not saying anything and then stopped, "This says something about whales spewing venom, and mountains, and fire," she followed the characters with her finger. "And this symbol is everywhere," she pulled her head back taking in the entire map.

"What does it mean?" Kief asked.

"Bird... big bird, like a hawk," she replied and then leaned in again following the characters with her finger and turning to her book. She was silent for a moment. Kief supposed she wasn't able to read the rest but he didn't want to interrupt her by asking.

Then she mumbled, "Drinking from the tree."

Realizing there was too much to remember, Kief pulled his journal from his satchel and quickly scribbled down all the words she was saying. Next to the words, he sketched the symbols as best he could. None of them made any sense.

"Where did you get this?" she asked.

"From my grandfather," Kief replied.

"Where did he get it?"

"I don't know. He's dead."

"Well that doesn't help. I don't know what these other symbols are," she said frustrated as she pointed her black-stained finger around the map. "I want to study it with some of my colleagues; leave it with me."

Kief paused, driven by curiosity, he almost agreed. But he knew he couldn't.

"I'm sorry I can't. But I can bring it back at another time to meet with you and the other professors," Kief offered.

"Very well then, stop by the clerk to schedule an appointment. I have other things to do. Shut the door on your way out," and she returned to her writings.

"Whales, venom, drinking from the tree, birds, what does it all mean?" Kief muttered as he walked back to his dorm room. Patin had fallen asleep with the book on his chest. Kief jumped up on his bed with the map. He reviewed the characters and symbols over and over until he could almost write them without looking.

A knock came at the door. It was Clarin.

"Guess he's tired," she said as she came into the room.

"Hasn't budged," Kief said putting the map in his trunk.

"Ok, well, then you come with me, I want to show you something."

Kief followed her pulling the door closed quietly so as not to wake Patin. As they walked down the stairs, Clarin talked casually about some of the professors he'd have his first year. He listened attentively; partly because he wanted to make a good first impression on his professors and partly because he liked hearing her talk. Her voice hadn't changed, soft and strong, like silk. She could sing wonderfully. He remembered her solo at the New Year Celebration before she left for the academy. For a small girl she had a big voice. And big eyes too; chocolate brown ones that Kief felt could see right through him.

She led him through the Mariner Section to a hall Luften hadn't taken them. A wide arched hallway with polished dark wood on the walls and ceiling reflected light from the rows of lamps mounted along both sides. There were no windows. In the center, carved into the stone floor, was the image of a large compass. The ceiling was covered with all the major constellations, some Kief recognized and others he didn't.

"This is Discovery Hall," Clarin smiled. "It runs directly north and south. At the far end," she pointed, "is the Northern Torch," the three-star constellation the sailors used in the northern hemisphere to find true north.

"And there's the South Star," Kief looked directly above him to a bright star carved in the ceiling.

Kief took a breath when he recognized the pictures and maps covering the walls. All the great explorers were there, from Barsalon to Traver to Indicon. Next to each explorer's portrait was a large map detailing their travels and discoveries. Kief followed Traver's path with his finger from Jarmond to the Fire Islands.

"This is where he encountered the Comba native tribe along with the jade jewels; the island was covered with them."

Kief's face shone with adulation. He hoped to one day share their fame. Clarin followed him down one side of the hall and up the other, smiling and nodding as Kief rehearsed to her their varied and remarkable journeys.

"You know a lot," she said.

"Oh, well, I just loved reading about them when I was a kid. I have a whole bookshelf full of their stories," he replied nonchalantly. Kief sat down on the long wooden bench that ran the center of the entire length of the hall.

"Maybe you'll be here one day," Clarin smiled.

"Ha! Maybe..." Kief replied not taking his eyes off the portraits.

Clarin sat down next to him. "So how's your father?"

"Ah, he's the same," Kief ran his fingers through his thick black hair trying to brush it off.

Clarin persisted, "At least he let you come to the academy."

"Yeah, he let me come alright. He doesn't really say much about it but I can tell he's disappointed in me," Kief looked down the hall acting like it was no big deal.

"Still wishing you'd go to the Engineering Academy?"

"Engineering, law, a skilled trade, anything that would keep me from chasing the sea," Kief replied with a sigh.

"He probably just wants you close because he loves you."

"Well that's a funny way to show your love, don't you think, trying to stop a boy's dreams," Kief came back a little sharp.

"He's paying for you to come here right? That says something."

Kief stood and walked up to a map of the Battle of the Island of Plat. It was one of the most ferocious battles in modern history. The marines of Jarmond had captured the Eng Renegade stronghold.

"They lost over seventy-five percent of their men," a voice came from down the hall. It was Luften. He walked up next to Kief and looked at the map with him. "You guys hungry?"

"I'm starved," Clarin jumped up off the bench.

"Me too," Kief said.

They stopped to get Patin on their way to the dining hall.

"Thanks for taking me there today," Kief said to Clarin.

"I thought you'd like it," she gave him an elbow and a smile

The meal choices were entirely different but every bit as tasty as the day before. Kief looked out at the ships as he ate.

"What a splendid view," he declared cheerfully.

"You're spry," Patin said still groggy from his long nap.

"This is all so extraordinary; don't you feel it?"

"Nobody feels what you feel! You're so itching to get onboard one of those ships... but I have it all figured out. I'll manage your expeditions from my big office and take half your profits. Think of it, I'll enjoy the benefits of your trade while sitting in my mansion with all my servants. Now that's the life," Patin said raising his glass.

"Clarin's just as excited," Kief turned to her.

"Yeah, I guess so," Clarin replied. "Though I can't very well set sail with a group of sailors at my command like you. Women are stuck running logistics at the ports or in the infirmary as nurses. Not quite as exciting, wouldn't you agree?"

"Who says you can't sail?" Kief challenged her.

"A lady can't be in command of a ship of men," Luften declared.

"Then she has a crew of woman," Kief replied.

"That would be a sight," Patin snickered.

"On my ship, I'd take Clarin over you any day," Kief smiled.

Patin just shoveled a spoonful of sweet potatoes into his mouth.

"Slow down Patin, the food's not going anywhere," Luften said but was cut short by a great vibration that shook the building. Dishes rattled, windows shuddered, and the chandeliers in the hall swung eerily. Before anyone spoke, a second tremor hit.

Clarin let out a little scream, "What is that?"

Kief set his cup on the shaky table. Luften sprang to the window. Two more rumbled past like waves in the ocean.

"Maybe one of the factories had an accident," Patin exclaimed as they jumped up and joined Luften.

In the distance, smoke was rising from buildings along the shoreline. By this time, the few others who had been dining gathered at the windows as well. Another blast sounded, closer this time, and more buildings began to smoke.

"Something's not right," Luften said grimly.

Uncharted

"Come on," Luften turned.

"But we haven't finished eating," Patin complained as he snatched up part of his dinner and followed Luften and the others swiftly out the door.

"Run to your rooms, grab your satchels, and meet me at my dorm."

"Where are we going?" Patin called after him but he didn't respond.

"Just do what Luften said, I'll meet you downstairs in the main hall," Clarin ordered her little brother and ran to her dorm.

Kief looked back at Clarin and then sprinted to their room. They grabbed their satchels leaving everything else behind.

"But, where are we going?" Patin continued asking.

"I don't know," Kief replied sharply, "We don't even know what's happening out there." Another tremor shook the building, this time with much more force, nearly knocking them to the ground. "That one was close!"

"Really close, let's go," Patin said frantically.

They ran down the hallway passing other frightened students rushing about.

Luften had just come out of his room "Follow me," he said as he pushed past them, his satchel slung over his shoulder, his leather hat atop his head.

They sprinted down the four flights of stairs, Patin trying to keep up. In the main hall, vases had fallen shattered on the ground and pictures were misaligned.

"Look at this place," Clarin said as she caught up with them.

"My map!" Kief blurted out realizing he hadn't put it back in his satchel. "I'll catch up with you," Kief turned and sprinted up the steps knocking into a few students who were scrambling down the stairs.

Explosions continued to hit, with more frequency and so strongly now that the stones under his feet were shaking. Reaching the fifth floor, a smoky haze filled the air. He ran down the empty hallway. In his dorm room, he flung open his chest. As he grabbed his map, a thunderous crash exploded across the hallway, spewing shards of wood and crumbled rock into his room. The blast knocked him to the ground. He felt a sharp sting in his arm. A piece of splintered wood was imbedded deep in his bicep. He bit his lip and yanked it out. Blood ran dripping off his elbow. Stuffing his map in his satchel, he grabbed a shirt from his trunk and wrapped it around his arm. It burned as he pressed on it. More blasts hit shaking the building. The smell of powder and burning wood was all around him. Down the hallway a gaping hole in the side of the academy stared at Kief. He ran toward it. The granite wall had been shattered and part of the floor was missing. Wooden beams and furniture burned as sunlight shone through the smoke in long uncanny rays. Through the hole Kief could see that the academy ships were on fire. And then he caught a partial glimpse of a vessel, the likes of which he'd never before seen. Smoke was blocking his view, but then he saw it, a blue flag painted on its hull with a yellow sun in the middle. It was the Gars! More cannon balls hit the school and Kief could hear the crashing of walls below. Sprinting down the hallway, his arm pulsing with pain, he clambered down the rumpled stairs. Out in the academy gardens he found his companions. Luften was talking to a man who had been at the harbor when the explosions had hit.

"It was a ship that looked like an enormous whale," he shouted. "It rose up out of the water and just started blasting the coastline with cannon fire!"

"It's the Gars," Kief told them disgustedly.

"What do you mean the Gars?" Patin said in disbelief.

"I saw the Gar flag painted on the side of one of the vessels. It was as plain as day. It's the Gars," Kief replied firmly. "I saw the whole thing through an enormous hole their cannons blew in the side of the academy—I was almost hit by one of 'em!"

"Oh, your arm!" Clarin said looking under his makeshift bandage. She pulled out her nursing kit which she had been trained to always have with her and washed his wound with alcohol pulling a few remaining slivers out of his arm. Kief clenched his teeth. "It's not bad," she said applying some gauze and wrapping a bandage around it.

Another explosion smashed into the wall of the building across the yard.

"We need to leave, now," Luften demanded.

"Leave? Leave where?" Patin cried out now in a full panic.

"Out of the city, we can't stay here," Luften said.

"Then home to Shaflann," Patin insisted.

"Another train doesn't depart until tomorrow morning, by then it'll probably be too late," replied Luften as two more explosions rocked the city. "We can go to my home, my dad will know what to do."

"Well, how can we get to your place?" Patin yelled above the pandemonium.

"There's a transport station on Cluff Street. Teamsters leave all the time hauling goods out on the Hodge Highway inland; they pass right by my home. If we hurry, we might be able to catch a ride," Luften pulled his hat down snug and broke into a run.

The entire city had erupted into a mass fear. People and horses dragging carriages, some of them empty, were running in every direction. Clouds of black smoke plumed upward, covering the city in an ominous shadow of destruction. The man's words describing the attack by the ships kept running through Kief's head. Somehow they seemed so familiar. He repeated the words, "A ship rose up out of the harbor like a whale." He stopped. Professor Elenda had translated, "...whales spewing venom." The map! They were the words from the map.

"How much further?" Patin shouted almost slamming into Kief.

"Just a few more streets," Luften hollered over his shoulder.

With a booming crash, two carriages collided in front of Kief and Patin. One spun out of control and toppled over as the other smashed into a lamp post and then continued on its frenzied path. The wheels of the overturned carriage spun freely in the air as the horses struggled to regain their feet. Kief dashed into the street. Luften hesitated; if they stopped they may not make it to the transport before the teamsters all left. But Kief was already calming the horses in the madness. Luften jumped up onto the carriage, yanking open the door. An elderly couple lay battered and cut on the door that was now against the ground.

"Take my hand," he reached in sympathetically. The old man helped his wife up. Luften grabbed her wrists and lifted her up and out of the carriage. "Help her down!" Luften hollered at Patin, who was just standing there looking lost.

"Thank you boys," the gentleman said weakly as Luften helped him out onto the ground.

Clarin rushed into the street, both the man and his wife were bleeding and bewildered, "Where's your home?" she asked.

"245 Hopenshaver Street," the dazed woman replied.

Luften looked at Clarin, "We don't have time, that's just around the corner, they should be alright from here."

"They won't make it through this," she insisted, gesturing at the commotion all around, "look at them, they can hardly walk!"

Luften sighed, "Let's see if we can get this carriage turned up then, Kief."

Heaving together they turned it upright. The horses whinnied and scraped theirs hoofs at the ground.

"Patin, get inside!" Luften yelled impatiently as Kief helped Clarin get the old couple up into the carriage.

Luften took the reins. Dodging in and out through the confusion he found the house and brought the horses to a stop. Clarin had begun attending to their injuries when Luften burst open the door, "We've got to go!"

"Just a moment Luften, I'm almost done!" Clarin said firmly.

Luften turned toward the street and waited.

"There," Clarin said, "now we can go." She piled out of the carriage with her companions and the four of them sprinted back out into the streets dodging the chaos.

"There's the transport station!" Clarin shouted as they approached Cluff Street.

Luften spotted a teamster trying to calm his skittish horses as he climbed into his rig.

"Sir, sir!" he shouted, waving his arms. The man continued to prepare as if he hadn't heard Luften. "Sir, we need a ride to Kosh. Can we jump onboard?"

The teamster glanced over the edge of the cart to see who was talking. "How many?" he asked in a rough voice.

"Four of us, we won't be any trouble. We just need to get to Kosh," he begged.

He released the brake and the spooked horses jerked his cart forward.

"My family, we need to get to my family!" Luften yelled, desperately running after him.

The man halted to yell at another teamster cutting into his path, "You better get on if you're coming with me," he hollered over his shoulder.

"Let's go," Luften motioned as he helped Clarin jump onto the back of the trans-cart.

Kief and Patin followed him, clinging to the cloth filled bags.

Once the teamster cleared the station, he broke his six-horse team into a full gallop. They chased a steady trail of dust from the fleeing exodus of trans-carts that led into the countryside. Now, away from the city, they could see the full extent of the destruction. The entire center section of Trite along the coastline was in flames, smoke billowing into the sky.

"Holpe's Island was attacked—and we saw the whole thing!" Patin stared in disbelief.

Kief had a suffocating feeling. Everything had turned in reverse. The sea and uncharted lands were further away than ever. The great ships of the academy were burning and would soon be at the bottom of the sea. His hopes and dreams a senseless scene of orange and black whirling in the air before him. Silently he sat, wondering with his friends at the horizon, as the cart rumbled along the Hodge Highway.

Farewell

Kief awoke with a start, the cart banging along on the rough road. It was early dawn; eclipsing the stars on the horizon, the faint glow of the sun lighted the quiet countryside. It was so still, surely yesterday was just a terrible dream. But he was atop a teamster's trans-cart traveling on the Hodge Highway; his arm sore and throbbing where he'd been hit with shard. Luften was awake, watching the endless fields of grain. Patin slept, half sitting, with his head resting on one of the sacks of fabric stacked on the cart. And Clarin was curled up, sleeping peacefully, her tangled hair still managing to glisten. Tiny spots of blood stained her hands and sleeves.

"Are we close?" Kief whispered to Luften not wanting to disturb Clarin.

"Getting there. The teamster won't pass through Kosh though, so we'll have to walk in from the main road."

"How far is it?"

"Not too far."

"Do you think news has reached your family?"

"Not likely, we've traveled here so fast I can't imagine anyone is ahead of us."

"I guess this means we're in a war," Kief said staring into the fields. Heads of grain drooped low from the heavy dew that sat on them.

"I'm sure the militias started preparing as soon as that first cannon hit Trite," Luften replied.

"It's going to take more than the militias."

"Yep. It's going to take every man and boy on this island to stop the Gars," Luften said pulling his hat off and rubbing his hands through his hair. "And their arsenal is the most advanced on Fundautum."

Patin stirred, "Did we fall asleep?"

"We did. It was lucky for us we caught a ride onboard a cloth trans-cart and not a cabbage one—it was almost as comfortable as my bed," Kief patted a bag of cloth next to him.

Patin took out his canteen and swallowed what water was left. "I'm thirsty," he said wiping his mouth. "We'll need to find some water."

"Sure, you go ahead and ask that teamster if he wouldn't mind stopping for you so you can get some water," Luften said not offering to share any of his own.

Patin just stared at him.

"You can have all the water you want when we get to my place."

Clarin stirred, stretching her slender arms above her head letting out a soft yawn, and then curling her body up tighter.

"Shhh!" Kief wrinkled his brow at Patin. "Stop complaining and let your sister sleep—we're going to be there soon enough."

The sun peaked over the horizon casting its warmth over the

weary refugees. Kief pulled out his map and studied the writings wondering about the translations Professor Elenda had given him.

"What is that?" Luften asked after a while.

"A map my grandfather left me after he died," Kief said rolling it up.

"What does it say?"

"I don't know," Kief replied.

"Not much good then is it?"

"I guess not," Kief said.

At the fork to Kosh, the teamster reined the horses off the road alongside a watering trough.

"Is this it?" Patin asked licking his parched lips.

"Yep, wake your sister and grab your satchel," Luften replied.

They jumped off the back of the cart and onto the dusty road. Luften adjusted his hat, "Time to move out."

"No water?" Patin moaned.

"You are welcome to drink up there with the horses, Patin. But I'm going to wait for fresh water at my house," Luften said as he headed down a road that seemed to lead to nowhere.

"Well how far is that?" Patin started after him.

Luften just let out a big sigh and kept walking, "If you move as fast as your mouth we should be there in no time!" he called over his shoulder.

Cows and horses grazed in the fields. The sun was already heating up the day and beads of sweat dripped down their faces and backs as they jogged down the road. Patin ended up eating most of the dust that trailed behind the rest of them.

"Why don't we just borrow one of those horses," he hollered. But no one was listening. As they came into town Patin mopped his wet brow with his palm, "and I thought Shaflann was small."

he remarked looking up and down the empty street.

"It's small—and quieter than I remember," Luften muttered.

They walked across Main Street and followed a narrow path a short distance to a solitary farm.

"Luften! Luften is home!" The front door burst open and out came an excited little boy.

"Adle," Luften hollered. He ran toward the small blond boy and scooped him up in his arms. A grin grew on Kief's face, it had hardly been a week since he'd left home, but the events of the past day made it seem like it had been years. He longed to be home and safe with his own brothers and for everything that was so wrong to be righted.

"Well hello there," Clarin smiled stooping down next to the bashful boy.

"Hello," he said shyly.

"Where's dad, Adle?" Luften asked.

"Inside," he tugged on Luften leading the way into the house.

"Oh Luften," his mother cried as they came through the doorway. She wiped her hands on her apron and squeezed him tightly.

"Luften my boy, you made it home safely," his father said in a thick accent Kief had never heard before.

"We've been worried about whether you'd heard the news. And here you are!" Mrs. Crawfd said. "And you brought some schoolmates, I see."

"Yes—but—you know about the attack?" Luften asked surprised.

"News came down right after it happened, a courier brought the dreadful report yesterday," Mr. Crawfd replied.

"Yesterday?" Luften asked puzzled, "We were just attacked yesterday near Dusk, how can anyone have traveled here faster than we did? What are you talking about?"

"The attack on Armp," his dad responded with a confused look on his face.

"Armp was attacked too?" Luften looked at Kief and then back at his father.

"What do you mean, 'too'?" Mr. Crawfd asked.

"Trite was attacked! Yesterday. The city was in flames when we left," Luften replied.

Mrs. Crawfd became distraught, "Oh, what are we to do? Are you okay? Are you hurt?"

"We're fine mother. Look at us—do we look hurt?"

Luften's dad was pacing the floor. He paused to look out the window at his fields of wheat.

"We must go," he turned resolutely to Luften.

Kief looked at Luften in surprise. He was sure it had been many years since Luften's family had come to Holpe's Island; judging by their well-tended fields and comfortable home.

"What? Go? Go where?" Luften was as taken aback as Kief at his dad's hasty conclusion.

"Back to the homeland," replied his father shaking his head. "Your mother and I have been discussing this since we received the news yesterday, but we couldn't make a decision until you came home. And now, with the attack on Trite, it's clear we have to go. The people of this land can't stop the Gars. They'll overrun the entire place. We should return home—to our home—now, before it's too late."

"But we can't run father, this is my home... and your home now too," Luften insisted, looking back out at his father's fields.

"I love our home here on Holpe's Island as much as you," his father walked to the window and looked out, "but it's useless to stay. Thousands will die and in the end we'll lose everything. We still have our home and family in Kritland. I think it's best to return, my boy."

"You all must be hungry," interrupted Luften's mother, obviously distressed by the matter.

"Thirsting to death," Patin sighed.

"Come, let me get you something," she motioned them into the kitchen. The smell of freshly cooked ham and biscuits reminded Kief how hungry he was and how long it had really been since he'd eaten last. Mr. Crawfd didn't join them. He sat heavily in his well-worn chair; his face creased with thought and worry.

As she led them into the kitchen, Mrs. Crawfd finally had a moment to notice how worn out and tattered everyone was. "Oh my dear, look at you," she said taking hold of Clarin's hand and leading her to the sink. "There's some soap—and let me get you a fresh towel to clean up."

Clarin scrubbed the dirt and dried specks of blood off her hands and arms.

"And you my boy, what happened? I thought you said no one was hurt Luften." She scolded him seeing Kief's bandaged arm.

Luften opened his mouth to protest when Kief interjected, "It's not bad at all, Mrs. Crawfd, Clarin fixed me up fine."

"Yes, come here Kief and let me take a look at that," Clarin motioned for Kief to come over to the sink as she finished drying her hands. Removing the bandage, she washed Kief's wound, "It's healing up nicely," she smiled looking pleased at her handiwork.

Kief noticed the cut had closed itself and there appeared to be no infection. Clarin pulled his arm up to the sink where she washed it and patted it dry with the towel before putting a fresh bandage on it.

"Another day and you won't even know it was there," Kief winked.

They sat around a cozy wooden table in the corner of the small, quaint kitchen. Tiny paintings, kitchen gadgets and glass vases brought from their home across the sea covered the walls and shelves. Mrs. Crawfd set a pitcher of water on the table and Patin downed two glasses letting out a sigh of satisfaction. She served them biscuits, ham and cheese, and fresh strawberries. Patin started in ravenously, on the food. Clarin nudged him to slow down.

"Oh, don't worry, my dear, there's plenty," Mrs. Crawfd smiled.

Patin gave Clarin a smug look and stuffed another half a biscuit into his mouth. Clarin rolled her eyes at him as Mrs. Crawfd put more slices of ham on the table.

There was too much to be said, and no way for anyone to know how to say it. And so they simply sat and ate in silence.

"Did people die?" Adle's little voice broke the tension.

"Adle, don't ask those kinds of questions," Mrs. Crawfd said, sharper than she'd expected.

"We left before the Gars came into the city," Luften replied patting his little brother's head, "but yes, I'm sure many died in the explosions and fires."

"Oh," whispered Adle as his innocent mind thought about what that meant.

"Luften, please…" Mrs. Crawfd protested.

Luften kissed his mother on the forehead and excused himself from the table, "Thank you for a wonderful meal, mother. I've missed your cooking."

"The safest way to High Valley will be on horseback," Mr. Crawfd said as Luften came back into the room. "I imagine the steam lines aren't running now. They can take a few of our horses, we won't need them all. And I suggest they leave as soon as possible. Who knows how quickly the Gar's infantry will move inland, but I wouldn't take any chances considering their speed thus far. We too must leave by dusk, Luften."

"By dusk!" Mrs. Crawfd cried overhearing Luften's dad from the kitchen above the clattering of the dishes she was cleaning, "how can we possibly leave by dusk?"

"Mrs. Crawfd, we don't have a choice," he called back firmly.

"But dad, where? The ports in Trite and Armp are overrun; no one can catch a ship there."

"We'll travel the countryside south-west to Jarmanea and catch a south-bound ship around Holpe's Island to Kritland."

"Surely they've attacked Jarmanea as well," Luften said.

"It's not likely. The cliffs are too high to hit the city with cannon fire and the port is too shallow to dock their armada. It's our best option, Luften. Your friends should make it to High Valley but I don't know how long they'll be safe there."

"Then you need to leave right away before the army passes through Trite and makes their way to Jarmanea. We'll help you and mom load your things."

His dad stopped, "What do you mean? You sound as if you aren't going with us?"

"I'm not."

The shattering of a dish was heard from the kitchen and his mother came through the door with a look of disbelief.

"Dad, my home is here," Luften said decidedly. "You and mom have your home in Kritland, but this is the only home I've ever known. I can't leave it now."

Luften's father stood silently a long while as a tear trickled down his weathered and worn cheek. But Kief could see from the look in Luften's eyes that he intended to stay.

"Luften, you are a man now. I can't force you to come to a

place you've never known to call home. This is where you belong. I see it in your eyes, I can respect that. My father said the same thing to me when I left so long ago for this land." He put his hands on Luften's shoulders squeezing him as he looked into his eyes, "We'll pray for your safety until this awful thing is over."

Luften's mother, overwhelmed by the decisions their family was being forced to make, threw her arms around Luften and held him tightly, sobbing into his shoulder.

"My love," Mr. Crawfd cleared his throat, "we'd better get a move on it or none of us will be going anywhere."

Mrs. Crawfd rushed out of the room.

"So you'll ride with your friends to High Valley?" Luften's dad turned to Kief.

"Uh…yes sir, we'll go there for now." Kief responded falteringly, "he'll be welcome in our home."

Kief had no idea what to do really; he only hoped his father would. He listened as Luften discussed with his father details of their escape. Mrs. Crawfd rushed back and forth between rooms haphazardly gathering treasured items in a sort of organized chaos. Clarin calmly followed her wrapping the fragile items in dish towels and linens. Patin, surprisingly, played with Adle distracting him from the difficulty that would surely lie ahead. The day will be over soon, Kief thought. And Mr. and Mrs. Crawfd and Adle will leave in their carriage in one direction. And we, along with Luften, will leave in another. And then, at his home, what would they do, where would they go? Would they end up fleeing across the sea as well? High Valley was secluded; maybe the militias from the other provinces would join forces in time to oust the Gars before they could take over Shaflann. Kief could only hope.

As the day passed on, the anxiety grew for everyone—in fear that the Gars were already moving inland and fear that they were moving toward Jarmanea. Kief helped Luften hitch the team to the family carriage while Clarin and Patin helped Mrs. Crawfd load it with the family's most precious things. Luften saddled his horse taking longer than was necessary; prolonging the time when he would have to say good-bye to his family. Mrs. Crawfd came out of her doorway for the last time, she turned and looked back. A flood of cherished memories overcame her and she broke down sobbing. Mr. Crawfd put his arm around her and walked her to the carriage. Luften opened the carriage door for his mother. With tears flowing down her cheeks, she hugged him not wanting to let go.

"I love you my dear," she whispered.

"I love you too mom. Don't worry, we'll be together again," he said softly in her ear.

"Watch out for each other, Luften. Be strong, be smart," Mr. Crawfd said hugging his son.

"I will dad," Luften squeezed his father, tears rolling down his cheeks.

As he and his mother climbed into the cart, Adle jumped up into his brother's arms crying and holding him. Luften's eyes filled with fresh tears, saying goodbye to his little brother was the hardest of all.

"I want to stay with you," he pleaded.

"It's too dangerous Adle; you're brave, but not big enough yet."

Luften lifted his little brother up and into the carriage and Mr. Crawfd clicked the horses forward down the lane.

"You take care of mom and dad, Adle."

"I will Luften," he hollered, "I'll find you!"

Luften watched the Crawfd cart roll down the lane and disappear into the horizon.

"I'm sorry Luften," Patin said.

"Not your fault," Luften replied wiping his eyes and walking back into the house. He came out a moment later carrying a pair of crescent side slingers—double barrel powder-fired weapons. He handed one to Kief along with a few crescents.

"And what do we need those for?" Patin objected.

"In case we cross paths with the army," Kief said putting the crescents in his satchel.

"Oh, we aren't going anywhere near that army!" Patin said.

"We might not have a choice," Clarin replied matter-of-factly.

"Let's get going," Luften said as he turned and somberly walked to their horses.

They rode hard for the rest of the day. When it was too dark and they were too tired to keep going, they found a secluded spot off the trail to camp.

Early the next morning they started back on their journey, stopping at the Montisse River to water their horses. By midday, they came to the outline of a tiny town in the distance.

"What town is that?" Clarin asked.

"Dayzier," Luften replied.

"Oh, we know Dayzier. We met a man there, a silver craftsman who makes jewelry," Patin shouted above the pounding hoofs of the horses.

"Good, let's pay him a visit and see if he's seen anything," Luften shouted back.

In town, where their path met up with the tracks to High Valley, a set of enormous gouges running alongside the tracks were torn into the ground.

"What happened here?" Patin asked.

"The Gars couldn't have come here that quickly, could they?"

Clarin turned to Kief.

"But what else could have made those tracks, they're huge," Patin pulled back on the reins as if that was as far as he was going to go.

"Come on," Kief prodded him, "There's only one way to find out. Mr. Homer will know."

They moved forward, their heads turning side to side, scanning the place. The town was deserted, not a soul in sight. Turning up the lane to Mr. Homer's house they were met with a ghastly sight. A lone figure was hanging by his neck from the tree in the front yard. Racing to the fence, Kief jumped off his horse and ran up the hill. His heart sunk when he saw it was him. Untying the rope he lowered his frail and empty body to the ground. Holding him in his arms, he stroked the old man's head. He noticed the trace of a faint smile on his face. Kief couldn't help but smile back, his own eyes blurry with tears.

The others circled around him starring in unbelief.

"Who would do something like this, to a defenseless old man?" Patin could hardly look at him.

"Monsters," Clarin said covering her mouth in shock.

"Let's get him buried," Luften said soberly.

They found a spade and laid the old man to rest in the shadow of the tree. A soft breeze moved through the branches as they stood silently, their heads bowed.

"We have to get to Shaflann before they do," Patin broke the silence in a tone of desperation.

"Well, we could use more supplies," Luften said, and turned to go inside.

"But we have to hurry," Patin urged him, following him into the house.

Kief couldn't get himself to go inside yet. He and Clarin stood next to the old man's grave looking out over the open prairie. A man carrying a bucket in each hand scurried down the lane that passed Homer's house toward town. Kief shouted out and ran toward him. But the man sped up his walk, sloshing water from the buckets. Kief finally caught up to him and when the man could see Kief was unarmed, he stopped.

"What happened?" he demanded.

Wide eyed, the man stuttered, "There were massive machines with big cannons on top and hundreds of soldiers on horses."

"Yes, but, why did they hang Mr. Homer?"

"They were searching the town for weapons. But crazy old Mr. Homer there," he pointed at the fresh mound of dirt where he lay, "he told them to leave or he'd sling them down! I thought maybe they'd leave the old man alone, what can a bent and worn man like him do against that huge armada of machinery anyway? But they didn't—they just marched right onto his house. Mr. Homer fired a few measly slugs out his window, and what do you know, that feisty old hoot killed two of them before they were able to grab him! But in the end," he shook his head, "they brought him out here and hanged him; I suppose to warn anyone who thought they might try resisting," he said hopelessly.

"What a fighter," Clarin looked back at his grave.

"Good for him," Kief said. He knew there was a reason, beyond the silver, that he liked the old man. "Single-handedly taking out two of the soldiers before they got him—I kind of wish I could have seen that. So, where are the other townsfolk?" Kief asked the man with the buckets.

"In hiding, where we should all be," he said his eyes darting around expecting the army to show up again at any moment.

"And the army, where is it now?"

He looked at Kief and Clarin and tightened his lips. Then he pointed towards the mountains, picked up his buckets and hurried down the path.

"The mountains?" Clarin looked at Kief puzzled. "Why would they go there?"

Kief shook his head and shrugged, "I have no idea."

"That man was scared stiff," Clarin said as they walked back up the hill.

Inside Mr. Homer's house, Kief wandered into his treasure room. The soldiers had destroyed everything and had taken all his masterpieces. Broken glass and debris was strewn all over the floor. Nothing of value remained. He saw the granite stone on the floor and picked it up. He remembered the old man's face with the funny tubular glasses on his head telling him to hang on to his stone. Kief told Luften about the soldiers and armored machines while he helped him pack up the supplies he'd gathered.

"Can we go now?" Patin's voice sounded loudly in the hallway.

Kief looked back at Homer's house as they rode down the lane. It didn't seem real. The old man hanged, his place ransacked; anger stirred in Kief's heart. This was not how things were supposed to be.

In town, the streets were empty, Kief and Luften were talking about the army's machines, when Patin burst out, "Someone's coming!"

Two riders were approaching on horseback. Grabbing their crescent slingers, Kief and Luften motioned for the other two to follow them as they ducked behind the nearest building.

"They're members of the Trite Militia." Luften said when he recognized their red and white uniforms, "I knew they'd be showing up soon."

"Hello," called the soldier in front as Luften came out to greet them, "I'm Captain Jonst of the Trite Militia!" He was leading the soldier in the rear by the reins, who was bent over and teetering atop his horse. "My comrade here, Sergeant Lind, has been injured and needs medical attention immediately. Can you direct me to the town physician?"

"I'm sorry Captain, we're not from this town but we can help you find someone," Luften offered.

Clarin jumped off her horse to examine the injured soldier.

"Are you aware of the invasions of Armp and Trite?" the captain asked. "We were headed to Suinville and then on up to High Valley to deliver a message from Governor Baldoon of Trite, when the Gars nearly killed the both of us! I need to get him patched up as soon as possible so we can be on our way, again."

"Yes, we were at Trite when it happened," Kief replied. "We're on our way home to High Valley and Shaflann to warn them right now."

"It's a very bad thing," he said. "Are you a nurse?" he asked turning to Clarin who had a concerted look on her face.

"I am," she replied. "And this man isn't going anywhere, he'll never make it."

"Oh, no, that won't do," the captain was clearly out of sorts. "It's of the upmost urgency," he insisted.

"I'm sorry but you're going to have to find another way to get your message there," Clarin said jerking the reins of the sergeant's horse from the captain.

Kief shot Luften a look of surprise at Clarin's boldness, "Can she do that?" he whispered. Luften just nodded and smiled.

Clarin turned the sergeant's horse around and started down the street of the barren town, calling out for a doctor. A few faces peered from their windows, but no one made any offer to help.

Exasperated she stomped her foot and yelled at Patin, who

was as dumbfounded as the rest of them at Clarin's impertinence, "Could you help just a little?" she pleaded.

At that the captain, along with Luften, Kief and Patin snapped to attention and began shouting out for help. Finally, a door opened slightly and a man's voice came from inside.

"Bring the soldier in here," he called.

Luften helped the captain take the soldier inside.

"We can deliver the message for you," Kief proposed to the captain when he returned.

He looked at Kief with penetrating eyes, scrutinizing him and his companions. He stared at them a good while.

"Very well," he finally agreed. "I guess I don't have much of choice. I must be on to Suinville alone to deliver my message there."

Reaching into his satchel he pulled out a letter tube and handed it to Kief. He grabbed it but the captain didn't let go. He shot Kief with a piercing stare, "You kids are nothing when compared to that army," he said. "Stay clear of them, and make sure this makes it to the governor. Our lives and possibly the future of Holpe's Island depend on it."

Kief swallowed hard. "We will," he replied.

"How big is this army?" Clarin asked.

"Oh," he said straightly, "it's unlike anything I've ever seen. Their transports are fully armored with cannons and slinger slots for the soldiers inside. They aren't powered by horse or steam; it's some sort of a combustion engine."

"Like the ship at the academy," Patin said amazed.

"Exactly," he pointed a finger at Patin. "The transports are traveling the road alongside the steam line track. Our best guess is that they're refueling the transport engines from tanks full of fuel, carried by the train."

"Yes, the man in town said they were heading toward the mountains—and the tracks go to High Valley. What could they possibly accomplish from the mountains?" Kief replied.

"We've been asking the same question. We're not sure; which is why it is so important that you deliver that letter," responded the captain.

"Don't you worry, we'll get this message to High Valley before they do," Kief assured him.

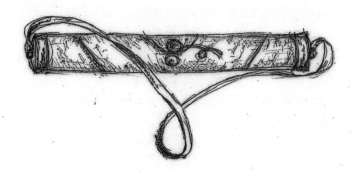

Couriers

They traveled late into the day following the disfigurations made in the road by the army and again found a secluded place to camp. Unloading his supplies from his saddlebags, Kief held the leather message tube in his hands. He wondered what was written in the message. If he read it, no one would know and how would it even matter if he did, he thought. Luften called out asking for the matches. The captain's riveting stare flashed into Kief's mind and he decided it was probably best to just deliver it to the governor. He stuffed the message tube back in his saddlebag.

After dinner, he walked with Clarin down to a nearby stream.

"What do you think is going to happen?" she stopped and knelt by the water to splash the dust off of her face.

"I don't know," Kief sat down on a rock next to her. "How does our militia stop those machines, we have nothing like them."

"Well, everything has a weakness, they just need to find it," Clarin replied running the cool water up her arms.

"I suppose. After everything we've seen the last couple of days, it still doesn't even seem real," Kief sighed looking up at the evening sky.

"I know," Clarin came over and squished next to him on the rock.

"And to think that no one in Shaflann knows what's happened and what's coming."

"I sure hope we can get there before the Gars do to deliver that message," Clarin reached down and pulled off her boots. Rolling her pants above her knees, she waded out into the stream.

"That looks like it feels good," Kief said.

"Oh yeah, I wish I could dip my whole body in."

"Maybe I'll join you," Kief slipped off his boots and waded out with her. "Ah, that does feel good," he said wiggling his toes in the cool water.

As he bent down to wash his face he slipped on a rock covered with moss and fell face first into the water. Clarin burst out laughing. Kief came up with a handful of water and splashed it at her.

"No!" She squealed throwing her arms in the air. At that, he splashed her again.

"Oh, that's it," she had a devious grin on her face as she started kicking walls of water at him. Giggling and dripping wet, they plopped back down on their rock together leaning against each others' backs to catch their breaths and dry off in the warm evening air. They sat quietly soaking in the warmth of each others' bodies.

"I can't imagine why they're going to High Valley," Clarin said trying to piece it together. "There's nothing up there but farm fields."

"It doesn't make any sense," Kief agreed. "Maybe the army's headed to Suinville and it just looks like they're going up the canyon. I'll bet they'll continue on to Jarmanea from there. It

would make more sense for them to capture the big lowland cities than the mountain villages don't you think?" Kief wondered.

"I hope not, poor Luften's family," Clarin shook her head as she pulled on her boots. Her hair brushed against Kief's arm. It was soft. "I'm exhausted," she sighed.

Kief lingered on the rock.

"Aren't you?" Clarin asked.

"I guess so," he said running a hand through his hair.

"Well then," she laughed, reaching out her hand to him, "we'd better go and get some sleep; we have another long day ahead of us tomorrow."

At early dawn, they were up and moving again. Toward the end of the day, they'd reached the mouth of the canyon.

"Looks like they're not going to Suinville," Luften pulled off his hat and wiped his brow with his sleeve.

"We can't go this way now, the army…" Patin objected as they started up the canyon.

"It's the only way to High Valley," Kief replied. "Really Patin, you've got to pull it together—I've never seen you back down from anyone."

"Words are one thing, slugs are something entirely different!"

"There's no talking yourself out of this one, that's for sure," Luften muttered.

Patin started in again, but Luften gave him a look that told him he'd better not.

In single file, they followed the road up the canyon alongside the tracks and the river; Patin bringing up the rear, still jumping at the slightest creak of a branch or flutter of a bird. They rode into Dusk. A faint rumbling hum rose in the air.

Patin yanked back on his horse's reins, "Do you hear that?"

In the same instant, everyone stopped their horses.

"Shhh," Luften hissed.

Patin insisted they move off the road.

"Would you be quiet," Luften growled gritting his teeth.

Patin clamped his mouth shut.

Kief tapped his heels to his horse's side moving him slowly forward. They continued cautiously on, Patin's fear of being left behind now keeping him extra close with the rest of them. Everyone's nerves were on edge. Nature had fallen silent all around so there was no sound to startle them; only the hum of the mysterious machines growing louder and louder. Kief could tell they were getting close, the vibrations from the roaring engines resonating in his chest and head. A noise like the sound of an immense river rolled down the canyon. The reverberations he was hearing along with the descriptions Kief had been given created an image of a menacing contrivance in his mind. He hoped that the picture he was creating in his head was more furious than the reality he was about to face.

When the noise became so loud that they knew the army was around the next bend, they found a spot to hide their horses and tied them to a tree. Hiding behind a rock, they caught their first glimpse of the army.

Two massive steel machines surrounded by soldiers on horseback were bringing up the tail-end of the procession. A pair of soldiers was perched atop manning two black cannons, one forward and one rearward. The machines were painted blue with a yellow sun, the Gar emblem, on the side. It was just like the painting on the hull of the ship Kief had seen through the hole it had torn in the academy wall. The paint was fresh, as if they'd been built specifically for the invasion of Holpe's Island. They were bigger than a train car with small slots like windows around all sides and four pairs of ribbed wheels that looked like they could crawl over any terrain. Kief could see soldiers moving around inside, a few slinger barrels stuck out through the slots. A plume of black smoke puffed up from a pipe sticking out the back in rhythm with the rumbling.

Kief touched his crescent slinger and then laughed, "My slinger against those things? It'd be like hunting bears with snow balls," he muttered to himself.

"Oh my," Patin heaved a fearful sigh. "There's no way we can get around that!"

Suddenly there was a noise behind them. Spinning around, they saw the steam train chugging up the canyon on the other side of the river.

"Back to the horses!" Luften ordered.

Bolting into the trees, they stood perfectly still next to their horses. Through the forest, the steam train came into view. In the engine car, soldiers with slingers stood on the lookout scanning the forest on both sides of the tracks. The train was pulling two flatbed cars. Each had two large tanks sitting on them.

"Do you think they saw us?" Patin whispered after it passed.

"They would've stopped if they had," Kief replied.

"Best to stay put for a moment," Luften motioned for them not to move. "There may be riders trailing behind the train."

They waited until they could hardly hear the train in the distance before they climbed on their horses and emerged from the grove. With dusk upon them, the canyon was shrouded in shadows. Kief spotted an eagle in the twilight. Probably the same eagle they'd seen when they came down the canyon—it seemed like ages ago now, Kief thought to himself.

"How many men do you think there are in those things?" Clarin asked.

"Maybe twenty, maybe thirty," Kief replied.

"It looks like they're some kind of transport for carrying their soldiers—and not just soldiers; did you see the size of those cannons?" Patin sputtered.

"We saw them," Luften responded tersely.

"Let's cross the river and skirt around them," Kief guided his companions to the river's edge.

"But the train is over there," Patin objected. "And those soldiers have slingers too."

"You wanna try and get around the transports and two hundred soldiers over here or just a handful over there?" Luften scowled.

"I see your point," Patin admitted.

Luckily it was late into Sun Rhythm and the river ran low. The water just touched the horses' underbellies as they plowed through the rushing river and up the bank on the other side.

Keeping to the trees, they came upon the train. It had stopped in a clearing though its engine was still running. Across the river and further up the path, the transports had stopped as well. The soldiers were dismounting, removing their gear and saddles from the horses.

"I think they've spotted us," Patin panicked, turning his horse to run.

"No, I think they're setting up camp for the evening," Luften said watching the army across the river.

"Let's circle around the train," Kief motioned them forward.

Just as they were passing it, Clarin whispered loudly, "Wait!"

"What?" Luften whispered sharply back. They were in too vulnerable a spot to stop now.

"Don't you remember the captain? He said they were refueling those transports with fuel that was being carried by the train."

"Yeah, and so?" Luften was annoyed at such a pointless

observation.

"Look," she said pointing to the transports and the train, "they're on opposite sides of the river right now. But see where the soldiers are setting up camp? The train joins back up with the transports there; now's our chance to sneak down, and see if we can drain the fuel from the tanks while the train is all alone."

"Wow! That's a crazy idea Clarin. But it's a good one—what do you think Kief?" Luften pulled his hat down snug on his head.

"My sister's lost her mind!" Patin interjected.

"I didn't ask you," Luften snapped.

"It's crazy alright," Kief replied smiling at her. "If they see us, we're dead for sure. But, I think we should do it."

"Come on, if we can stall them, it would give High Valley and Shaflann more time to prepare," Clarin persuaded.

Kief knew there was no army at High Valley that could be ready to fight at a moment's notice. A day or two could make all the difference for the townspeople. And maybe by that time the Holpe's Island militias would be assembled and ready to attack from behind. It was certainly worth a try anyway.

"Ok, Luften and I will sneak down and open the valves, you two wait here and keep a lookout," Kief directed.

"Yeah, what are we looking for?" Patin replied sarcastically, "something dangerous like a BIG ARMY!"

"Something like that," Kief smirked. His adrenaline started pumping and he was actually excited to carry out such a risky move.

"You're all lunatics," Patin muttered as Kief and Luften dismounted and disappeared into the trees.

With their crescent slingers in hand, they crept through the underbrush toward the train. Kief stepped carefully. He tried to calm his breathing; every shadow giving him a start as he squinted in the darkness. Making their way through the forest to the tracks, they crouched together behind the cover of a large pine tree. Two soldiers stood near the front of the train, each holding a heavy slinger strapped over their shoulder. A single lantern from inside the main cabin cast its glow out the open door, the long shadows of the soldiers extending into the forest. A third soldier with a lantern walked straight toward them. They froze as he came up to the tree where they were hiding. They raised their slingers and prepared to make a break for it.

He stood a few paces away and they got an up-close look at the enemy. Atop his head was a blue helmet that came down both sides of his face covering his ears. On the left side was the emblem of the sun that was on the transports. His broad shoulders were covered with shiny metal plates that looked more for decoration than protection. Slung over his left shoulder diagonal across his big chest was a thick gold strap filled with spare crescents for his heavy slinger. Kief quickly counted the crescents; there were nine which gave him eighteen shots. That was a whole lot more than Kief's own two shots and his one extra crescent in his satchel. Over his right shoulder was the leather strap of his heavy crescent side slinger which hung under his arm. The soldier's jacket and pants, tailored to fit him perfectly, were also blue elaborately decorated with yellow trimmings. Around his waist was strapped a dagger as well as other weapon-looking things that Kief didn't recognize.

When the soldier was so close that they could see his eyes, Kief recoiled ready to bolt. But the soldier stopped, relieved himself, and then continued back to circling around the train.

"Shew, that was close!" Kief whispered, his heartbeat thudding in his ears.

"Yeah, just watch where you step," Luften joked.

Kief and Luften sat crouched for some time evaluating their chances of the plan actually working. There were four tanks in total, two on the first car and two on the second car. Their diameter was nearly as wide as the train car and they were a good arm's length taller than Kief. Attached at the base of each of the tanks was a long hose coiled up on the deck.

"Looks like there's a valve at the end of each of those hoses," Luften concluded. "If we turn the valve and drape it over the edge to the ground, the fuel should drain out quietly."

"I guess it's now or never," Kief said, shrugging his shoulders, and they moved toward the steam train.

Before they were clear of the brush, one of the soldiers hollered. Kief stopped dead in his tracks, fearing he'd been spotted. Then, the two soldiers that had been standing next to the line, climbed aboard and it began to slowly chug forward.

"Looks like the train is crossing back over the river to join up with the army," Luften said.

"Come on!" Kief called.

They ran to catch the moving train. Kief jumped up on the first car and Luften the second as it began to pick up speed. Wasting no time, Kief twisted open the valve. It was stiff but turned easily. The translucent fuel glistened in the moonlight as it gushed out of the hose and onto the ground. Hanging the end of the hose over the back edge of the car, he moved to the second tank and turned open the valve. The sound of the assault transports grew louder as the steam train approached the army. Kief tried to stay hidden from the guards riding up front in the engine car. With his tanks draining, he crossed over to the second car where Luften was having trouble opening the second valve.

"What's going on?" Kief asked in a panic, "We've gotta go, the train's about to cross back over the river!"

"The valve is open but nothing is coming out," Luften responded.

"Leave it—let's just go!"

"Knock on the tank," Luften asked.

Kief knocked, there was a hollow echo, "It's empty already."

The rumbling of the transports was nearly upon them. They looked up to see that the train had begun to cross the small bridge over the river.

"Jump!" Luften called out.

They leaped off the back. The train was going fast enough, now, that they were knocked down as soon as their feet touched the ground and they tumbled through the fuel soaked grass. Picking themselves up they looked back and watched the train meet up with the army. In the moonlight, they could see three of the transports and at least fifty men and their horses.

They retreated quickly back into the forest to find their friends. Kief was right on Luften's heels as they worked their way through the brush. It wouldn't take long for the Gars to discover that someone had drained their fuel supply. The thought of a hundred angry soldiers chasing them doubled their pace. They called out as loudly as they dared in the dark forest trying to find Patin and Clarin. The sound of horses coming through the brush, made them stop. They stooped down in a low spot and raised their slingers.

"Kief, Luften," Clarin's soft voice penetrated the darkness.

"Over here," Kief called quietly.

"We have to get out of here fast," Luften grabbed his horse's reins from Patin.

"Did you do it?" Patin asked anxiously looking around.

"We did it alright," Kief answered swinging up on his horse. He looked at Clarin, "We found their weakness."

Clarin smiled and then noticed the shine on their clothes, "What did you do—take a shower in it?"

"You could say that," Kief replied wiping at his arms.

They rode at a swift clip through the forest circling around the soldiers, the double moons Dot and Otoo lighting their way. The transport engines began to shut down one by one. With the engines silenced, the conversation and commotion of the soldiers filled the air and then it all fell quiet with a few men shouting. They were too far away to hear what they were saying but it didn't really matter, they were speaking a different language anyway.

"They must have discovered the fuel," Luften said, "They'll be looking for us now."

"Follow me," Kief clicked his horse and led them across the mountainside.

Eventually they came to a clearing where Kief guided them back across the river to the main path. Once on the path, they kicked their horses into a gallop not looking back. The sound of the soldiers searching for them faded behind them.

After riding for some time, both riders and horses were exhausted. They agreed they were far enough ahead to stop and rest for awhile. Riding up a small adjoining canyon, they found a place to hide and rest. They situated themselves on their blankets under the stars. Moonlight cascaded through the trees as the branches moved in the wind. Kief looked up at the South Star shining brightly. It split a patch of clouds drifting slowly through the dark sky.

"What a day," Patin sighed for once having nothing left to complain about.

Kief felt like they had been running for weeks and it was far from over. Again he thought about the message they were carrying and wondered what it said. He was growing more curious. Had he not been so tired he probably would have retrieved it from his saddlebag. Guess he'd know soon enough, he thought. It sounded like the militia was putting together a plan and he wished he could be part of it.

His mind grew heavy and he could no longer keep a coherent train of thought. It wandered off, thinking of Clarin who was resting quietly a few steps from him. He could hardly hear her breathing. The last thing he remembered was hearing Patin shifting and groaning trying to get comfortable. And then he drifted off into a heavy sleep.

The rumbling of transports startled Kief awake.

"They're moving again!"

Clarin and Luften sat up quickly but Patin stirred and then rolled over.

"Patin, wake up!" Clarin said shaking her brother.

He slowly opened his eyes and then sprung upright, "Are they coming?"

"Yes, they're coming! And we have to go—again," Kief couldn't help smiling as he strapped his blanket onto the back of his horse. "You keep things interesting that's for sure, Patin."

"What?" Patin looked at his friends blankly.

"Nothing, just get your things and let's get outta here," Luften said shaking his head.

Riding hard, they didn't hear or see the army again. When they reached the valley, Kief veered them off the main path to the city of High Valley and started to follow the old Tubin Road up to Shaflann Bucken.

"Where are you going?" Clarin asked stopping her horse.

"The army's stranded, they aren't going anywhere," Kief reasoned. "We have time to warn our families first, and then we'll be back by Dusk."

"But the captain said to deliver it immediately," Luften objected.

"I know, I know. It won't take long. We'll warn our families and then ride right back down to High Valley after."

It made sense to Patin, he had no protests, but Clarin stayed stubbornly where she was. "It wouldn't take long to deliver it either—and we could be to Shaflann long before the day is over." She put her hands on her hips.

"Come on Clarin, I want to see you home safely..."

"I want to see me home safely!" Patin butt in.

"Oh, yes, of course—you too," Kief allowed. "Luften and I will come back down as soon as you two are home."

"I'm torn," Luften said sarcastically, "I agree with Clarin that the message should be delivered now, but I hate not to see Patin delivered home safely, either."

"There," Patin said smugly, "Let's go home, Clarin."

Clarin just glared at her little brother.

Luften sighed, "Well, what are we waiting for, Kief. Let's get these two home and then we'll ride back down."

Reluctantly Clarin followed Kief to Shaflann. Finally feeling safe Patin became his old self again, citing facts about nothing important to Luften; and Luften didn't mind—because at least he wasn't whining. Crossing Tubin Bridge, Patin told Luften all about Kief's jumps off the bridge. And for the first time Luften sided with Patin; he thought Kief was crazy too.

Gilend Hill

They came to Kief's home first. Clarin insisted they stop and Kief obliged her this time, she wanted to hear what Mr. Stadd had to say. Needless to say, his family was shocked at their arrival and the news of the invasion; the burning city, Luften having to say goodbye to his family, Homer's death, the message for the governor, and the daring feat of draining the fuel tanks in the canyon.

"You kids did that?" Mr. Stadd asked incredulously.

"It was Clarin's idea," Patin blurted out.

"Well, it was a very good idea," Mr. Stadd sat back in his chair, his forehead wrinkled in concentration. "How could this be? And you're sure it's the Gars?"

"I saw their flag, dad, and the ships..."

"Oh, right, their flag—of course. And the submersible ships, that sounds like something the Gars would invent." Mr. Stadd sat for a moment tapping his finger on the arm of the chair. Then he leaned forward, "We need to get everyone assembled and hold a town meeting. It's certainly going to take more than the

High Valley Militia to stop them. Patin, Clarin, your parents just got home a few days ago—luckily for them, the Gars must not have reached Condull before they left. Go home and tell them what's happened and that we'll have a town meeting at Dusk's 2nd Cadence in the arena.

"Kief, you and Luften run and tell Director Kir-Trad and ask him to open the arena for the meeting. I'm going to Mayor Chatton's. You two meet me there," he said.

"Wait, dad... the message," Kief pulled the letter tube from his satchel.

Mr. Stadd paused, "Bring the message to Mayor Chatton's, he'll get it down to the governor."

"Of course, I should have thought of that!" he turned to Luften.

"That should work," Luften agreed.

Clarin turned to leave with Patin, "So I'll see you at the arena," she waved.

"See you in a bit," Kief said.

He and Luften left right away for the school. Passing the academic houses, they crossed the yard to the Director's Mansion. Up the wide stone steps, Kief knocked on the heavy door.

After a moment, the house keeper opened the tiny leaded window situated just above the knocker in the middle of the door and peered out, "Yes, can I help you?"

"Is the director in? We need to see him, it's an emergency," Kief asked.

The house keeper huffed, "Very well, come in and have a seat. I'll call him." He pulled open the door and let them inside.

They sat on one of the sumptuous couches and waited anxiously for the director to come. Luften looked around at the elaborately papered walls hung with beautiful paintings and ornate lamps and

finishings. Decorative moldings and cornices over the doors and windows defined the room.

"Nice place," Luften mumbled.

After what felt like a very long wait, the director strolled down a wide hallway to the waiting room. He was already dressed for a quiet evening at home, in his orange silk robe and rabbit-fur slippers. Kief and Luften stood as he entered the room.

"You're back from the academy, did it just not suit you—what seems to be the problem Kief?" he asked stroking the lapels of his robe with his finely manicured hands.

"The Gars have attacked the Island, Mr. Kir-Trad!"

"The Gars attacking us, how do you know this?" he replied skeptically.

"When we were there—at the Merchant Academy! They attacked Trite, the academy; the whole city was in flames. There's an army coming up Temblin Canyon right now. They'll reach High Valley within days," Kief exclaimed.

"Here, in days?" Mr. Kir-Trad sat down in one of the big chairs, thinking. "Sit," he said, "let's see if we can't figure out a reasonable way to approach this conundrum."

Kief and Luften sat back down, "My dad thinks we should hold an emergency town meeting in the arena." Kief said catching his breath. "He's going to talk with the mayor right now."

"Oh, now there's a start. Yes, the mayor will definitely know whether a town meeting is in order. But, this evening? Perhaps tomorrow when he has had time to talk with his ministers and plan a course of action."

"But sir, you should've seen what they did to Trite! And they took all the weapons from the townsfolk in Dayzier," he insisted.

"Well, Dayzier is such a tiny little dot of a town... but that's beside the point," he waved his hand shooing his distracted

thought away.

"But, Mr. Kir-Trad, we really need as much time to prepare as we can get," Kief appealed.

"Ah, very well then, I'll alert the academy warden and have him open the arena. You boys go on home now."

"Thank you, director," Kief replied.

"He's a strange man," Luften said as they mounted their horses.

"He's a little quirky like that, but I really liked every class I had with him. He knows so much about everything. He's a bit pious but I don't mind. Tarc sure does, though!" Kief laughed at the thought of Tarc mimicking him.

On their way to the mayor's, Kief and Luften knocked on doors telling the townsfolk of the meeting. By the time they reached his home, Kief's dad was just finishing discussing the crisis with the mayor.

"Let's be careful and not do anything rash; the High Valley Militia, even with all the support we could garner, doesn't have the strength to oppose the Gars, you know. We'll need to come to a rational solution so that people don't get hurt. It's my job to make sure that everyone's safety is first and foremost."

"Yes, of course, Mr. Mayor."

"Oh, hello boys," the mayor said turning to Kief and Luften as they entered the room, "I understand you have a message for the governor."

"Yes," Kief responded reaching into his satchel and handing the letter tube to Mayor Chatton, finally relieved to have passed on the message.

Taking the tube the mayor praised them, "Well done, your father here has told me how brave you boys have been. I'm very impressed with your valiance. We'll be sure to get this to

the governor right away," he said smacking the tube in his hand. "I'll meet you at the arena with my ministers, Mr. Stadd?" he said turning to Kief's dad.

Mr. Stadd shook the mayor's hand firmly, "Yes, Mr. Mayor. Thank you."

By the time they left the mayor's house word had already spread like wild fire on a dry prairie; the streets were filled with people making their way to the arena. There was so much commotion in the streets, it seemed like midday at the market; clopping horses' hooves and the rattle of cart wheels, and people shouting above it all. At the arena, everyone was crowding at the entrance. Kief's heart thudded with excitement that they'd arrived in time to warn the town. Now he was doubly pleased that they'd drained the fuel from the tanks. What a great idea, Clarin, he thought as he pushed his way through the crowd.

Inside, they gathered onto the main floor and up in the stands, some already carrying side slingers ready to defend themselves. The mayor and his ministers were all there along with Director Kir-Trad and other town officials.

Mr. Stadd found Bonds, the mine superintendant, and recounted everything that had happened to Kief and his friends. Bonds was Kief's favorite.

"Good to see you again Kief," Bonds smiled heartily as he shook Kief's hand, "though unfortunate under such circumstances."

"There you are," Clarin grabbed Kief's arm.

"Clarin, you made it," he smiled at her. "Where's Tarc? I haven't seen him yet."

"Yeah, I don't know. Patin and I stopped at his house, but no one was home." She squeezed in next to him on the bench. The arena was as full as it was at any urt match.

"Quiet down everyone, please quiet down," Mayor Chatton

raised his hands and shouted above the noise of the crowd.

"I guess our idiot officials are gonna tell us what to do," Bonds grumbled out of the corner of his mouth.

Kief snickered. Bonds was never short of something to say about their officials; how they were always looking out for themselves and nobody else. Kief didn't really see it that way. He knew they were full of themselves, but what official wasn't. Shaflann Bucken was a nice town and they kept it running smoothly.

"As you have all heard, there have been several unconfirmed attacks against our Confederation of Holpe's Island. It has been rumored that the invaders are the Gars—though no one has verified that yet either."

Kief and Luften looked at each other, jaws dropped in disbelief.

"Unbelievable," Clarin whispered.

The mayor continued, "I think it best that we refrain from any action until we understand if these accounts are correct, who this is, and exactly what they want."

The arena grew loud again as they talked amongst themselves.

"What does he mean wait?" Kief nudged his dad. "We rushed here so we had time to prepare; now we're going to do nothing."

"If it's the Gars, we can be certain of their reason, they want our land," someone shouted from high up in the arena.

At this, the crowd erupted in disorder.

"If they do to us what I heard they did to Trite, there won't be anything left of Shaflann," another joined in.

"We don't know that," the mayor bellowed above the confusion. "Negotiating is the best option. The High Valley Militia along with every one of us isn't enough to stand up to them, talking is our only choice at this point."

"I agree with the mayor," said Minister Sland. He raised his hands to calm the crowd.

"Here, here," shouted the other ministers clapping and nodding in approval.

"Mr. Mayor," Kief's dad interrupted. "It's clear that the invaders—and we can be certain it was the Gars—had no intentions of negotiating with Trite before they destroyed the city and took thousands of lives."

"Well, Mr. Stadd," the mayor looked down his nose condescendingly, "we can't be certain exactly what happened now, can we. I'm sure whatever negotiations there were would not have been made known to just anyone before the attack. You know how young people can exaggerate," he shot an insolent smile at Kief. "It's nothing personal young man. I simply think we're being a little too hasty. We haven't received an official account."

Kief knew there was obvious animosity between his dad and the mayor since the mayoral elections two years earlier; Mr. Stadd had been a strong supporter of the incumbent. And now it seemed the mayor felt the same way toward Kief as he did his father.

"That's absurd," Bonds growled to Mr. Stadd loud enough for everyone around them to hear. "How can we just assume they tried to talk with the authorities in Trite? We've done nothing to incite their attack."

The eruptions from the arena became frenzied as men began waving their slingers in the air and shouting to fight the Gars.

"Calm down folks! As I discussed with Mr. Stadd earlier today, your safety is paramount to my concern! Isn't that so Mr. Stadd?"

Kief's dad nodded.

Bonds moaned, "And here we go. Watch this..."

"Exactly. We're in no position to fight!" he yelled emphatically,

"We have brave men, to be sure," he gestured to the men waving their slingers around the arena, "but you'll be no match for a trained army. Our only option is to attempt a peaceful negotiation."

"I wonder what a peaceful negotiation looks like to the Gars; giving them our land?" Kief said sarcastically to his dad.

He gave his son a defeated half-grin.

Mayor Chatton continued, "We should shortly hear from Governor Mon-Dirk's emissary. I suggest we not make a decision at this point and follow the lead of High Valley.

"Now, let's everyone return to our homes and wait. We'll send a dispatch to High Valley to determine their plans and hopefully have word by tomorrow at Dawn."

Before Mr. Stadd could counter the mayor, the crowd began to disperse and file out of the arena.

"And poof!" Bonds burst his fists open like an explosion, smearing a big grin across his face, eyes wide, "Magic."

How'd he do that, Kief wondered as he followed his dad to where the mayor and his ministers were seated.

"Gentlemen, we must encourage Governor Mon-Dirk to prepare his militia and the townspeople to fight," Mr. Stadd tried to persuade. "The Gars weren't merciful to Trite, why would they treat us any differently?"

"We can't stand against them!" the mayor retorted sharply. "My ministers and I," he said piously, composing himself, "feel the best approach is negotiation. That will be our recommendation to High Valley. Now then, we need to prepare our dispatch," he excused himself curtly.

"That's ludicrous; bowing down to the Gars," Bonds was irate.

"So that's it?" Kief asked his dad, dumbfounded.

"Mr. Stadd, the four of us barely escaped Trite and we had

something of a head start. Here, we're trapped by the mountains, there's nowhere to go," Luften said.

"Nowhere but up," Kief replied. He had explored the mountains so much; he knew at least that would be an advantage against the Gars and their giant machines.

"Yes, yes, I'm at a loss," Mr. Stadd frowned. "I guess we'll go home and figure something out."

"I've never seen my dad like that, Clarin," Kief said as he walked her home.

"I have a feeling we're going to see a lot of things we've never seen before," she sighed.

"Right, like who'd have ever thought to see me sneak straight into a hostile army's camp, carrying nothing more than a little crescent slinger to defend myself, and ruin their evening," he laughed, "that was a great idea, Clarin."

"Thanks," she smiled.

At home, Kief's dad called the family around the long oak kitchen table.

"Well," he sighed, "that meeting went nothing like I had hoped. I'm afraid the mayor proved me right tonight—I have no reason to respect that man." He sighed again, "He made no effort to help our town defend itself. Based on what Kief and Luften have told us, I fully expect that the Gars will attack without hesitation. I'll do what I can to persuade the Governor of High Valley to fight, but I certainly don't carry any weight there and with our own town leaders pushing for negotiations..."

"So what do we do, dad?" Atela asked biting her lower lip.

"We need to be ready to leave. If the Gars attack High Valley, we'll know we have to go."

"But where daddy?" Myri tugged on his arm.

"Oh Myri, we'll have to go through the mountains and make

our way all the way east to Point Shar. Maybe by that time, Councilman Kyedon will have gained enough support from the other council members to organize a central army to oppose the Gars. If not," he said sadly, "we may have to flee the island."

"Why is no one fighting dad?" Balt asked.

"We should fight Balt, and I'm hoping the regional militias are doing the best they can to gather together, but the Gars attacked with such surprise it's hard to gain the upper hand after the fact. And, if the Gars accept High Valley's surrender, that movement could lead to the downfall of the entire island."

"Does the mayor really believe he can negotiate with the Gars?" Mrs. Stadd asked astonished at their decision.

"Yes, he does, and all his ministers with him."

"So, what are we waiting for?" she started pulling a few essential items from the pantry, "Balt, Curchin, run out to the barn and bring in a few crates and then you two run upstairs and start packing. And Klar, we need to go down and pick up my mother tomorrow."

"Yes, I was planning on leaving at Day to do that."

Kief couldn't believe that for the second time, in just about as many days he was sitting around a kitchen table talking of leaving home. He had hoped they would be safe in Shaflann and that the militia would have been taking care of things by now. When he thought about it, he didn't really know what he had expected to happen. He just wanted it to all go away. He didn't want to be packing to leave his home for anywhere but the academy—he didn't have anything to pack anyway, almost everything he owned was blown to bits and probably at the bottom of a pile of rubble that used to be the academy. And how was his mom so optimistic; even as they were facing leaving their home and making what was sure to be a grueling journey to the coast. He'd never known her

to be intimidated by a challenge, but this was unlike anything he'd ever imagined.

Kief went upstairs. He stood looking around the room, watching his brothers pack. They talked casually about what they should take, almost like they were going to be going on some great adventure. Kief decided they were just too young to really know what they were up against. But he knew. He'd seen it first hand; and it was no adventure. He didn't say anything though—he'd let them have their innocence as long as they could.

His brothers finished packing and went downstairs. Kief was sitting on his bed talking to Luften when he heard a knock at their front door.

A moment later Tarc walked into his room, "I leave for the day and the whole town falls apart."

"Where have you been?" Kief jumped up glad to see him.

"Down in High Valley at my cousins', we just returned. What a day to pick for a visit, huh? Who's this?" he asked pointing at Luften.

"This is Luften, from the academy."

"Tarc is it?" Luften shook his hand.

"Yeah. This is crazy! When they said the Gars had attacked Trite, I didn't believe them. I guess you saw the whole thing?"

Kief excitedly told Tarc all about it. This was something Tarc could get into. He listened intently as Kief recounted everything.

"Nice move draining those tanks," Tarc clenched his fists and swung at the air, "So what do you think? We can take 'em, right?"

"If we can get High Valley to fight, but the mayor wants to wait and try to negotiate with them."

"What's that going to do?" Tarc protested.

"Exactly. Dad says we should make a break for the mountains

if they attack High Valley. We've been packing all evening. You and your mom should probably do the same thing and then stop back by in the morning."

"Running like a rabbit doesn't suit me, but I guess it's our only option if the army is as big as you say," Tarc scowled. "Mom and I will be ready. I should get word to my cousins tomorrow as well," he said and rushed out the door.

It was well after Dark before they all lay down for a short sleep. Luften made his bed on the wool rug in Kief's room. Kief lay awake for some time thinking about escaping through the mountains. It could take weeks. There were plenty of game and wild berries in the forest to survive on until they made it down to the eastern plains. The army would never find them in the woods.

At breakfast the next morning, Bonds stopped by. Mr. Stadd answered the door, "What's the word?"

"A message arrived early this morning, the governor has agreed to surrender!" Bonds shook his head. "A carriage with a surrender embassy is making its way toward the army now." He stepped in and Mr. Stadd closed the door behind him. "They carry an invitation to the Gars' Commander to enter the city and meet at Town Center to discuss the terms of a truce agreement!"

"Oh, that's disturbing indeed," Mr. Stadd exhaled as he walked back into the kitchen.

"So?" Kief looked at Bonds.

"Surrender," Bonds replied pulling out a chair and sitting down with the most disgusted look on his face, "They're delivering the surrender proposal shortly."

"I don't believe it!" Luften ran his fingers through his hair in complete dismay.

"So where's the embassy now?" Kief asked.

"Driving to Temblin Canyon as we speak."

There was a brief silence in the room then Mr. Stadd turned to Bonds, "We need to know how the embassy is received by the army."

Kief knew what that meant. If the messengers were killed or captured, then it would be clear that the Gars weren't interested in negotiating. If there was an exchange and the messengers were permitted to return to the city, it would mean the Gars had accepted the invitation.

"Dad," Kief jumped out of his seat, "Luften and I can ride down Tubin road to Gilend Hill; from there we can see all the way down to the mouth of the canyon."

"Yes, you should be able to see how the embassy is received and still be at a safe distance," Bonds thought it was a good idea.

"Well, considering your stunt the other evening. Just get back here as soon as you know something."

"We will, c'mon Luften."

Kief sprinted up the stairs to get his spectascope and they ran out the back door to the barn. As they readied their horses, Tarc came around the corner.

"Morning Kief, Luften. Mom's ready, what's the plan?"

"Bonds just brought notice that High Valley is surrendering," Luften said jerking his saddle off the rail. "They've sent out a surrender embassy to meet the army."

"So they're going to raise the red flag are they? Cowards," Tarc said feeling the same indignation.

"Yeah, hard to believe isn't it?" Kief threw his saddle on Natch. "We're riding to Gilend Hill now to have a look. Take that horse there, it's one of Luften's, his name is Sarjen," Kief pointed to a gray speckled stallion.

"Oh he's a beaut," Tarc said admiring the large, calm, horse.

"He's yours," Luften said, already taking a liking to Tarc's directness.

"Really? ... Thanks," Tarc said overjoyed to finally have his own horse. "How come you never did anything like that for me, Kief? And here I thought you were my best friend—but I guess it's Luften," he slapped Luften on the back.

He smiled, "The saddle's over there on the left, the dark one with the silver boot loops."

Tarc took a moment to stroke his new steed.

"Ok," Luften prodded, "You'll have time to get acquainted later, hurry and saddle him up so we can get going."

"Right," Tarc led Sarjen out of the stable and strapped on his saddle.

They galloped down Tubin Road. Natch led out in long strides; he was the fastest horse in the mountains. Kief rubbed his neck happy to be riding him again.

How stupid of High Valley, trying to negotiate with the Gars! They half deserve it if they are attacked, he thought. As he passed a few townsfolk rushing around in obvious confusion he realized it was their leaders, not them, that had made the foolish decision. It sure wasn't fair for them to have to pay the price of their leaders' idiocy. Kief was glad his father wasn't going to hang around.

At the top of Gilend Hill, they saw the army coming through the mouth of Temblin Canyon.

"Wow," Tarc exclaimed, "would ya look at that!"

Riding up the canyon they had caught glimpses of the army but now it was in full view and it was a menacing sight! The assault transports were ominous even from a distance. They were surrounded with tents and hundreds of soldiers, their horses gathered in one location, saddles off, and grazing.

"That's a strange place to set up camp, right there in the open with no protection," Luften commented.

"Do they look like they need protection?" Tarc joked.

"They must finally be out of fuel and waiting for the train to return," Kief said.

"Or maybe they're preparing to attack the city," Luften replied.

"Well, if they're out of fuel," Kief frowned, "now would be the best time for the militia to attack."

"I'm ready," Tarc puffed out his chest and beat it a few times with his fists.

They sat on a rock overlooking the valley watching the army. There wasn't much activity for awhile and then they noticed a carriage coming from High Valley toward the canyon. Kief turned his spectascope on it.

"What do you see?" Tarc asked impatiently.

"It's the messenger carriage alright. I can see the Governor's Crest on the side."

The sound of horses coming down the trail behind them made them jump. Kief almost dropped his spectascope.

"Your dad told us you were here," Sefrana whispered.

"Sheesh, could you have picked a better time to sneak up on us like that?" Tarc criticized.

"What do you mean sneak? We rode down the trail plain as day. You were just so intent that you didn't hear us till we were almost right on top of you," Patin retorted. "So what's going on?"

"What's it look like?" Tarc grumbled.

"I don't know, Kief's the one with the spectascope," he shrugged his shoulders sarcastically.

"Our leaders are bowing to the Gars," Luften replied nicer than usual; but he wasn't looking at Patin, he couldn't keep his eyes off Sefrana.

They climbed off their horses and Sefrana introduced herself.

Luften stuttered a feeble hello. Kief had to admit, her red curls and blue eyes could leave any boy speechless. But she'd always been just one of the guys to them. Patin, Tarc and Kief watched in amusement.

"So… where're you from?" Sefrana asked before the silence became too awkward.

"Kosh…it's a small town outside of…mmm…Trite."

"And your family, are they still in Kosh?"

"No, they escaped to Jarmanea," he began to recover, "they'll be boarding a ship for Kritland. That's my father's homeland."

"I guess you don't know if they made it?" her tone dropped.

"My father's a smart man, he'll get them there."

"I hope so, this is all so terrible. Thanks for getting these three home," she reached out and squeezed his arm.

Luften blushed.

Kief had seen enough, he returned to looking through his spectascope. As the governor's carriage drew near the army, a group of twenty or so soldiers rode out to meet it. Circling the carriage they pointed their heavy slingers at the embassy. The carriage door opened and a man stepped down.

"C'mon, details, Kief" Tarc prodded.

"Someone's stepping out of the carriage," Kief replied focusing. He paused, "It can't be…"

"What can't be," Tarc was ready to rip the spectascope from his hands.

"It almost looks like the governor!"

"No way," Patin exclaimed, "they'd never send the governor, they'll kill him."

"The army's leader... and two soldiers are approaching him."

They strained their eyes hoping somehow to see what Kief was describing.

"They're dismounting now... The leader is walking toward the governor..."

"Oh don't watch Kief," Sefrana tensed, "They're going to kill the governor!"

"It's not possible!" Kief uttered in astonishment.

"What's not possible?" Patin asked, now as close to him as Tarc.

"The Gar leader just gave the governor a big hug!"

"What are you talking about?" Luften replied, "Let me see that!"

Kief handed Luften the spectascope. Tarc and Patin watched it reaching out their hands, befuddled that they weren't next. Luften peered through the lens.

"It's as if they were long time friends." He passed the spectascope to Tarc.

"I guess they want to negotiate," Patin said.

"Negotiate, they're not just negotiating. They look like they're getting ready to have a big fat reunion!" Tarc fumed.

"Ok, maybe the governor offered them a truce to save the city; maybe he did a good thing, right?" Sefrana tried to find something positive about it.

"Surrendering your city to the Gars isn't a good thing," Luften said straightly.

"But if you save everyone in the city..."

Tarc cut her off, "Better to be dead than live under Gar rule."

Kief stared at the stranded army. "Now is the perfect time to strike," he muttered. Why did they surrender? Why did the governor come out to greet them like that? None of it made sense.

"What's happening now?" Luften asked Tarc who was fixed on the army with the spectascope.

"The governor has climbed back in his carriage and it looks like they're headed back to the city."

"C'mon," Kief grabbed Natch's reins and jumped back on his horse, "Let's go tell my dad."

The hammering hoofs of their horses echoed in the canyon as they raced across Tubin Bridge. Kief's heart pounded in his chest. The rushing wind cooled his sweating brow. He had an eerie chill as he thought on the events that were unfolding.

At home, Kief gave his dad and Bonds the news.

"Send the governor, they wouldn't risk that," Mr. Stadd was baffled.

"That's what we thought and we waited for the worst but then the Gar leader hugged him!" Kief said, still not believing what he'd seen.

"Mon-Dirk, that scum," Bonds cursed. "Give the city away with a cheerful hug, that's an official for you. He's trying to get something out of it, mark my words," he pounded his fist on the table.

Kief's dad stared out the window in shock at the news.

"What do we do now, dad?" Kief asked.

"I don't know what to do. Here we were, preparing for a flight and now it looks as if they've really accepted the governor's offer—whatever that was." Mr. Stadd paused, "Bonds, you and I need to go see the mayor. I want to know what surrender means for us."

"Thank you boys... and ladies," Bonds said making a short bow to the girls. "If we save this land, it'll be because of people like you," he patted Kief on the shoulder.

"Yes, thank you," Mr. Stadd rushed out the door, "We'll be back soon."

"Good luck dad," Kief called as they walked down the path.

"What are we going to do?" Sefrana asked desperately as the door closed.

"Well, if they aren't going to attack, maybe there's no reason to run," Patin said.

"We need to fight," Luften insisted. "Where are the other militias? We gave them plenty of time for at least the provinces on this side of the island to have united. We're losing precious time."

"I agree, we need to hit them now while they're just sitting there!" Tarc punched the palm of his hand.

Sefrana pulled nervously on her red locks.

"Tarc and Luften are right," Clarin agreed. "The longer we wait, the more entrenched they'll become."

"But what can we do?" Patin said already feeling defeated. "High Valley has surrendered and our mayor will soon follow. The Gars have essentially won without firing a slug."

"Not if I can help it," Tarc pounded his fist on his thigh.

Preparations

The Gars sat idle for seven days waiting for more fuel to arrive. And no sign of the militias appeared. When the steam train returned with fuel, the army, with no one to resist them, quickly overtook the city of High Valley. A few days later, more troops arrived, their leaders taking up command posts in Town Center. The governor and his council maintained their positions but they now answered to the Gar commander. Astonishingly, there were very few clashes. Commerce, while tightly monitored, for the most part seemed to carry on as usual. The Gars had positioned soldiers in every part of town with curfews established from dusk to dawn. Those found loitering or socializing after their business had been conducted, or on the streets after dark were arrested. Any who resisted arrest were slugged; which proved to be a cruel, but effective mode of keeping order and snuffed out any ideas one might have of organizing an opposition.

The people of Shaflann waited daily for their fate to arrive. But after a week, when no one had come from either the militia or the Gars, a few shops in town reopened as they learned that commerce continued in High Valley. Sefrana's father was one of the first to reopen, his earnings were already meager as it was. To stay closed any longer would deplete what little savings he had to live on. He sold dishes, platters and pitchers, and seasonal items for celebrations throughout the year.

Kief and Luften circled around behind the store and hid their horses in the trees. Even though the Gars hadn't occupied Shaflann, they didn't want anyone knowing that they were meeting.

They climbed the back steps quickly to the second floor where Sefrana and her father had a small home above their store. She was sitting at a make-shift kitchen table built out of the leftover crates from the store when they came in.

"Did you see the others?" she asked in a bit of a panic.

"No," Kief replied.

Luften smiled at Sefrana and tipped his hat. She smiled back. Natch whinnied outside.

"That must be them now," Kief said setting the games he'd brought for a decoy on the table.

Loud, clomping footsteps came up the stairs and Tarc burst in like he was arriving at his own party. Patin and Clarin came in behind him and pulled the door shut.

"Yep, I'd know that sound anywhere," Kief laughed, "Only Tarc can make that much noise coming up a flight of stairs."

"And coming through a door," Patin added.

"Not really a good time to play games, do you think?" Tarc said noticing the games Kief had brought.

"Actually, I wouldn't mind a game or two," Clarin sat down next to Kief.

"Our alibi—my dad suggested it," Kief smiled smugly.

"Ah, good idea," Tarc nodded as he stomped to the table and pulled up a chair.

"Ok," Sefrana punched Tarc in the arm, "This is supposed to be a secret meeting because the Gars will arrest anyone 'socializing'— and my father might have customers downstairs."

"Well, first of all, your father doesn't have customers downstairs— have you seen the streets lately? And secondly, I don't care who hears me, I'm not afraid of the Gars," Tarc replied as he returned a little punch at Sefrana's arm.

"I heard they've been locking people up who speak out against their regime. They're afraid to say anything in High Valley," Patin said.

"And it's only going to get worse if we don't do something," Clarin added.

"C'mon, who are we fooling? What can we do?" Sefrana asked looking around the table at her friends.

"It's obvious the six of us can't go up against the whole Gar army," Patin agreed.

"Maybe we could secretly rally people," Clarin suggested.

"It's too risky," Luften cautioned, "we wouldn't know who we could trust. With the town leaders against a resistance, anyone could be an informant."

"What if we ride to Condull and get their help?" Kief asked. "We're isolated up here in the mountains, who knows what's going on around the rest of the island."

"Yeah, but what if their leaders are big cowards like ours?" Tarc folded his arms across his chest, "We'll be in the same situation we're in now."

"Councilman Mar Kyedon is from Condull. My dad told me he's been trying to organize a centralized army for the island for years now," Kief said.

"Well maybe that's our best option then," Sefrana said.

"Traveling there won't do much to speed their march if they're coming here," Luften replied.

"So we just wait," Tarc dropped both hands loudly on the table. "It's a good thing we snuck over here all quiet like to decide to wait!"

"You call that quiet," Sefrana rolled her eyes.

"...Isn't that what we've been doing for a week now anyway?" Kief was with Tarc. It wasn't much of a plan. He opened a game tube and rolled out the playing canvas on the table, "Maybe we hide out in the woods at dark and pick them off one at a time, day after day."

"You mean kill them?" Sefrana shot a disapproving look at him.

"Yes, kill them," Kief responded, fiddling with one of the game pieces, "that's what war is."

"I know that... but we're not soldiers," Sefrana replied looking around the table for support.

"Or we're all soldiers now," Luften said siding with Kief.

"That's right, we're all soldiers," Tarc agreed, "and if any of you can't handle that, it's probably best to get out now."

"I'm out," Patin started to stand.

"Easy there Tarc," Kief said motioning for Patin to sit back down, "Sefrana has a point. We don't know the first thing about fighting. Our plan has to take that into account no matter how much courage we may have."

"How hard can it be?" Tarc continued, "I'm ready."

Sefrana smiled, "Yes, we're quite the group of formidable

soldiers! What are we going to fight them with, rocks?"

"A rock would suit me just fine, I'd bash a few..." Tarc sat back in his chair exasperated but getting the point.

"She's right, our first step is arms," Kief said.

"Well, I wasn't suggesting that," Sefrana tried to clarify.

Kief continued, "We need to gather as much as we can as quickly as possible. Before the Gars decide to make it up here to Shaflann"

"I think my dad's old slinger is around somewhere, I'll see if I can find it," Tarc replied excitedly.

"The rest of you do the same," Luften pointed around the table.

Patin spoke up, "Yeah, my dad did mention that the Gars were searching all the homes in High Valley confiscating weapons—like they did in Dayzier."

"So, they'll do the same when they get here," Luften said.

"Right, hiding them at home isn't a good idea," Kief agreed.

"And here in the store isn't good either," responded Sefrana worried about what they'd do to her father if they found an arsenal hidden in his store.

"The cave!" Tarc blurted out, "They'll never find them there."

"That's perfect," Kief smiled. "Tomorrow morning then, we'll ride to the cave and stash them there. We'll meet at the West Fire Tower just after dawn."

"And bring as much powder and slugs as you can find," Luften added. "There won't be anything left after the Gars get here."

Somehow, hiding slingers at the cave made Kief feel like they were at least doing something. But he would give anything to be back at the academy. By now he would have had his first voyage aboard a merchant ship. It was part of the opening week's activities for new students. He knew it would be a long time before he

would see the sea again. And sail... that was unattainable, now.

"Anyone for a game of Nundun?" Clarin interrupted his thoughts.

"Sure," Kief agreed. Clarin always had a way of setting him at ease.

They played until midday, laughing and joking, forgetting about the impending doom that awaited them. By lunchtime, they were feeling much more relaxed. But it didn't last; as they came down the back steps they heard a commotion out front. They ran around the side of the building just in time to see Drade and Ellison ride past them shouting, "They're coming, they're coming!"

Luften dashed past Kief, "The Gars are coming?" he called out, standing alone in the empty street.

"They're on their way, now!" they turned and rode off, their cries bouncing off the buildings.

"Ride to your homes—quickly!" Kief ordered his friends. "Get your slingers, powder, and slugs and meet back at the tower, now!"

"We don't have time," Patin cried out in a panic.

"Just do it," Tarc snapped at him.

Kief and Luften rode hard for home. They were both on the ground before their horses had stopped. Bolting across the yard and clearing the porch steps altogether, they burst into the house.

"Dad, mom! The Gars are coming!" Kief shouted.

His mom came running into the kitchen, "What?"

"Drade and Ellison just rode through town warning everyone. Where's dad?"

"He's at the mayor's house – again – trying to persuade him to do something besides wait."

"Come on Luften, we've gotta warn dad," they flew out the

back door. But Mr. Stadd rode around the side of the house as they were running across the yard. "Dad, did you hear?"

"Yes, I heard, where's your mother and your brothers and sisters?" he asked short of breath.

"They're inside. Luften and I are headed to the cave to hide our slingers. They confiscated everyone's weapons in High Valley," Kief told his dad.

"I don't know why we didn't think of that earlier—here, take mine, too."

They followed Mr. Stadd back into the house.

"Is everyone here?" he asked nearly running into Mrs. Stadd as he flew into the kitchen.

"Yes," she said distressed, "they're in their rooms."

"Kief, Luften, come with me," Mr. Stadd said running upstairs.

He had several slingers both 'side' and 'shoulder'. He gathered most of his collection, a box of powder, and a bag full of slugs. They grabbed the ones Luften had given them and carried everything down to the kitchen.

"Please be careful, boys," Kief's mom pleaded.

"They should have plenty of time to get up there and back before the army gets here," Mr. Stadd replied kissing her on the forehead, "they're just leaving High Valley now."

"Don't worry mom," Kief assured her, "we'll hurry and be back before they even know we were gone."

They followed his dad out to the barn. He grabbed both sets of saddlebags and threw them onto their horses. Loading the bags with the arms, he told them to stick to the trees on their return if the army, by chance, arrived before they did.

When they reached the tower, the others were already there waiting.

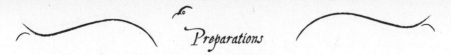
Tarc looked at Kief's bulging saddlebags, "Now we're talking," he smiled, "what do you have, a cannon in there?"

"Dad sent all his slingers with me," he patted the load of weapons, "we should be good with these."

They galloped up the dirt path toward the woods, crossing the stream and then moved quickly into the forest ducking and dodging branches. At the cave they unloaded their stash.

"Let's take them back to the Throne Room; we can hide them on the ledge along the rear wall," Kief said as he lit a lantern and led them in.

He and Tarc had named it the Throne Room because in the light of the lanterns, the spires that hung from the ceiling glistened like crystal chandeliers in a hall fit for royalty.

"Wow, this is the perfect hideaway," Luften gaped as they made their way through the tunnel.

"It goes way back into the mountain," Tarc was proud of their discovery even though it was Kief's grandpa—and the eagle that had led them to it.

When they reached the Throne Room, Tarc and Patin lit the lanterns they had scattered throughout. The flickering light cast a lively spectacle of dancing shadows on the cave walls and the formations glistened on the ceiling. Kief jumped up on the ledge and the others handed him the bags of arms. Untying them, he pulled out the slingers one by one and stacked them on the rocky outcropping.

Among them he noticed his father's small double slinger. Turning it over in his hand, he remembered the first time he'd fired it. It was near the lake where they fished. They'd found an old tree stump there that made the perfect target. It hadn't taken long before he was able to hit the stump with every shot.

He hesitated to add the small slinger to the pile. A concealed weapon may come in handy, he thought. He stuffed it into his satchel, along with a few slugs, and then filled a little pouch full of powder. He placed the powder boxes and slug bags next to the slingers and then covered them all with a cloth from the bottom of one of the saddlebags.

"Okay, that's good," he said jumping down from the ledge.

No one was in a hurry to leave the peace and silence of the cave. It was a stark contrast to the volatile world that awaited them outside.

"Well," Kief finally said, "we'd better get going," he dowsed the lantern next to him.

The horses were whinnying when they came out. Kief could tell Natch sensed something was coming. His ears were shifty and his gait was more like a prance. Kief rubbed his neck trying to calm him. Natch snorted.

"Tomorrow morning, everyone meet at Sefrana's store, if you can get out without being noticed," Kief said as they separated. "And don't arrive at the same time," he called after them.

At home, he and Luften could hear the approaching army. Kief's heart thumped in his chest. He stroked Natch and led him into the stall.

"Everything's going to be alright," he said reassuring him as much as himself.

Kief's dad was standing at the kitchen door when they came up the steps. He locked the door behind them though he knew it was a futile attempt to keep the approaching menace out. Upstairs they joined the rest of the family who were all peering out the big picture window in Kief's room.

Mrs. Stadd gasped as the full army came into view, "There must be over a hundred of them."

"They have cannon carts too," Kief's dad said, pointing to

an iron barrel extending from one of the carts. They watched like rabbits being hunted, standing still hoping they wouldn't be spotted, listening intently for anything out of order. The army marched past their street. The road to Shaflann had been too steep and narrow for the heavy transports so they traveled by horseback with carts fitted for war pulled by teams of horses.

"Where're they going?" Curchin asked. "They already passed town."

"Huh, the school is the only thing up this way," Kief replied as he stared after the train of soldiers.

"I suppose the school yard would be a good place to set up camp, maybe that's their plan," Mr. Stadd said.

"How would they know the school's up there?" Curchin wondered.

When the army disappeared up the street, Kief and Luften were the first ones to dash down the stairs and out the front door into the yard. Kief's dad, stopped in the doorway with the others.

"Dad, tell them to get back in here," Atela whispered.

"They're fine," Mr. Stadd assured her. "Kief," he motioned to him, "you and Luften cut through the woods to the school and see what they're doing. And if anyone spots you, get back here double time."

"Will do," Kief nodded. He was excited and surprised that his dad was showing so much confidence in him taking such dangerous risks. In all his adventures before going to the academy, his dad never seemed to appreciate Kief's boldness. It reminded him of the time his father went to great lengths, at considerable risk to the rescuers, to save two miners that were trapped in a collapsed tunnel. But maybe that was just it—saving lives was worth the risk, adventures were not. Regardless, this whole thing was bringing out a side of his dad that Kief didn't recognize.

"Curchin and Balt, get back inside!" Mr. Stadd ordered the boys who had snuck out the kitchen door and were running to catch up with their older brother.

"Aw," they moaned, slouching their shoulders and ambling back in the house.

"Dad, what are you doing sending them off like that?" Atela scolded him as he shut the door.

"Considering what they've already done, I think they'll be fine," he squeezed her shoulder.

Atela shot a pleading glance at her mom.

"They'll be alright," she said.

They crept through the groves between the houses moving in short intervals. The army sure didn't worry about keeping their arrival a surprise and they clearly weren't attempting to conceal their position. But then again, why would they? There was no army to challenge them. At least Kief and Luften didn't need to worry about the noise they were making above the clamor of the army, just that they were hidden.

Curchin was right, they followed them straight to the school yard, a big rectangular grassy area surrounded by the six academic houses. Three houses ran along one side and three on the other with the Director Kir-Trad's home at the far end. The academic houses were similar in construction to the other houses in Shaflann, tall and circular, only much larger. The director's house was a square brick mansion at the far end. Just beyond the Mathematics House, Kief and Luften hunched low in the trees and watched. The soldiers unloaded gear from their horses and carts and began to set up camp. Within moments, they had erected over twenty circular tents spread out across the yard.

"That guy there with the gold stripe over his shoulder must be a commander, he seems to be the one giving all the orders," Kief

whispered to Luften.

He was a tall and thin soldier, gray hair giving away his age with a stern voice.

"I wish you had your spectascope right about now," Luften mouthed quietly.

"How'd I forget it," Kief growled.

Two soldiers walked toward them.

"There's no way they can see us!" Luften pulled back preparing to run.

"No, hang tight, and be still," Kief put a reassuring hand on his shoulder.

The soldiers approached the edge of the forest just a few paces from where they were hiding. They held their breaths. They were talking in Saandonese, but appeared to be checking out the area for setting something up. Kief wished he could understand what it was. After a while they walked back into the yard.

They watched for a moment more and then Kief saw something that caused him to forget he was in hiding.

"What?" he blurted out.

"Shhh!" Luften put an angry finger to his mouth.

"That's Director Kir-Trad," Kief whispered furiously, pointing at a man walking with the commander.

"What's he doing?"

"I don't know," Kief stared.

Most upsetting to Kief was that Kir-Trad didn't seem tense or frightened. He followed the commander around the camp as if he were part of the command. When Kief saw him give orders to the troops, he nearly lost it.

"Great, another one in cahoots. Where do these guys come from?" Luften couldn't believe it.

"Well, we know who told the army about the school. My dad

isn't going to believe this," Kief turned in disgust. "I've seen enough, let's get out of here."

They crawled back into the forest and worked their way home. Kief was now convinced they'd all been deceived by their leaders into not fighting the Gars.

His dad was shocked and angry when he heard about Kir-Trad.

"We've waited long enough. It's time we leave for Condull," Mr. Stadd said decidedly.

"But, I don't want to leave our home daddy," Myri cried.

"I don't want to leave either," he hugged her.

"And now the question becomes, do we go alone or invite others to come with us?" Mrs. Stadd asked. "And you need to go get my mother."

"Yes, I've been mulling that over in my mind for some time now. Of course we'll talk to Tarc and his mother, and Bonds, and there are a few others I trust, but it's just too risky to tell too many," he replied. "And whoever is going with us will need to be ready to leave the day after tomorrow.

"If we can make it to Shootern Pass, just over Mount Plaunch, we'll be safe and I won't worry anymore. The thing that concerns me the most is that we'll need to leave in small groups of just two or three so as to not attract attention. Kief and Curchin know the way up to Mt. Plaunch—they've been up there plenty of times, so they can each lead a group."

"Wake up," Luften shook Kief. "Remember we're meeting the others at the store this morning."

Kief sat up rubbing his face, "Oh! I completely forgot! I've had so little sleep... Are we late?" He jumped out of bed and scrambled around trying to get his pants on.

"No," Luften laughed at him, "you can take your time getting those pants on."

"Where are you two going?" his mom demanded as they came into the kitchen.

"Sefrana's store," Kief replied straightly.

She scowled pointing her finger, "I wish you wouldn't go out snooping around, we don't know what these soldiers will do."

"Where's dad?" Kief changed the subject.

"He left early to see Bonds, he should be back soon."

Kief grabbed a few muffins from the table and tossed some to Luften.

"Ok, well we'll be back by lunch, I just want to make sure my friends are all set. Everything's going to be okay; we'll make it out of here just fine."

Riding into town a group of soldiers marched up and down the abandoned streets. Kief and Luften did the best they could to look like they had business to attend to. Behind the store, Clarin stood at the top of the stairs, motioning for them to hurry up and keep quiet.

"Well all of this wasn't in the plan now was it?" Tarc said as they came in.

"We never had a plan, remember," Patin rolled his eyes.

"What are we going to do?" Sefrana paced, her arms straight down at her sides.

"I know, did you see the size of those soldiers? They're huge!" Patin said.

"But they're human aren't they? They'll bleed just like the rest of us," Tarc responded sharply.

"Luften and I saw Kir-Trad helping the army yesterday. He's a traitor too," Kief said. "My dad thinks with the town officials working hand-in-hand with the Gars, it's just best to flee to

Condull for help. We're leaving tomorrow up Mount Plaunch through Shootern Pass to the lowlands."

"Open up in there," a voice yelled. They froze. "I say open up in there," the voice came again.

"They're downstairs," Clarin whispered.

Patin stepped quietly to the front window. He peeked through the shutters and stared down into the street.

"Well what do you see?" Tarc asked impatiently.

"Four soldiers; one of them is talking in perfect Jarmondon."

"Yeah, we can hear that," Tarc replied. "We all speak Jarmondon in case you've forgotten."

"Or a version of it," Clarin cocked her head at Tarc.

The shop door opened and the treading of soldier's boots on the wood floor sounded below. They strained their ears to make out what was being said. No one made a move.

"What if they come up here? What do we do?" Patin started hyperventilating as he glanced around the tiny apartment for a place to hide.

"Relax and play the game," Luften replied annoyed, "at least we have that planned."

Eventually the soldiers moved on to the next store.

"I'll go down and see what they wanted," Sefrana opened the trap door in the floor and climbed down a ladder into the back storage room.

"What do you think they're doing?" Patin asked.

"Well, they're certainly not buying new dishes to cozy up their camp, that's for sure," Tarc mumbled.

Patin looked out the window again.

The trap door opened in the floor and up came Sefrana.

"So what did your father say?" Patin asked anxiously.

"He said the soldiers told him that his store was now the

property of the 'Kingdom of Gar'. They had the audacity to permit him to continue to operate the store on behalf of the kingdom. He has to pay half of his earnings to the Gars each week. If he doesn't submit half, the operation of his store will be turned over to someone who will and we will be left with nothing."

"What? That's insane, who do they think they are? They barge in your store, they don't even buy dishes, and then they want half of whatever your dad sells," Tarc growled.

"It doesn't matter anyway. He's leaving it tomorrow," Patin looked at Sefrana.

"I hope he'll go… " she frowned uncertain if her stubborn dad would be willing to leave.

"Go home and tell your families about our plan," Kief stood. "Get prepared and keep it quiet, it's obvious there are few we can trust. Let's meet back here again at Dusk to get a count and arrange the groups. I'll talk with my father and let you know what he says. We'll leave tomorrow."

Visitor

When Kief placed his saddle on the rail, he noticed his dad's saddle wasn't there; Stiemer's stall was empty.

"Oh good, dad isn't back yet. He must be still at Bonds, planning. Let's go over."

Leaving their horses, they went on foot. Bonds' house wasn't far, just a few streets further north of theirs. Sometimes Kief and his dad used to swing by on their way to the mine and ride together with Bonds.

Kief couldn't wait to start their journey. Bonds would be going with them and probably a few of the other miners as well. They were a tough bunch and since they still didn't know if the Gars had invaded Condull, Kief couldn't think of any he'd rather have with them on their journey.

Through the trees they could just make out Bonds' house. It was a squatty little thing, a main level and a bedroom above in the conic roof. It was the house Bonds and his young bride had lived in when they were first married. He was a widower at a young age and never remarried holding on to her memory by staying in their home. As the mine superintendant, Bonds certainly had the money to buy a bigger place but those kinds of things weren't important to him. And he couldn't let go of her memory, always telling Kief they'd meet up together again.

When the house came into full view, however, Kief's excitement evaporated. Five soldiers stood on the front porch. Kief motioned for Luften to follow him and they cut through the woods two houses down to approach Bonds' home from the rear.

"No! There are guards at the back door too," Kief cursed. "What do we do?"

"We'd better wait and watch from here," Luften cautioned seeing Kief was about to dart across the yard into the house.

"They're probably just talking to dad and Bonds, do you think?"

"I don't know Kief; anything's possible with the Gars."

The image of Homer hanging from the tree suddenly flashed through Kief's mind, but he pushed it abruptly away. The back door opened and out walked a soldier. Pulling the door closed behind him he said something to the soldiers with a nasty smirk on his face. Kief wanted to wipe it off with a slug through his teeth. He knew they were up to no good. They continued talking, strutting around to the front of the house.

"Come on," Kief said stepping out from their hiding spot.

"Wait, there might be more," Luften called out, but Kief was already halfway to the house. Luften crouched down and followed

him across the clearing.

Kief peered in the window and listened, "I don't see any soldiers. It's just Bonds sitting on the couch." Kief pulled the door latch.

"Who's there," Bonds turned toward them.

His face and shirt were covered in blood. He was holding the broken picture of his sweetheart; shattered glass strewn on the floor.

"What happened?" Kief rushed to his side, "And where's my dad?"

"They took your father, Kief."

"What?" He sprang to the front door, flinging it open. The soldiers were gone.

"I don't know," Bonds wiped the blood still dripping from his nose with his sleeve. "We were here talking when the soldiers started banging on the door. They called me by name and asked for Mr. Stadd. When I tried to shut the door on them they shoved their way in and started beating us with their clubs. Then they took your father. They asked me all kinds of questions about a resistance but I told them nothin'."

"Bonds, I have to go find my dad."

"Go Kief, I'll be alright. But you watch out. There's no way they could have known about your father unless someone had told them."

"Kir-Trad," Kief seethed in anger.

In the cover of the forest, they raced to the school grounds searching the yard from front to back. They saw nothing. As they neared the director's house, the back door opened. It was Kir-Trad! He was wearing one of his finely tailored suits; a pleased look spread across his face. He pulled out a chair at the table in his garden, and started writing in the book he was carrying.

"Come on," Kief stepped out from the trees.

"Are you crazy?" Luften grabbed his arm.

Kief jerked it free and marched toward him, fists clenched at his side. At first Kir-Trad didn't notice them, but when he did, he greeted them as if nothing was out of the ordinary.

"Well, hello Kief, it's nice of you to pay me a visit. And you brought your friend again," he set his book aside.

"Where's my father?" Kief demanded pounding his fists on the table so hard it made Kir-Trad recoil his pretty hands to his chest.

"Please, sit down Kief," he recovered calmly smoothing the pages of his book. "Your father's been taken in for questioning. I'm sorry, but what he's been up to is out-right rebellious. The Gars simply want to ensure he won't be a threat to everyone's security."

"A threat to everyone's security," Kief barked. "It's the Gars that are a threat."

Kir-Trad let out a long sigh, "The Gars have come in very peacefully; just as we assured everyone they would. There was no reason for your father's rallying for war now, was there?" Kir-Trad said insipidly. "As long as we cooperate, no one will be hurt."

"Tell that to Bonds," Kief replied with a ferocious snarl. "The soldiers roughed him up real bad."

"Well, was Bonds cooperating? If you cooperate, you don't have to worry about a thing."

Luften grabbed Kief's arm to keep him from attacking Kir-Trad.

"Where did they take my father?" he yelled more insistently.

"I can't tell you Kief. One, because I'm not allowed; and two, because look at yourself. That passion you're exhibiting right now would drive you to do something terribly rash. Go home. Give it some time, all will be fine. Soon you'll see the wisdom of it."

"He's right," Luften said pulling on Kief's arm. They could hear soldiers approaching from the side of the house, "We should go home and give it some time."

Kief glared at Kir-Trad as they withdrew back into the forest. Kir-Trad picked up his book and stood to leave. As he did so, a folded slip of paper drifted to the ground unnoticed by him.

Kir-Trad hollered over his shoulder at them as he met up with the guards, "You'll see Kief, give it time, you'll see."

Kief paused. Luften, reading his mind, shook his head no. But as soon as Kir-Trad disappeared around the corner of the house, Kief darted back out into the open and retrieved the paper.

"Hurry Kief," Luften called out quietly.

Kief made it back to the cover of the forest just as Kir-Trad and the Gars came back into view.

"That man is a demon traitor!" he clenched his fist crinkling the paper in his hand.

"Yep, I'm sure Kir-Trad told the Gars all about your father," Luften said grimly, "and his appeal to set up a resistance. They'll start picking up others they suspect will cause trouble too. We have to be careful now, Kief."

"We have to find my dad and get him out—that's what we have to do!"

"Yes, but we need to be smart about it," Luften reasoned. "Getting ourselves killed trying to free him won't be good for anyone."

"Nobody here is dying, but Kir-Trad."

Kief stormed home through the forest. He was so mad he hardly noticed the swarm of soldiers going in and out of houses along the way. The cries of children and women screaming were finally what caught his attention. He watched in disgust as a soldier walking out the door, with his arms full of ammunitions, shoved a man to the ground. Slingers and powder boxes were being stacked on a cart in the middle of the street.

Luften stopped, "They're going door-to-door collecting weapons just as we'd expected."

Kief still had Kir-Trad's paper clenched in his fist. He stuffed it into his pocket and ran with Luften the rest of the way home. Another cart stacked full of more slingers and powder sat in the street beyond Kief's home.

"It looks like they've already been here, Kief," Luften hesitated.

Kief burst through the front door. He didn't care if there were any soldiers inside. In fact he half-hoped there were a few—he'd kill 'em all.

"Kief! You nearly scared us to death, bursting through the door like that!" his mother cried.

"I thought dad was coming back with you—where is he?" Balt sprang up from the couch. "We need him. Did you see they're barging in everyone's houses and taking their slingers?"

"Where's daddy?" Myri repeated.

"They took him," Kief said, the words barely audible through his clenched teeth.

His mother and Atela both covered their mouths with their hands and started to cry.

"What do you mean they took him—where?" Curchin's eyes were wide with fear.

"I don't know but we'll find him," Kief promised.

"I don't need you arrested too," his mother said wiping her cheeks. "I need you here, with us," she said firmly.

"Yeah, five of them just left. They just marched right in here and tore everything apart, even pushed Myri down," Curchin said putting his arm around her. "We need you here."

"You're right, I promise I won't be stupid, but I've got to try and figure out what we can do to get them to release dad, too."

Kief convinced his mother that he had to meet his friends back at Sefrana's store at Dusk to at least let them know what had happened. When he got there he told them about his father being arrested.

"Kief, I'm sorry about your dad, but I think that's our cue to stop the unnecessary risk we're taking of meeting together like this." Patin said as sympathetically as he could muster in his own state of self-preservation.

"What are you saying, Patin?" Clarin glared at him. "That's about the most insensitive, stupid thing I've ever heard come out of your mouth!"

"I'm saying that's it! This is stupid. We could all get arrested—or worse killed. I have a few good years left. I want to live them peacefully. Even if I have to do it by giving the Gars half of everything I have." Patin got up, "I'm going home."

"No!" Clarin shoved him back in his chair, "first of all, you have nothing to give to the Gars, so that's a moot point. Secondly, the Gars just want you to believe there will be peace under their rule, but there will be no such thing. And thirdly, you will have no good years left if you don't stay right here where you are and use that smart little brain of yours to help us find Kief's father. If you don't, I'll slug you myself!"

The others stared in disbelief at Patin and Clarin's heated exchange.

"Whew!" Tarc sighed. "I sure am glad you said it, Clarin—that was a lot nicer than I would have put it."

Sefrana cleared her throat, "My father heard from some of the other storekeepers that they were taking the prisoners to High Valley—to the city jail," she offered quietly.

Kief's heart jumped, "He's in High Valley..."

"Ok, everyone, I'm just saying," Patin put his hands in the air cautiously, "that my dad said they have troops everywhere in the city, and more than twice as needed around the jail. You get a thousand paces from that place and they'll slug you dead."

Kief dropped in a chair with a desperate sigh, "There has to be some way to get him out."

Silence filled the room. It seemed impossible to rescue Kief's father. And it seemed quite possible that they'd be living under Gar rule indefinitely.

Luften suddenly remembered the note, "Did you get a chance to see what that paper said, from Kir-Trad's notebook?"

Kief pulled the waded paper from his pocket.

"You went to see Kir-Trad," Patin looked at them like they were idiots.

"You just keep opening that trap of yours, don't you Patin. Go on, what does it say," Tarc pushed.

"To the Honorable Governor Mon-Dirk,"

"Psh!" Tarc and Clarin laughed simultaneously.

"We regret to inform you and all of Holpe's Island that our cherished country has been barbarously attacked by the nation of the Gars. They struck at Trite and Armp without warning and have succeeded in overthrowing both cities. Their militias have retreated southward to Jarmanea where they hope to regroup and move to Suinville to strike the Gars there. We intercepted a message that the Gars are moving on to High Valley. Employ your militia and any volunteers you can muster to stop them from coming into the valley. If our attempts to retake Suinville are successful, which we believe they will be, we'll move up

Temblin Canyon and attack the army from the rear. With your troops striking in the front, we have a much greater chance of defeating our invaders and establishing peace once again for our people. Move with haste as time is short. Most sincerely, Governor Baldoon of Trite."

"Let me see that," Luften snatched the letter from Kief. "This must be the letter we delivered to Mayor Chatton."

"Looks like Governor Mon-Dirk never received it," Patin said turning to Kief with an accusing stare.

"Mmm... you don't remember the warm welcome the Gars received from Mon-Dirk?" Kief was usually patient with him, but he was about ready to punch Patin himself. "I'm thinking this," he waved the paper in front of him, "wouldn't have done much good anyway."

"So," Tarc fumed, "had we resisted the Gars when they were stranded at the mouth of Temblin Canyon, the militia would be here by now to help."

"Yeah, and we can also be certain that the Gars were aware of the militia's plans to attack – via this letter – and that they prepared counter-attacks," replied Clarin.

"This is just all so wrong, we can't trust anyone," Kief exclaimed.

Tarc glared at Patin.

"Hey, don't look at me," Patin said. "I get it. That's what I've been saying all along. If anything gets out, it could mean the capture and death of us all."

Sefrana turned to Luften, "That's good news for you, I'm sure your family is alright, then."

"Thanks," Luften said, sincerely.

"What I still don't understand is why the Gars attacked us," Sefrana said.

"It's obvious, they want our beautiful land, their place is a dump," Tarc replied.

"No, that's not it. Try reading a little," Patin came back sharply. "I haven't just been sitting around fretting about all this like you guys think. I found a history book in my dad's library and read all about the Gars."

"Sounds like fun! Please, enlighten us," Tarc poked.

"Ancient prophecies say the Saans were chosen to protect Fundautum from evil."

"And they're doin' a mighty fine job at that now aren't they," Tarc mocked.

Patin continued in his usual conceited manner—which none of them had seen in some time and were actually glad to see, "And the Saans from Gar believe it's their right to rule the world."

"Okay, so it's a bunch of crazy people who want our land," Tarc replied, "All the more reason to stop them."

Kief grinned as some of the tension in the room diffused. He turned to Patin, "So, you see why we gotta do something, right? Come on, we need that brain of yours. Help us figure out what to do."

"Alright, alright..." Patin conceded nodding his head reluctantly like he'd just volunteered to fight the entire army by himself.

Clarin scooted up close to Patin and put an arm around his shoulder. Grinning she shook him, "That's my brother."

* * *

After several more meetings at Sefrana's and a secretive trip braved by Kief and Luften down to High Valley, they still had no feasible plan to free Kief's father. On one particular day, returning from their meeting, Kief and Luften came home to the front door left wide open. Three soldiers were walking away from the house back toward the school. Kief quietly raced up the front path, so as not to alert their attention, and into the house. His mother was sitting in the front room crying. Kief's brothers and sisters were gathered around her on the floor in tears too. Luften stood silently in the open doorway. Kief felt a gripping pain in his chest.

"What is it mom?" was all he could squeeze out of his tightening throat.

She tried to speak through her sobs, but couldn't.

"Mom..." he fell to his knees next to her.

With trembling hands she handed him a note.

"To the Stadd Family," he read, *"Your father and husband, Klar Stadd, was sentenced to death for rebellion against the Kingdom of Gar."* By now Kief's chest was heaving violently as he finished, *"He was hanged this morning with sixteen other guilty persons. The bodies of the infidels were burned. Let this be a lesson to all; insurrection will not be tolerated and is punishable by death!"*

Kief struggled to breath. His hands shook as he crushed the paper into a tiny ball. Throwing it against the wall, he sprang for the door.

"No," Luften blocked the way.

"Move," Kief shoved him.

Luften braced himself in the doorway holding firm in front of Kief, "No Kief, it won't do any good."

"It'll do me good," Kief locked Luften in an urt move and prepared to throw him out of the way.

Curchin ran to push the door shut and grabbed Kief, "Don't Kief, they'll kill you too."

Kief struggled to break free.

Atela started screaming, "Stop it, stop it, stop it!"

Kief stopped struggling and Luften and Curchin slowly loosened their grip. He started banging on the door with his fists shouting curses at the Gars and Kir-Trad and Mon-Dirk and himself. Then he collapsed on the floor and sobbed uncontrollably.

For days, no one ate or slept. Friends secretly came to their home to offer their pity as the news spread. Kief kept watch day after day on the kitchen door hoping that his father would come walking in. But he never did, and the reality of life without him began to take hold. Kief's mother couldn't keep it together. She constantly worried about Kief and his friends and their secret meetings, but he had to keep going to them. They were the only thing that was keeping him sane right then. Luften finally talked with Kief about the situation and suggested his mother and siblings go and live with Kief's grandmother in High Valley for awhile. It was a good idea. If the soldiers did find out about their meetings, they would have no reason to believe that his mother or family knew anything about them. They would be safe from any ties to Kief's 'rebellion'.

Curchin and Kief somberly hitched Stiemer and Daz to the carriage. It took much longer than it should have and Stiemer kept whinnying.

Kief rubbed his drooping head and pulled his ear close to his mouth, "I miss him too, boy," he whispered. He buried his face in Stiemer's neck smearing the tears from his cheeks.

While Kief tried to conceal his anger under a facade of feigned acceptance, Balt continued to have fits of rage. As he threw his trunk into the back of the carriage he smacked his shin against the wheel. Screaming, he grabbed a broken branch off the ground and smashed it angrily against a tree trunk until there was nothing but a stub left in his hand. His mother waited until he was finished before she approached and hugged him tightly to her.

The others continued loading undistracted as the fits had become a common occurrence. Kief saddled Natch and tied him to the back of the carriage. He took his father's place at the reins. Luften followed on his horse.

Kief allowed himself one glance back at the picturesque scene of the stone house in the woods. He remembered moving to Shaflann Bucken and seeing their home for the first time, he and his brothers had cheered and shouted so loudly that the neighbors had stepped outside to see what the problem was. He remembered the look on his mother's face when his father inserted the key and opened the front door extending his hand for hers and bowing. She was elated beyond words. Mr. Stadd could hardly contain his excitement as well, as he led them from room to room. Balt just about died waiting to get to their room which was on the top floor—and the last room they would see.

Kief snapped the reins. Now it was all gone. His heart ached deeply.

The Gars permitted travel between Shaflann and High Valley, but they had posts all along the route.

Reaching the checkpoint on Dondor Road the guard demanded, "State your name and business!"

"Stadd family visiting family in High Valley," Kief replied doing all he could to restrain himself from jumping out of the carriage and killing the guards with his bare hands.

One of the guards reached for Natch's lead tied to the back of the carriage, "The commander's horse is lame, this one will do."

Kief exploded out of his seat. Instantly, four soldiers pointed their slingers at him.

"Do you want to live and give us your horse or die and give us your horse," one of the soldiers said with a dangerous grin.

Kief stood defiantly, his legs ready to spring. Luften motioned for him to sit. His mother grabbed his hand and pulled his rigid frame down into the seat.

"Wise choice. You're free to pass," the guard ushered them forward.

Kief didn't move, he just kept glaring at them. Luften rode out front and grabbed Stiemer's bridle. Kief could hear Natch whinny as they rode away. He clenched his fists, his knuckles turning white, but his mother's tight grip on his arm kept him from flying out of the carriage. She needed him to keep his head. He looked back at Natch.

"I'll get you boy, I'll get you," he swore under his breath.

Somehow Natch seemed to understand, he followed the soldiers calmly as they led him around the back of the tent that served as the make-shift guards post. Kief slipped his hand into his satchel and clutched the small crescent slinger he had hidden there. With two slugs he could only get two of them and that was only if he shot straight. He couldn't even see straight in that moment, it was no good. As he released his grip from the slinger his hand brushed against the pouch that held his stone. It was hot when he grabbed it. It felt like it was glowing.

But as soon as Luften led them around the bend and out of the soldiers' sight, the heat began to fade. It had distracted him just long enough for Luften to get them away from the soldiers. Half way down the mountain Kief tried to get Luften to take his family the rest of the way so he could go back to get Natch. His mother had to beg him, telling him she couldn't survive another loss. He suddenly became aware that his anger was reaching a breaking point. He didn't know how much longer he could keep from flying into a rage.

Once in High Valley, they got their first glimpse of how the city had changed since the Gars had arrived. The pristine city was now a mess. It was clear that people lived in constant fear. Soldiers were everywhere and, fortunately for Kief, none of them harassed his family as they drove down the street.

At his grandma's, it fell to Kief to give her the awful news. Kief hated retelling the story as his grandmother wept, and in his current state he barely made it through the entire account.

When they had brought their belongings and settled in a little, Kief wandered into his grandfather's study. His grandma had left everything where it was on the day he died. His navigation charts were still on his desk next to his compass, his altimant and spectascope on the shelf, the telescope near the window. Kief sat down in the chair next to the window where he'd sat so many times as his grandpa worked. He grabbed the altimant off the shelf and peered through the sights adjusting the rise. His grandma walked in and sat down next to him.

"That was always your favorite toy," she smiled. "You loved turning all those knobs. I'd come in here and watch you—but, you never even knew. You were off on some real adventure."

Kief smiled and set it back on the shelf. "Do you miss him?"

"I miss him every day. When you're together with someone as long as your grandpa and I were, they become a part of you."

"I guess you'll be glad to see him again one day."

"One day," she squeezed his arm and paused, "I'm so sorry about your father, Kief."

Kief reached into his satchel. "Grandma, where did grandpa get this stone?" he dumped it out of its pouch.

She reached out and stroked its smooth surface, "His father

gave it to him before he died and so on and so forth. It has been passed down for generations along with the map."

"But what is it?"

"Your grandpa didn't talk much about it. He kept it hidden for years. And then one evening after we'd gone to bed, he awoke and came in here. When he came back into the bedroom he was all in a panic saying we had to leave the house immediately. That we were in danger, and someone was after the stone. I threw a few things in a bag while grandpa readied the horse, and we rode for Shaflann with barely a moon to light the way."

"Is that the time you and grandpa stayed with us for two weeks? You said it was grandpa's poor health and that he needed the mountain air."

"Yes, he told me not to tell anyone why we'd left."

"But grandpa was in poor health."

"Yes he was. It wasn't long after that that he passed."

"So, that must have been when he hid the stone in the cave?"

"He said the stone led him to it."

"That doesn't make any sense," Kief turned the stone over in his hand, but slipped it back in its pouch when Luften walked in.

"You ready to go?" Luften asked.

Kief's grandmother pulled him close to give him a hug, "Be careful, Kief," she whispered. "With that stone in your pocket, it's not only the Gars you need to be worried about."

Surprised he pulled away to look her in the eye. She was dead serious.

Kief said goodbye to his family and promised his mom he wouldn't get into trouble. Taking his father's horse, he and Luften left for Shaflann. Luften asked Kief if he knew of any small trail they could take back home that the soldiers wouldn't know about.

There was the trail that followed the steam line up the mountain. No soldiers would be there. It was a rugged and overgrown path that was seldom used since the tracks for the steam line had been put in. Kief didn't want the trouble of taking the old trail—it would take them much longer, but when Luften insisted, he relented. He knew why Luften was being so stubborn about it, and maybe he was right. He really wasn't holding it together very well. Sometimes when Balt would throw his fits, Kief wished he could too. But he didn't have that luxury. He had to hold it together—for his mom, for Balt, for himself. He was half-afraid if he fell into a rage he'd never come back out. It was all so unfair. The dreams he'd carefully woven all his growing up years just kept unraveling until it seemed there was no piece of them left. He was losing grasp of everything—and everyone. All he had left was a stone and a map he couldn't make sense of in his satchel, and his friends. He wondered how much longer it would be until his friends would be taken from him. And now, from what his grandmother had whispered, he had to worry about losing the stone and his map too—the only tangible things remaining that reminded him that he had family that loved him.

If only he could get Natch back. Whatever he did, though, the soldiers would know it was him. The only solution he had was to steal Natch and make a run for the mountains. But then he'd really be alone. He didn't know what to do.

A distant screech in the sky drew his eyes upward. A dark eagle circled.

"Look at that," he pointed it out to Luften. Every time he saw those eagles he couldn't help but wonder at their magnificence. And for a brief moment the eagle took Kief's mind off everything.

But it didn't last nearly long enough. A loud commotion ahead in Town Center brought his attention back to his reality.

From the side street they'd been taking, they could see the town square. It was filled with soldiers marching in perfect unison in their elaborate blue and yellow uniforms; stomping their feet and slapping their shoulder slingers to attention. They looked like they were practicing more for a parade than for battle. What arrogant idiots! Taking by brutal force and deceit the lands of a quiet and innocent people and then marching around as if they should be celebrated! He stopped. Beyond the pageantry of the soldiers, workers were constructing something that looked like a stage with a podium in the center. A large banner hung over the podium flaunting the Gar emblem.

"What are they up to now?" Luften turned to Kief.

"I have no idea," Kief shook his head slowly.

Then they noticed the placards that hung on all of the lampposts. Luften dismounted to read one of them.

"What's it say?" Kief asked, his eyes studying the stage.

"It says there's going to be a celebration in the square proclaiming High Valley as the new world capital of Gar."

"What?" Kief protested, "The 'Gar' capital!"

"It says that all power will flow from High Valley."

"How in the world did they decide that this little city in the middle of the mountains would be a good spot to set up their place of power?"

"I don't know, but the Gars' top general is coming to speak on the 23rd day of Harvest Rhythm," Luften continued to read.

"They must really think we're special," Kief smirked.

The marching soldiers turned with a loud stomp and faced the podium.

Luften pulled himself up onto his horse, "You ready?"

Kief didn't respond, his eyes were fixed on the square.

"What... ?" Luften asked.

He just kept staring at the stage and sweeping the square with his eyes. Maybe he really was going crazy, but he didn't care.

He turned to Luften, a smile spread across his face, "Come on!"

"I should be happy about it, but I'm not sure if that smile on your face is such a good thing right now..." Luften mumbled.

Kief led them quickly through town. When they reached the fields, Kief kicked his horse into a full gallop. Halfway to the mountains where there was no one in sight, Kief stopped and divulged the plans spinning around in his head. He had finally discovered a way that their little band of friends could fight the Gars.

"It's an excellent idea, Kief, but you know it's grounds for treason according to the Gars and they'd kill us for sure if they found out."

"But don't you see, that's why it's so perfect! They won't know until it's too late," Kief laughed confidently.

"Yeah, I'm just not sure everyone is really on board with this whole 'let's fight the Gars' idea. It's a big risk whenever you have a fair-weather friend... to trust them with your life like that."

"Hey, I've known those guys for a long time... " he defended.

Luften put his hands up in surrender, "I know you have, but you haven't known them in war. War does things to people. We should at least swear them to a pact of secrecy or something."

Kief paused, "You're right—it wouldn't hurt. Maybe we could come up with some sort of a name too, I have the perfect one." He got a big grin on his face again, turned and clicked his dad's horse.

The entire way up to Shaflann he and Luften talked the details of the plan. In all the time Luften had stayed with them they really hadn't talked that much. He was smart, and Kief liked him.

They came up with an oath of allegiance and secrecy for their group. Kief even invented a secret handshake that he couldn't wait to show Tarc.

Luften laughed, "Ok, if it makes you feel more legitimate."

"Oh, it does," Kief replied sarcastically. He didn't know when they would use it but, he needed all the legitimizing he could get for his group of 'nobodies' that were crazy enough to try and fight an army!

They had planned to meet at Sefrana's store after he took his family to High Valley, so they rode straight there. Everyone was waiting in somber silence when Kief and Luften burst through the door. Patin looked up shocked. Sefrana stood and hugged Kief and asked him if he was doing okay, but he just smiled and said he was fine.

"What's going on?" Tarc asked what everyone was thinking.

Kief pulled up his stool. The meagerly furnished apartment offered sparse seating, but everyone had managed to find a favorite something for sitting—the squatty stool was Kief's. He let Luften tell them all about the happenings in High Valley.

Patin interrupted, "I don't get it—you're smiling about that?" he asked Kief.

"Yes! The general is coming, it's time to strike," Kief declared as if he had a secret army at his command, ready for battle.

"Strike? Strike with what?" Patin asked in utter bewilderment, "Let's see, one, two... " he started to count, "six. There are six of us and a few more side slingers. Even if there were a hundred of us, it wouldn't be close to their numbers. And then there's that assault transport thing they have, slingers are no match for even one of those!"

"True, but I have a plan!"

The Plan

"But before I tell you, we need to enter into a pact of secrecy."

"What do we need to do that for?" Tarc objected, "You know we're all in this together."

"Yeah I know," Kief said, "but what if there are other people that want to join us?"

"Like who? I don't even know if I want to join us," Patin said bluntly.

"Shush," Sefrana smacked him.

Kief continued, "We've already talked plenty," he gestured at

Patin, "the dangers of what we're doing. Luften and I think it's best to make sure our plans are kept secret. Anybody who wants to join us has to make a promise of secrecy. And we should be the first." He paused for dramatic effect, "How about calling ourselves The Dark Eagles," he said, adding mystery to his voice.

"Oh, that's superb," Tarc smiled, "do we get some kind of uniform or something?"

Kief laughed, "Will a secret eagle handshake do? I thought of it as we were riding up here—you're gonna love it," Kief reached across the table to Tarc. "Make three talons by holding your index and middle finger together for one talon, your ring and little finger together for another, and then your thumb for the last. Each person's thumb talon splits the two finger talons of the other's hand between the middle and ring fingers in the eagle grip. See that?"

They clumsily worked with their fingers until they figured it out. Luften took Clarin's hand and Sefrana grabbed Patin's.

"That's it," Kief smiled at his cleverness.

"I feel safer already," Patin said sarcastically.

"Shut up Patin," Tarc glared, "I like it."

"Now for the pact," Kief said, "on your feet." Their chairs scratched loudly against the floor as they stood. Kief turned to Luften, "Go ahead."

Luften cleared his throat, "Raise your right fist in the air and repeat after me: I, say your name," they repeated their names, "do swear my loyalty to The Dark Eagles in defending our country against the invading enemy until peace and freedom are restored. I do further promise to maintain the secrecy of The Dark Eagles along with all their plots to restore freedom."

An unexpected stillness came over the group. Even Patin and Tarc stood quiet. Luften was right, it was a good thing, Kief thought. Now they were united together.

Lowering their arms, Tarc broke the silence, "Well, now we have a team, let's hear this plan."

"Okay," Kief grinned. He couldn't wait to tell them the plan and see the reaction on their faces. "So, they're building the stage in Town Center where the general will deliver his big speech and it looks like the entire battalion of High Valley will be there."

"A whole battalion...shouldn't be a problem for us," Patin continued to poke.

Sefrana smacked him again, "Be quiet and let Kief talk."

Kief continued, "The train tracks pass right next to the stage. My plan is to release from up here in Shaflann, a train car full of explosive powder down the tracks—that will detonate when it reaches the stage! We could take them all out with just one car full of explosives."

"Woa hoa," Tarc exclaimed loudly slapping both hands on the table, "that's fantastic!"

"Keep it down," Sefrana hushed him.

"That's brilliant," Clarin smiled.

It was the perfect plan. And best of all, it was possible, everyone agreed—even Patin. It was something they could pull off.

"That's a lot of people we'll kill," Sefrana spoke hesitantly.

"What's the problem with that," Tarc asked bluntly, "it's the enemy."

"But they're people."

"Not in my book," Tarc shot back.

"They'd kill us without hesitation," Luften said.

"They haven't yet," she countered.

Luften rolled his eyes at Kief for help who jumped in, "Sefrana, they made their decision to die when they invaded our country. It's right for us to defend ourselves."

"He's right Sefrana," Clarin added. "Kief lost his father. Any one of us or someone of our families could be next."

Sefrana looked pensively at the door that led to her father's bedroom and then slowly nodded. Luften gave Kief a look of concern. He could tell that Luften was both attracted to her gentleness, and bothered by it at the same time. She had always been the peacemaker; her ability to keep Tarc and Patin from killing each other was remarkable. Luften was right though, Kief thought about his plan, war does change people.

"Just one little hitch, where do we get the explosives?" Patin spoke up, "Our whole plan hinges on that."

"I know, I was wondering that myself, but I worked that one out too. The powder house—up at the mine," Kief replied.

"Are you crazy? Have you seen how many guards they have up there? I thought the idea was to avoid confrontation," Patin said.

"Yeah, but I have my father's key," he rubbed his fingers together as if he were holding the treasured item. "I'll be able to get into the powder house as if I'm working on mine duties. Bonds told me that the guards have old man Jimbs working, pushing a cart full of supplies around for them all day long. Throughout the day, I'll slip a few powder boxes under his cart. When he goes out behind the mine house to fetch more water for them, we'll have him hide the powder just inside the edge of the forest there. And then one of you will be there to pick them up."

"And you're sure we can trust this Jimbs, right Kief?" Luften asked.

"Oh yeah," Tarc had grown up with the miners and knew most of them well, "old man Jimbs is as good as they come."

Patin started calculating the numbers in his head, "Two boxes a day won't be nearly enough to fill an entire train car in time for the general's speech."

"I know. We're going to have to make more than one trip per day, maybe four or five," Kief replied.

"And where do we put them?" Sefrana asked.

"In the old loading station there are a few rundown cars. One of them has a broken coupling, which is perfect because we won't need the coupling and they can't use the car. I know because I helped my dad put it there. I figure we stack the powder right in the car—no one ever goes in there," he reasoned.

A faint creaking on the back stairs brought instant silence to the room. They froze but heard nothing more. Luften crept to the door and peaked through the crack.

"No one's there," he whispered, "it must have been the wind."

Still no one moved for some moments seized with fear, their ears acutely tuned to the door.

"So once the car's loaded," Tarc didn't care much for sitting in fear, "how do we get it down to Town Center?"

"It's downhill the whole way to High Valley," Patin whispered angrily, not quite ready to assume they were safe.

Clarin patted his balled up fists, "And what about the fuse?" She asked Kief, "It'll need to be timed too."

"We can ride the car to Krem Hill just past Dondor Bridge and ignite the fuse," Kief explained. "It's the last hill before entering the valley. It should have plenty of momentum from there to plow straight into town."

"So based on the distance from Krem Hill to Town Center," Patin estimated, "we'll probably need a five stroke igniter."

Igniters were used at the mine to set off timed explosions in the tunnel. Standard igniters were between three and eight strokes. For timed explosives longer than that, the igniters were custom

built.

"We have to be precise on the detonation, though," Luften interjected. "If it's too short, it will go off before the car reaches the army. Too long, and they'll have time to extinguish it before it goes off."

"Luften's right," Patin conceded, "we'll need to test it somehow."

"Ok, Patin, you and Luften come up with a way to test the timing." They stared at each other, working together – alone – wasn't part of the bargain. But before either of them could object, Kief had gone on with the planning, "And Tarc, Sefrana, Clarin, and I will work on getting the powder stored in the car," he said, feeling pleased that they had worked through the entire plan.

"So when do we start?" Clarin asked.

"Now," Tarc answered for Kief. "Today's the 1st day of Harvest Rhythm, that gives us twenty-two days."

Clarin, Sefrana, and Tarc rode with Kief to his house, leaving Luften and Patin to figure out how to get along.

Kief walked into the quiet kitchen; the place that had been so full of warmth just a few short weeks ago was now empty and cold and repulsively painful. He wanted to leave.

"Where's the key?" Tarc asked matter-of-factly.

"It's upstairs, let me get it."

"We'll go with you," Sefrana pulled at Tarc's sleeve.

"I know," he mouthed and yanked back his arm.

His bedroom was as painful as the kitchen. His brother's neatly made beds... But it would never be the same, not without his father. In his trunk he found his dad's keys next to his scoop sail and explorer's journal. This adventure he wouldn't be recording, though—at least not until it was over. He paused, this is an adventure of sorts, he thought to himself.

"Do we need anything else?" Tarc hurried him along.

"Nope, not at this point," Kief placed the keys in his satchel.

They left and rode for the mine. Production had restarted a few weeks earlier and the miners were under the same demands as the store owners—produce and give half to the Gars or they'd be replaced and left with nothing. Kief had worked a few shifts before his dad was arrested, but he hadn't been back since.

They easily blended in with the miners coming and going. At the old loading station, they slipped behind it and tied up their horses. The door was locked, but one of the back windows was broken out. Kief climbed through and the others followed. A sparrow chirped from the rafters, protecting her nest of eggs.

There were five old cars in the loading station. "This is it," Kief pointed to the one with the broken coupling, "come help me push it a few paces to make sure the wheels haven't seized up."

Kief removed the chalks that braced the wheels and they gave it a heave. It moved slightly, enough to convince them that the wheels were working fine. He replaced the chalks and they climbed up into the train car to inspect it. It was a wide compartment with sliding doors on both sides as well as rotating doors at the front and rear platforms. On the rear platform, a ladder led to the roof of the car.

"This should be plenty of room," Tarc said. "It's going to take at least a hundred boxes of powder to make a blast big enough to take down the stage and wipe out that battalion."

Suddenly, the front door shook violently as if someone were trying to break in. A guard started yelling in Saandonese.

"What do we do?" Sefrana panicked.

"We get out of here," Clarin said jumping out of the car.

Again, the guard shouted and shook the door. Through the cracks in the wall they could see at least three soldiers. Shadows

flashed in front of the shafts of light as the soldiers moved around to the back.

"Hurry!" Kief said as they scrambled out of the broken window.

Stealthily they led their horses around the other side of the station. By the time the guards reached the rear, they were back at the front. Mounting up, they joined a group of miners riding down the canyon.

"Don't look back," Kief ordered, "keep your heads forward."

But no calls came and they never looked back. When they reached the bottom of the canyon they broke off from the rest of the miners.

"What was that?" Sefrana gasped.

"Too close is what that was," Tarc replied, "there are guards everywhere and they seem to be watching everything."

"We're going to have to do this one person at a time, it'll draw less attention," Kief resolved. "Tomorrow morning we can start. I'll report to the mine early and help Sim at the board. He refuels the mine lanterns at the powder house first thing. I'll set up a routine of refilling the lamps for him. Each time I'm there, I'll take a few boxes and hide them on Jimbs' cart."

"And Sefrana and I can be little forest fairies," Clarin laughed. "Tarc, we'll let you load them into the car."

"Gladly, I can't wait to blow those yellow bellies to Dot," Tarc declared.

Early in the morning Kief left alone for the mine. Clouds gathered overhead as he rode up Dunton Canyon. He could taste the coming rain on his lips as the breeze blew against his face. Every time he passed a group of soldiers, he would look anxiously for Natch. But there was no sign of him.

Passing the old loading station, Kief came to the stables. He put Stiemer inside and walked up to the main mine house which was next to the powder house. Beyond them was the smelter where they purified the mined silver. The tunnels to the mine itself were further up the canyon. Over a hundred tunnels had been dug into the mountains on both sides of the canyon. Each was marked with a number and a flag; blue flag signifying the tunnel was open and active. Kief reported to 'the board', a long, wooden counter where the miners picked up their safety equipment every day.

Rain began to come down just as he slipped inside the door.

"Blast," he mumbled to himself, "I can't put the powder out in this rain."

Sim was at the board, preparing the safety gear.

"Good morning," Kief greeted him as he had always done.

"Morning Kief, you sure you're ready to start working again?"

Kief looked at him astonished, he didn't think he'd ever heard Sim tell him good morning, and certainly it was the first time he'd ever shown he cared.

"I'm ready," he replied cautiously.

"Very sorry to hear about your father, he was a good man," he looked around guardedly as he whispered.

"Thanks, Sim."

"Looks like rain; it'll be a short one though," he spoke normally, now, as if they'd always talked of the weather. "The sun is already peaking through the clouds to the east," Sim said looking out the window as he cleaned a pair of goggles.

"I hope so," Kief muttered moving behind the board.

Sim continued with his work and Kief did an inventory of the lanterns.

"Huh, a number of these lanterns are low on fuel, Sim. I'll go ahead and take them out and fill them."

"Is our refueling barrel empty again?" Sim asked.

"Uh... no, it still has some fuel. The walking and fresh air will do me some good."

That was a stupid thing to say, he ridiculed himself, 'the walking and fresh air will do me good'. Who says that?

"Suit yourself, you'll get a shower along with your fresh air," Sim chuckled which he rarely did.

"I suppose so," Kief let out a short laugh and picked up two lanterns.

Thundering clouds echoed the pounding in Kief's heart. Any moment, lightning would strike. Two guards walked out of the powder house intent on business, Kief walked by unnoticed. He went back to the room with the oil barrels to refuel the lamps. Turning the corner, he ran – literally – into Jimbs.

"Hey Jimbs."

"Well hello, Kief," Jimbs steadied himself. He was so bent with age if he didn't have his cart to push around; Kief figured he'd just topple right over and onto his head. "I'm sorry about your father, how are you?"

"I'm making it, thanks."

"Of course," he sympathized in his raspy, old voice.

"Jimbs," Kief leaned in close, "I need your help."

"Why, sure, anything for you, Kief," he smiled an almost toothless smile.

"I'm taking two powder boxes out of the cage and placing them under your cart. I need you to wheel them out back when you go to get water and hide them behind one of the trees. Can you do that for me?"

"Humph! You gonna blow up those despicable pigs? Yep, I'd be glad to help," he cackled.

"Now, Jimbs, if you don't know what's going on here, you

can claim your innocence—you can just tell them I made you do it. So no more figuring what we're doing, and not a word to anyone!"

"Your secret's safe with me. Who wants to talk to an old man like me anyway? Still... not a word," and old man Jimbs locked his mouth shut with an imaginary key and tossed it over his shoulder.

Kief smiled, no wonder he liked Jimbs so much.

"Oh, and could you wait till the rain lets up before you set them out? I'm not sure how water tight they are. I'll be right back."

Kief peeked around the corner to make sure the way was clear and then slipped back to the powder cage. Taking the keys from his satchel, he unlocked the latch and pulled open the cage. Fortunately it didn't squeak. His dad had kept the mine in tip top shape. The storage area was huge and they restocked it regularly. Hundreds of small wooden boxes stood stacked in neat rows, and fifteen to twenty large barrels full of explosive powder were lined against the back wall. He grabbed two boxes from the rear of the room. As he locked the cage, he heard the front door open. He could hear the soldiers coming up the hallway. He didn't have time to get the powder boxes to Jimbs and ducked into the oil room just as the soldiers turned the corner. One of them began barking at Jimbs in broken Jarmondon. Following their orders, he pushed his cart to the door. Kief slid the powder boxes under the old worn table in the oil room and waited silently. Approaching footsteps thumped loudly in his ears. He looked at the open window behind him, prepared to jump. He held his breath. They stopped, turned, and walked back out. Kief retrieved the boxes of powder just as he heard the front door open again. It was Jimbs. He hoped he was alone. The cart came around the corner

followed by Jimbs' bent body.

"Shew—it's you," Kief sighed leaning against the wall.

"Put them in," Jimbs said with enthusiasm as he opened the small door on the side of his cart.

Kief ran to retrieve the powder boxes. He shoved them inside and closed it up. With a wink, Jimbs turned the cart around and pushed it out the door. Kief filled the empty lanterns and carried them back to the mine house where he worked until Day. Sim offered Kief some of his lunch which he accepted graciously, he was starving.

"Hello Kief, some of the men told me you were here," it was Bonds.

"Bonds," Kief jumped up and shook his hand warmly.

"You doing okay Kief? If only I..."

"If only nothing, Bonds," Kief said firmly, "If only the Gars hadn't invaded Holpe's Island."

"Well, we'll make things right again," he said reassuringly.

"Yes we will."

"Kief, keep things low key around here," Bonds talked as if he knew something was up, "there are soldiers all over this place. They're like rats on garbage; when they smelled the silver, they descended in droves."

"Thanks Bonds," Kief gave Bonds a long look in the eyes.

"So," he said nonchalantly, "I heard you moved your family down to High Valley. Let me know if you need a place to stay or food or anything."

"I will," he nodded and shook Bonds hand again. He was like the uncle Kief never had.

After work, Kief returned to Tarc's house where he and Luften had been staying since they'd taken his family to High Valley. When he came in, Sefrana and Clarin were sitting with Tarc at the

table, big smiles on their faces.

"Did you get them?" Kief asked.

"Of course. Sefrana and Clarin delivered the boxes and I put them in the car," Tarc replied proudly, "what'd you expect?"

"I guess that's what I expected," Kief grinned.

Secret Mission

"Bonds invited me for dinner," Kief told them, his heartbeat picking up. He wasn't accustomed to lying.

"Don't stay out too late," Sefrana had taken to mothering Kief since he was on his own.

Kief made like he was going towards Bonds' but as soon as he was out of his friends' sight he cut back and rode for the cave. Alone in the forest, the solitude filled his soul. He wasn't exactly sure about his secret mission, but then he would fill with emotion again and any doubts he had would disappear.

At the cave, he lit a lantern and walked back to the throne room. He remembered the first time he and Tarc ventured into the small tunnel near the back of the cave. That was one of his most favorite adventures ever; coils of rope slung over their shoulders, head lamps shining in the darkness. Deep in the cave there was an opening in the wall that dropped off into a big cavern. They had used their ropes and harnesses to climb to the bottom where they discovered an underground river. Kief laughed out loud when he thought about Tarc almost falling in when he tried to catch a fish with his bare hands. The river was full of them. He wished he were on an exploration right then.

Kief climbed up on the ledge where they'd stashed the weapons. He found his dad's small shoulder slinger, accurate but lightweight so he could be swift on his feet. Sorting through the slugs, he found the smoothest ones in the batch to fly straight. He filled a small flask with powder and placed it, along with the slugs, in his satchel. He covered the rest of the weapons again to protect them from the moisture in the cave and jumped down. Following the long tunnel out, he became more sober as he thought about what he was about to do.

Outside, Stiemer had fallen asleep, a front leg bent, eyes closed. Kief slid the shoulder slinger under his saddlebags and saddle to conceal it from the soldiers.

The sun was beginning to set behind the mountain. In town, the streets were quiet. A few guards were out but they didn't pay attention to Kief. He rode to his house and put Stiemer in the barn for the evening. After lighting the lamp in the kitchen, Kief walked upstairs and lit the lamps in his parents' room. The last project his mother had been working on, a dress for Myri, still lay on her sewing table. She sewed most of their clothes and was an expert seamstress. He could admit now that his sisters had the prettiest dresses in town. He wished his mom was there to help him, but then she wouldn't have approved of what he was about to do anyway. Kief opened her trunk and sorted through the material. Soon he had a pile of black fabric stacked on the floor. Returning the pieces he didn't need, he closed the trunk and spread the fabric out on the floor. Finding her scissors he began to make cuts. First, he cut a long thin piece with two eyeholes. He tied it around his face while looking in the mirror. It was wide enough that it covered his eyebrows and extended down to his cheekbones. Untying it, he placed it on his parents' bed.

Next, he cut a large square piece and folded it in half diagonally. Again he stood in front of the mirror, tying the triangular part over his mouth and nose. For his head, he cut a long strip which covered the top and tied in the back hanging like a tail. Opening his father's wardrobe, he removed his long black riding coat, boots, and black riding gloves. He set them on the bed with the other pieces.

Going upstairs to his own trunk he pulled out his brown work pants. He wished he had black ones but brown would have to do. In his parents' room he removed the clothes he was wearing. After pulling on the brown pants, he slipped on his father's boots. They were a close fit. He tied the cloth over his eyes and the black bandana over his face. The short tail from his headpiece hung down his back. Buttoning up his father's black coat, he stood in front of the mirror staring at the figure before him. He couldn't recognize himself. He looked at his silver eagle ring and mumbled dark eagles before putting on the gloves. The tip of the black bandana extended below his chin in a point, almost like a beak. Only the whites of his eyes were visible.

From the beginning, he had tried hard to suppress his need for revenge. At first he thought carrying out the plan would be enough, but when he saw Kir-Trad earlier that day, for the first time since his father's death, without a speck of remorse, he knew he couldn't let it rest. He had taken his father, his horse, and his freedom. Now he would pay.

Slinging his satchel over his head, and grasping the shoulder slinger in front of him, Kief ran from the house into the trees. His vision was impaired somewhat; he should have paid attention and made the eyeholes bigger. His breathing was amplified under the bandana.

As darkness fell, he had to slow his pace to find his way through the trees. He went over and over in his mind what he needed to do; aim, pull the trigger, and leave. That was it. He had extra slugs in case he didn't kill him with the first shot. Two guards appeared on the road ahead. Kief stopped, but they walked by without noticing him in the forest. His confidence grew, dressed in black as he was, he would never be found out.

At the school, he warily made his way to the mansion. He could tell someone was sitting at the table in the garden behind the house. It had to be Kir-Trad he was always at that table writing in his book. Kief didn't know how he could possibly have that much to write about considering the weasely life he led.

He stopped to load his shoulder slinger. As he poured the

powder into the catch he had a sudden fear that the slinger wouldn't work. He'd actually never fired it. He had always gone for the big one with more power when he was with his father. Then he breathed a sigh of relief, of course, his father had fired it; it would work. Slinger loaded he crept forward, careful where he stepped. With lanterns lit throughout the soldiers' camp, the yard was bright. Kief reached a good spot to fire from behind a big, downed pine tree. Now that he was closer he could see clearly—it was Kir-Trad. He was studying a large paper he had spread out on the table.

Kief took a breath and raised the slinger to his shoulder. Visions of his father's death flashed through his mind, his hanging, his burning; all because of Kir-Trad. The soldiers would have never known anything about his father if it weren't for Kir-Trad. By now, they would be in the lowlands on their way to Condull, together as a family. He shoved his roaming thoughts out of his mind so he could concentrate. He was anxious to get this over with. Peering down the barrel he lined the cross hatch on Kir-Trad's chest. He had a clear shot.

Touching the trigger he tried to squeeze it but something stopped him. His hesitation caused him to hesitate even more. He started to tremble as he tried to convince himself to pull the trigger. He shook his hand trying to calm down. Fighting his uncertainty for a moment, he finally gave up and lowered the slinger. It was like he'd just finished an urt match, he was breathing so hard. He waited to see if he could find the nerve to slug him, but the back door opened and two soldiers walked down the steps. One of them was the commander with the gold band on his arm that Kief had seen with Kir-Trad before. They were followed by... "Mayor Chatton," he muttered as the figure stepped into the light.

They gathered around Kir-Trad and started talking, pointing at the paper. One of the soldiers talked something about tanks and that the general wanted six of them, Mayor Chatton ensuring that the steel would arrive the following week. The other soldier insisted work must begin immediately to have it operating in time.

Kief had to know what they were looking at. Leaning his slinger against the tree, he took out his spectascope. Focusing in on the table he tried to see the papers, but from his angle he couldn't see anything. Stuffing his spectascope in his satchel, he climbed the pine tree next to him. About a third of the way up, he had a clear view through the branches and stopped. Positioning himself he focused his spectascope in on the papers. He could see what looked like drawings of trees surrounding a large rectangle in the center. At first he thought it was the school yard with the forest around it but then he made out the words 'chatra fields'.

It was the chatra orchards in High Valley and the thing in the middle was the boiler house. One of the soldiers was pointing at something else next to the boiler but Kief couldn't see what it was. When he moved his arm, Kief could make out another large building next to the boiler house; a building he knew wasn't currently there. There were six circles surrounding the buildings as well. Those must be the tanks, he thought. Concentrating on the papers, Kief hadn't noticed how far to one side he was leaning. His foot slipped knocking a large pinecone to the ground. All eyes shot to the spot where Kief was hiding in the forest. The soldiers aimed their loaded slingers and moved cautiously in his direction. Kief held perfectly still, trying to control his breathing. He hoped they would assume it was a squirrel or tree rascal. They passed right below him. Kief thought about descending and making a break for it but he couldn't tell where the soldiers were. Mayor

Chatton returned to the house. Kir-Trad stayed. He seemed to be looking right at him. Kief turned his face, not wanting his eyes to reflect the lamplight. When the soldiers returned, they stopped at the bottom of his tree; they'd found his dad's shoulder slinger. Kief's heart sunk. He felt their eyes staring straight up at him, but he didn't dare look down. He was certain they'd spotted him and chose to say nothing. Walking back to Kir-Trad they set the slinger on the table and rolled up the paper. One of the soldiers ordered the other to get a squad and search the forest. Kief had to get out of there and fast.

As soon as the soldier left, Kief scrambled down the tree. He was sure Kir-Trad heard him but at that point he didn't care. He sprinted through the forest and by the time he made it to his house he felt he'd lost his pursuers.

He nearly flew out of his boots when he found Luften and Tarc sitting at the kitchen table waiting for him.

"That's some garb you've got on there, Kief, where'd you get it?" Tarc said, as Kief closed and locked the door behind him.

"Dowse the lamps," Kief said frantically.

Luften and Tarc turned off the lamps. Kief ran up the stairs to his parents' room to do the same.

"What's going on?" Tarc asked panting heavily behind him.

He and Luften joined Kief at the window. At first, they saw nothing. And then four soldiers appeared out of the darkness. They had their slingers out, their heads were swiveling back and forth in search of something—or someone.

"They're not looking for you are they Kief?" Luften asked.

"I'm afraid so," Kief pulled down his mask.

The soldiers approached the front door. They were listening. If they heard anything, Kief knew they'd barge through the door.

"What do we do if they come in," Tarc whispered.

Kief pointed up without saying anything. One of the soldiers was clicking the door latch trying to open it. It was locked.

"Did you lock the backdoor?" Luften mouthed.

"Yes," Kief replied.

A soldier clicked the latch and rattled the kitchen door. It was locked as well. They sat there in the dark, frozen…waiting. Kief had his small crescent slinger in his satchel but that was it. Tarc and Luften had nothing. Trying to fight would be useless. Kief could lead them upstairs and out his bedroom window to the tree next to the house. But he was sure they'd be spotted.

Talking started out front again. Four more soldiers had shown up. The eight soldiers stood conversing for a moment pointing one way and then another. And as quickly as they had appeared, they disappeared down the street. Kief counted to make sure all eight were there. He, Tarc, and Luften didn't move for a long while. They sat silently in his parents' bedroom, Tarc occasionally peering out the window.

"I think they're gone for good," Tarc said. Then he turned to Kief, "What were you doing?"

Kief stuttered.

"Come on, out with," Tarc was excited to hear.

"I was spying on Kir-Trad," Kief lied.

"What did you see?" Luften asked.

He told them about the mayor, the soldiers, and the drawings he'd seen.

"What could they possibly be building in the chatra fields?" Tarc was confused.

"You say the mayor runs a steel business and they're shipping in a load of steel?" Luften tried to put it together.

"Yeah, my dad once told me that the mayor is a partner in one of the largest steel businesses on Holpe's Island," Kief replied.

"They must be using the boiler and machinery for something other than the chatra," Luften wondered.

Tarc was staring at Kief's black get-up, "You've gotta make me one of those."

Kief grinned but didn't say anything. Maybe his failed mission to kill Kir-Trad would turn into a discovery that would help them.

"So what now?" Luften asked.

"We stay put until morning. It's too risky to leave," Kief replied and walked upstairs in the dark.

He hid his disguise in his trunk under his scoop sail. Kir-Trad had seen him come down from the tree all dressed in black. He would make the connection if the mask were ever found there.

They bunked down in Kief's room for the evening, but sleep didn't come easy for any of them as they trained their ears to the slightest noise outside.

Patin's Find

By the end of the week, they had successfully placed eighteen powder boxes in the train car. Gathered together again in the upper room of Sefrana's store, they were discussing their strategy when Patin barged through the door. He dropped a heavy book loudly on the table, "I know what the Gars are building in the chatra fields!"

Clarin came in behind him and closed the door.

"Doesn't anyone around here know what quiet means?" Sefrana asked disgusted, "We are, after all, supposed to be meeting secretly!"

Nobody paid much attention.

Tarc turned the book and read the cover, "The Complete Book of Botany... exciting. I hardly doubt the Gars are here for a botany experiment."

Patin jerked it back and opened it to a place he had marked, "They're going to make fuel from the chatra."

"What?" Tarc was flabbergasted, "how can you make fuel from a plant?"

"It's pretty easy really," Patin replied.

"Please, professor, enlighten us," Tarc said.

All eyes were fixed on Patin as he explained, "Chatra is loaded with sugar, which is obvious because we grow it to make sugar. But it also ferments quickly in a way that creates high levels of alcohol. No other plant has the same properties as chatra. Using a simple distillation process, you can remove the water and make pure alcohol which can be used as fuel," Patin sat back full of himself.

"So they're building a distillation tower at the chatra presses," Luften's eyes widened.

"And the tanks are for storing the fuel. Impressive, Patin," Kief cheered.

Patin smiled proudly.

Tarc punched him, "Finally, that brain of yours is coming in handy."

"That's the reason they're so interested in High Valley," Kief shook his finger at no one in particular.

"To fuel their war machines!" Clarin chimed in with Kief.

"Now how do we stop them?" Tarc pounded the table with his fist. "We're barely making a dent in filling our train car... "

"First things first," Clarin interrupted. "One mission at a time."

"Clarin's right. We need to focus on this one first. So how are your plans coming with timing the distance to Town Center?" Kief turned to Luften.

"We're going to do a test run," Patin answered, enjoying being the center of attention. "We'll release a track repair cart and see how long it takes to reach the bottom."

"But they're so much smaller than a train car, the time won't be the same," Sefrana pointed out.

"Yeah, but we can't test a real car," Luften replied.

"What about the guards?" Kief asked.

"We need to distract them while someone releases the repair cart," Luften replied.

"We're going to make it look like negligence on the part of the soldiers," Patin was getting attention greedy.

"I'd be glad to hit them with something," Tarc leaned back with a smirk.

Luften continued, "Either a diversion or we do it at dark after the guards leave."

"Oh, no guards at dark?" Kief asked.

"Nope, so it's probably best to do it then, no one will be there to see it," Luften made the decision. "Sorry Tarc, no taking out

soldiers for now."

Tarc was getting antsy, the 23rd couldn't come fast enough for him.

"And who are the lucky riders that get to take the cart down the mountain to Krem Hill," Clarin looked around the room.

There was a quiet pause.

"It'll have to be me," Patin lowered his head and volunteered reluctantly. "We all know I worked for track maintenance last Sun Rhythm. I'm the only one who knows how to release it."

"Alright Patin," Tarc slapped him on the back.

"Okay," Kief nodded, trying to conceal his doubts, "I believe you're the best choice we have."

Nobody believed Kief, not even Patin, but they weren't going to say anything because in a way he was right, he was the best choice they had.

"I'll go with Patin," Luften offered after an awkward silence.

"Won't you need to be at Town Center to time the cart's arrival?" Clarin asked Luften.

"What about curfew, you'll be arrested," Sefrana looked straight at Luften with her big blue eyes.

"I'll hide," Luften stammered.

Kief, Tarc and Clarin watched the exchange with amusement.

"It'll need to be somewhere high enough where you can see the cart on Krem Hill," Patin added, completely oblivious.

"The time tower's the tallest building," Clarin proposed. "It'll be dark though, I don't know how you'll see it."

"Wait for a double moon," Tarc spoke up, "you'll have no problem seeing it then."

"Do we have a double moon before the 23rd?" Patin looked around but no one knew.

"I'll go down and check, we have a rhythm chart in the

store," Sefrana slid back her chair and disappeared through the hatchway.

"I don't know how you'll get in there," Patin looked at Luften. "The tower is next to the governor's office. I'm sure it's packed with soldiers."

The floor hatchway opened and Sefrana returned, "We have a double full moon on the 10th of Harvest Rhythm."

"That's three days from now," Patin slipped into a panic as Sefrana dropped the hatchway door with a thud.

"Relax Patin, that's plenty of time," Luften said.

"Ooo... I have an idea," Clarin waved her hand, "we can catch a tree rascal and put it in the cart before we send it off. The guards in the square will think it released the cart."

"I like it!" Patin put up his hand to slap Clarin's, but missed. He lowered his hand sheepishly, "Those little varmints are always up to mischief," he mumbled.

"Dad has some old traps. Patin and I will set them tonight."

"Well, don't be surprised if you find a Gar in it in the morning," Tarc joked.

Bang-bang-bang!

"Open up in there!" guards shouted outside the door.

"Hurry, get a game," Sefrana whispered frantically. Clarin grabbed one off the shelf and they quickly spread it on the table.

"Open up immediately!" the voice barked again nearly breaking down the door.

"Relax," Luften prepared them, "they don't know what we've been doing in here, don't give it away."

Kief walked over and unlatched the door. Three soldiers barged into the room pushing him aside.

"What's going on up here?"

"Just playing a few games," Kief's heart was racing, but he

answered as composed as he could muster.

It was the same guard that had stopped at all the shops a few weeks earlier.

He glared at Kief, "What's your name?"

"Kief Stadd," he answered defiantly.

"Your father must have been Klar Stadd. That makes you the son of an infidel. He deserved his punishment. I would have hung the whole family if I were in command," he hissed hitting Kief in the chest knocking him back. "And your ridiculous mother, you should have seen her face when I gave her the news," he goaded.

Kief snapped and charged the soldier. Instantly the soldier hit him across the face with a club, nearly breaking his nose and knocking him to the floor. Kief wiped the blood with his arm.

They pointed their slingers at him, "On your feet boy, you're under arrest for assaulting a soldier."

"No," Sefrana cried out.

A soldier pointed his slinger at her while the others forced Kief out the door. Sefrana stood boldly still staring him down.

Mounting their horses the soldiers made Kief walk to their camp. His friends watched helplessly from the kitchen window as they led him away. Thoughts raced through his head, the promise he'd made to his mother, Curchin begging him to be there for them, Balt's fits of rage. He saw himself hanging from a tree; there would be no explosion, no revenge. Kief regretted his stupidity and cursed his temper.

When they reached the school yard, they shoved him inside one of the tents and chained him to a chair. Then they left him alone. He waited and waited, but no one came back inside. He tried to reach the slinger in his satchel, but decided against it; he'd been stupid enough for one day.

Darkness fell and he heard the changing of the guards outside his tent. It was getting cold, he could smell the dew settling on the dirt and grass. Drunken soldiers sung a few tents away. It went on late into the evening. His arms started to ache. He shifted them back and forth to get some circulation going. The camp fell silent. Kief shivered. Eventually he dozed off.

He awoke with a jolt. A man stood in front of him, the morning sun streaming through the open tent flap. Kief blinked his eyes and looked up. Professor Kir-Trad stared down at him, soldiers stood on both sides of the tent. He was holding a shoulder slinger in his hand. He spoke to the soldiers in Saandonese and they unshackled Kief.

Kir-Trad shook his head pitifully, "Kief my boy. I told you not to let your impulsive passions drive you to do something rash."

Kief kept quiet.

Kir-Trad said something else to the guards and they walked out.

"We're going to let you go this first time, or is it the second?" he glanced down at the slinger in his hands.

Kief recognized his father's slinger they'd found at the tree.

"But this is the last time I can protect you. I can't have you attacking the men who are trying to maintain peace."

Kief's blood boiled. He wanted to strangle Kir-Trad right then and there. It would almost be worth it, even if he was hung. Instead he nodded pretending to accept the warning.

"I expected more out of you. You come from such a noble bloodline—Saans, you know, through your mother. Certain things should have been passed on to you. But maybe you aren't the one."

Kief kept quiet. He realized he was talking about the stone. How did he know? His heart was thumping so loud he worried it would give him away. The stone was in his satchel. The soldiers had never searched him.

"Maybe the blood of your father has corrupted you," Kir-Trad stepped to the side inviting him to walk out of the tent. As he passed, Kir-Trad whispered in his ear, "I told you to give it time and you will see the wisdom in what is happening."

Kief didn't look back, he walked straight for the forest. A dark eagle screamed, circling above the camp. If only I had wings to fly away, Kief thought, and stepped into the trees.

Kir-Trad knew it was his slinger. He couldn't afford any more mistakes. He sprinted to Sefrana's store hoping to find his friends there. Sure enough they were. He'd never been happier to be in that little apartment above the store. He settled onto his stool and related his strange evening—leaving out the part about his dad's slinger.

"That's odd he would just let you go like that," Luften said.

"If I've told you once, I've told you a thousand times… keep your cool and don't do anything stupid," Tarc repeated what he'd said to Kief during every urt match, "but I think I've told you a thousand times."

"I know, that was unacceptable, I could have gotten us all killed."

As they walked out to leave, Kief kept back to talk with Clarin. He wished it was under pleasanter circumstances.

"Do you think Patin can handle his mission?"

"You're asking me this? You can't even handle playing a game without getting arrested. But, you know Patin," she replied, "whatever he sets his mind to, he does."

"Ow, that hurt," Kief stabbed his hand at his heart, and then continued, "but he's never set his mind to anything quite like this."

"I admit, he's drawn to merchant sailing for the money not the adventure, but he does have a bold side to him. Why do you think he loves hanging out with you? I don't blame him," she winked and walked out the door.

Kief tripped as he followed her down the stairs.

Clarin turned around, "For some, even going down stairs can be an adventure," she smiled.

Reckoning

Luften and Patin followed an old overgrown trail through the forest to the maintenance platform. The path switched back and forth down the mountainside through the trees. The trap wiggled from side to side on the back of Patin's horse, the rascal sliding around inside the cage.

"That thing sure is quiet, are you positive it's still in there?" Luften glanced back.

"He's quiet because he can't see us. If we took the cloth off, he'd screech so loud, the whole army would know where we are."

"Well that little critter is going to have the ride of its life," Luften chuckled, "I'll bet it'll do some screeching then!"

"Yeah, you'll hear it coming long before you see it," Patin laughed.

When the trail eventually leveled out, they made a long cut across the edge of a mountain meadow. The sweet smell of the

Harvest Rhythm flowers and grasses rode across the breeze.

Patin sighed, "Out here it doesn't seem like anything has changed."

"Yeah," Luften replied.

"You just don't say much of anything do you, Luften?"

"Nope, not if I don't have to."

They rode a short while longer and then Patin pointed, "That's it, see that clearing up ahead? Just beyond it and to the left are the tracks and the maintenance platform."

Luften pulled back on his reins, "Then I guess we wait here until it's dark and the guards have left."

They found a shady spot to sit and eat their dinner; deer jerky, hard cheese and some crackers. Food had become a good deal scarcer since the Gars had moved in, and where there had always been plenty of fresh foods before, now the farmers were not allowed to sell their produce to the locals until after the armies had had their fill; and there was never much left over.

"I've had about all of this I can take," Patin yanked on the hard jerky.

"It's better than having an empty belly," Luften replied curtly.

"Sometimes I'm not so sure," Patin picked a piece of mold off his cheese.

They washed down the dry crackers with a flask full of water and lay back on the ground to wait. Tall pines pointed skyward; billowing white clouds drifted across a brilliant blue sky. Luften tipped his hat down over his eyes and exhaled a heavy sigh.

"So, what do we do now?" Patin asked.

"We wait until sunset," Luften replied.

Patin draped his arm over his eyes and listened to the wind through the trees.

"Patin! Patin wake up," Luften said shaking him.

"What? What?" Patin sat up in alarm.

"We fell asleep," Luften stood and smashed his hat onto his head.

"Not good," Patin jabbered. "What time is it?" he asked desperately, seeing the setting sun.

"A few strokes before Dusk," Luften returned his time piece to his satchel, "I have to leave now if I'm to make curfew," he said hastily as he untied Odin.

"Okay," Patin panted, "cut to the right there and follow the opening through the trees. It hooks up with the path that takes you down to High Valley."

"I've been on it with Kief," Luften said impatiently. "Is your horse ready?"

"Yeah, leave him tied on Krem Hill near the tracks for me," Patin handed him the reins.

"Oh! Where's your time piece? We need to synchronize them," Luften said almost forgetting. He pulled his back out of his satchel.

"Right," Patin fumbled around trying to find his. "There! Okay, what do you have?"

They set their time pieces exactly.

"Remember, release the cart at Dark, straight on. I'll be watching from the tower."

"Okay. Good luck Luften."

"And to you Patin," he tipped his hat to him and rode off. At Krem Hill he left Patin's horse tied to a tree and clicked his horse into a gallop all the way to High Valley. As soon as he came onto one of the main streets, he stepped his horse in behind a group of tired farmers riding slowly, heads hanging low, after a long day's work. Luften was glad his own father left. He had loved his farm and was proud of his hard work. He wouldn't want to see his father beaten down like that.

In town, he broke off from the farmers and rode to the public stables. The number of travelers had diminished significantly and most of the stalls were empty.

He removed Odin's bridle and rubbed his neck, "I'll be back in the morning, boy, don't wait up for me," he whispered.

After giving him some hay, Luften hurried to Town Center just as the sun reached the edge of the mountains. As he passed by the stage, he could see that they were almost finished. There were a few soldiers patrolling the area but the almost non-existent resistance that they'd encountered left them rather lackadaisical. Good, he thought.

Two soldiers stood at each side of the entrance to the tower. Luften mingled in with a crowd of people. He pulled the rim of his hat down over his eyes. He waited until the guards were distracted, which didn't take long, and slipped inside the doorway unnoticed. He started up the stairs quickly, but soon discovered that they went on and on; he was worn-out much sooner than the stairway ended. Except for an occasional opening in the wall where the setting sun shone through, the passage was dark. Eventually he came to the end; a lone door stood in front of him. He checked it. It was locked. The faint sound of someone coming echoed through the stairway.

Luften pulled a knife and long metal tool from his satchel. He slid the tool between the thick oak boards of the door and inserted the knife into the lock. He jiggled them about, until the latch clicked and the door lock released. Pushing it open quickly, in case it squeaked, he ducked inside and closed the door behind him. He held the latch open to keep the lock from clicking loudly. Once he was safely inside, he looked around. He was surrounded by the massive gears, cables, and pulleys that made up the time tower mechanism. Working his way through the maze of metal, he found a nook just large enough to squeeze into.

As the noise grew closer and louder, he could tell there were at least two people coming up the stairway. They were speaking the now familiar Saandonese language, which meant only one thing: they were the soldiers he'd slipped past downstairs. Luften held his breath when they stuck the key in the door, and didn't breathe again until they'd searched the room and left, locking the door behind them. A red winged gull on the window ledge cooed. Luften looked down at his time piece; it was approaching Dusk's 1st Cadence. Curfew was on. He had two cadences to wait before Patin launched the maintenance cart. He climbed down from his hiding place within the gears and leaned back against the rock wall of the tower, making himself as comfortable as he could.

Patin crawled quietly under the cover of the pines near the maintenance platform where he hid until the sun sank below the mountains. The three guards on the platform sat lazily, every now and again exchanging a comment. Patin watched the double moons creep out from behind the ridgeline while he waited patiently for them to come down the steps. Dot, and then before it had cleared the mountain, Otoo began to show its face, casting their ethereal glow across the land. Double moons illuminated the land nearly as brightly as the sun on a stormy day. Patin could easily see the landscape and the buildings of High Valley.

Around Dusk's 2nd Cadence the guards, who would have normally left their post by then, still remained. Patin began to grow nervous. Finally, about twenty strokes before Dark, they climbed down, mounted their horses, and rode off. Patin waited until he couldn't hear them anymore and then crawled out from his hiding spot under the tree, brushing off the dry pine needles that clung to his elbows and belly. He crept cautiously. Edging up the steps, he peeked onto the platform. No one was there. Scanning the perimeter and seeing he was alone, he climbed back down and over to the trees where he had hidden the rascal cage.

Lugging the cage up the steps to one of the carts, he placed it on the floor and stepped inside. Maintenance carts sat on a switch track adjacent to the main track, and fit three men comfortably. The cart walls were elbow high with four poles, one in each corner, which held up the metal rain canopy overhead.

"Okay little fella, are you ready to go for a ride?" Patin whispered.

He opened the gate and switched the tracks. The metal lever had already turned cold in the dark. Pulling on it, he released the brake and the cart began to move slowly down the track. A big grin stretched across his face, ecstatic at his success so far. Air rushed through his hair as the cart gradually picked up speed rolling down the moonlit landscape. Maintenance carts were meant for slower speeds, but Patin didn't have time for a leisurely ride. He resisted the uncontrollable urge to pull back on the brake and let the cart shoot down the mountain. Rounding the last corner before Dondor Bridge, he applied the brakes lightly. Then, on the final straightaway, he released them again and let the cart fly. The rascal began to screech and scramble around inside its cage. Land dropped away on both sides as they shot out across the bridge. His hands gripped the brake lever, his knuckles turning white, as the small cart clattered every bone in his body. He wondered if he would catch flight and sail off to the canyon floor. But by the time he'd reached midway across the bridge he saw he wasn't

going to die and was able to relax. He loosened his grip and watched the Dondor River glistening in the moonlight far below.

"Wahoo!" Patin let out a cry of glee.

Applying the brake, he slowed the cart to a stop on Krem Hill. He sat for a moment in the darkness, his hands trembling and looked back across the bridge from where he'd come. The rascal had stopped screeching and was sitting quietly in its cage.

"I did it," he exclaimed in wonderment, "I did it!"

He looked around half hoping to find someone who had seen his victory, but there was no one, just his horse. He had done it.

He was so pleased with himself, he laughed out loud, "If only Kief could have seen that!" He smacked the little rascal's cage.

Patin checked his clock, "It's time," he said.

He placed an apple on the floor, opened the cage, and took the cover off its head. The rascal crawled out going straight for the treat. Patin dumped the cage onto the ground and quickly closed the door of the maintenance cart. He released the brake. The rascal was busy enjoying the apple and didn't even know that the cart was picking up speed again...

As the test time drew near, Luften stared out his window atop the time tower. The tracks glistened in the light of the moons. He could see clearly where they cut through the forest on Krem Hill. He peered into his spectascope, nothing yet. Down in the town square it was empty with the exception of two soldiers who stood watch in front of the Governor's House. His time piece clicked away the last few strokes.

"Okay Patin, it's time. Let her fly," Luften counted out the pulses and didn't get to ten before he caught sight of the cart. "That's it, Patin! Way to go!"

Luften marked the time and followed the cart with his spectascope down the hill. It picked up more and more speed as it approached the bottom of the hill. Reaching the valley, it raced through the farm fields toward the city. Luften saw a few lamps flicker on as the cart rumbled by some of the homes. Then he heard the screeching cry of the rascal. He chuckled to himself as he thought of the little guy hanging on for dear life. He checked the time, four strokes and counting. The cart raced into town and up toward Town Center, gradually losing speed. It slowed and came to a stop about fifty paces from the stage. Two guards ran over with their heavy slingers raised. Luften watched as they approached the cart. One of them shouted and they both fired their slingers. The poor tree rascal had jumped up on the side of the cart and was preparing to make a run for it when he was shot and fell dead on the ground.

More guards came running at the sound of the slingers going off. Twenty to thirty soldiers stood around talking, looking at the cart and the dead tree rascal; the two guards who saw it all happen explaining it to the others. They would point at the cart and then down at the tree rascal and back at the cart again. Eventually, they returned to their posts, leaving the cart sitting where it had stopped.

"Five strokes, ten pulses," Luften said as he removed a pencil and book from his satchel and recorded the time.

He smiled in satisfaction; their test had been a success.

"Way to go Patin," he repeated as he placed his book and pencil back into his satchel and lay down exhausted but happy on the stone floor.

The tower bell chimed loudly signaling Dawn's 1st Cadence. Luften shot up to the sound vibrating through his body. Fortunately for him, the chimes didn't sound during the evening cadences. Collecting himself he peered out of the tower and down at the people bustling about, all guards at their posts. A few were back at the maintenance cart apparently discussing what had occurred during dark.

Luften listened to make sure there were no guards coming up the stairs, and then opened the door and stepped out. Pulling it closed behind him he walked cautiously down the stairs. When he reached the bottom, he paused briefly and peered out before stepping into the square.

He strolled casually across the streets to the stables and found Odin well rested and as anxious to return to Shaflann as he was. Throwing on his saddle, he mounted up and rode out of town toward the farmlands. As he neared the fields, a few guards stood between him and his escape. He kept his face forward, avoiding eye contact with them. One of them shouted out to him. Luften turned, his heart racing, he tried to not look alarmed.

"Where are you going this morning?" The soldier asked in his halted Jarmondon.

Luften struggled for an answer, "Riding out to the fields," he blurted.

He knew the next question would be for more details which he didn't have. Luckily, a commander called to the soldier and he turned and walked away, leaving Luften alone in the street. He started again at a steady pace, a gallop would make the soldiers suspicious. When he felt he was far enough into the fields, he kicked Odin.

"Ha! Giddup!" he coaxed.

He stole one look behind him through his trail of dust and saw

Chapter Fifteen

no one following him. His heart thumped with excitement as he approached the mountains.

By the 11th day of Harvest Rhythm, they had moved forty-two boxes of explosive powder into the old train car; they needed another fifty-eight. During lunch break, Kief walked up to the rocky ledge overlooking the canyon behind the mine house. It was his and his dad's favorite place to eat and talk. He hadn't been back since their last lunch together before he left for the academy. To Kief's surprise, someone was already sitting there. His back was toward him when he came through the trees, a stocky blond haired boy about Kief's size. He spun around when he heard Kief approaching. It was Flinch! His old rival from school.

"You work here now?" Kief asked surprised.

"Yeah, what are you doing here?" Flinch replied coldly and turned back to looking out at the canyon.

Kief sat down on the rock ledge a few paces from Flinch and dangled his feet over, "Same thing as you, eating my lunch."

Flinch just kept eating. Kief unpacked the food Tarc's mom had prepared for him.

"I started working in the smelter a few weeks back," Flinch confessed. "Things have been tough at home, we need the money."

Kief tried to be amiable, "You on break?"

"Yeah, someone told me about this spot my first day. I've eaten lunch here ever since," Flinch replied, his eyes fixed on the landscape.

"Something huh."

"Sorry about your father," he said as if he had been thinking

about it.

"Thanks Flinch," Kief replied, surprised at his sincerity.

Flinch had changed.

"I can't take any more of this doing nothing."

"Me neither," Kief replied eyeing him.

"It's not like you to take any of this sitting down. You sure didn't with me... " he continued.

"Yeah, but what can any of us do?" Kief threw out a line.

"Well something, anything. I'm not going down without a fight—that's for sure. Our sorry mayor and governor just rolled over showing their coward bellies to the Gars. Why wouldn't they fight?" he said flinging a rock over the edge.

"They're getting something out of it; they're all tied in with the Gars."

"You bet they are," Flinch said flatly. "Traitors," he grumbled, "and no one seems to want to do anything either. But your dad did," he looked at Kief.

Kief stared at him. Flinch was a great fighter; he knew that from personal experience. He'd be a terrific asset.

Suddenly he had a strong hunch that he could trust him. "I've heard of a group that's forming a resistance to fight the Gars, you interested in joining them?" Kief asked.

"Absolutely!" Flinch replied with that intense stare Kief had seen so many times before.

"They make you swear to keep the group secret, and to be willing to give your life," Kief continued to prod.

"Sure. I'm already there, freedom or death for me, that's the way I see it."

That was good enough for Kief. He put his lunch down and stood.

"Stand up Flinch," Kief said.

Flinch looked confused. He stood up ready to square off for a match.

"Raise your right fist in the air and repeat after me. Kief tried to remember the words Luften had said, "I, say your name," Flinch followed along, "do swear my loyalty to The Dark Eagles in defending our country against the invading enemy until peace and freedom are restored. I do further promise to maintain the secrecy of The Dark Eagles along with all their plots to restore freedom."

Flinch lowered his fist, "I take it you're part of the group?"

"Yep, and now you are too."

"So, is there anyone else that's part of this group—or is it just you and me?"

"Gotta start somewhere," Kief joked and slapped him on the back.

A slight smile lifted on Flinch's stone face.

"We're meeting this evening at Dusk. Do you know Sefrana's father who has the pottery store in town?"

"Yeah."

"We meet in their apartment above the store, stairs are in the back. Oh and one more thing," Kief shook Flinch's hand showing him the secret handshake.

Flinch grabbed his satchel, "See you there," he called and headed back to work.

Kief sat back down in the quiet and enjoyed the rest of his lunch. For not having much it was a better lunch than most were eating; a pork sandwich on fresh bread with carrots, an apple, and a sweet roll. Tarc's mom was resourceful. She'd always grown her own vegetables and fruit and they raised pigs every year. Kief would help Tarc slaughter them. It was a messy job, and he didn't like it much but Tarc didn't seem to mind.

Of all people to join them, Kief thought, Flinch. There certainly was no one Kief would rather have fighting on his side. Flinch was relentless.

"Not much of a group," Flinch mumbled to himself as he tied his horse next to the five other horses behind Sefrana's store.

He knocked on the door.

"Yes," Luften said blocking the way to the stranger facing him.

"Hey, I'm here for the meeting at Dusk."

"Who told you that?" Luften asked.

"Kief," Flinch replied.

"I don't know what you're talking about," he came back and started to close the door.

"Will this help?" Flinch reached in and grabbed his hand in the eagle grip.

"What?" Luften uttered. He opened the door and invited him in.

"Hey Flinch," Tarc called out excited to see him.

Flinch told them about seeing Kief at the mine and his invitation to join them.

"So who's in charge?" Flinch asked.

"Kief," Clarin replied without hesitation.

"Well no one really," Patin said, "but Kief had the idea."

"This idea?" Flinch said looking around the room at the small group of kids who'd gone to school with him.

"Sit down, we'll tell you all about it," Tarc glanced around the room. "Here," he turned over the firewood bucket and patted it.

Kief came through the door.

"Finally," Tarc said. "Where've you been?"

"Sorry, I was at Bonds' for dinner."

"Yeah, we've heard that before," Tarc teased.

"No seriously, this time I was. You can ask Bonds."

"I believe you," Tarc waved his hand shushing him.

"So, what was the time?" Kief asked forgetting about Flinch. It seemed like he'd been with them since the beginning. "Did you get it?" he asked.

"You should have seen me and that little rascal fly! It was every bit as amazing as your jumps off Tubin bridge," he bragged.

"Five strokes ten pulses," Luften interrupted. "It came a little short of the stage but a heavily loaded train car should reach it no problem."

"Okay, then we go with a five stroke igniter," Tarc said.

Another week passed, and by the 17th day of Harvest Rhythm, they had stowed seventy powder boxes in the train car. Only six days until the general's speech. Kief rode up Dunton Canyon as he'd done the past few weeks, but his anxiety was beginning to grow. The constant watching over his shoulder was wearing on him.

"Good day Kief," Sim said as he walked in.

"Hello Sim."

"Going to spend the day running back and forth filling lanterns again, huh?"

"I suppose so," he said nonchalantly as he picked up a pair of lanterns and walked to the powder house. Jimbs was working outside.

"Morning Jimbs."

"How are we Kief, another delivery?"

"Yep, another one."

He drew in close to Kief, "I'd say you have enough at this point to blow up the entire mountain," he said under his breath.

"Getting close," Kief grinned.

"Be in shortly," Jimbs nodded.

Kief walked to the door and was harassed for no reason by two soldiers standing outside. One of them hit him in the back of the head with his club. It knocked him forward but he maintained his balance stumbling through the door. Kief remembered the last time he'd challenged a soldier and restrained himself from reacting. He was fuming inside. He wanted to rip the club out of his hand and beat them both. The soldiers followed him laughing, but stopped at the doors. Kief went back to fill the lanterns. He heard the doors open and the soldiers leave. He was glad. He didn't want them around when Jimbs came in. Shortly after, the doors opened again and Kief heard the squeaking of Jimbs' cart.

"Hey Jimbs, let me get the package."

Returning with the boxes he placed them on Jimbs' cart.

"You okay Kief? I heard 'em. I don't like 'em, don't like 'em at all," Jimbs said shaking a boney and bent finger at him. "Get 'em all, Kief."

He nodded without saying anything. He loved Jimbs.

Kief walked out the door. There across the way, Natch was tied up in front of the main house. Without thinking, Kief ran over to him, wrapping his arms around his neck. Natch's ears went straight up and he neighed with excitement.

"Easy boy, we don't want to attract the guards," he whispered.

His eyes fell on Natch's lead rope tied to the rail. He reached for it.

"Stupid soldiers, don't even know how to tie a quick release," he fiddled.

Untying the knot, he took a step toward the forest and then

stopped. He turned back to Natch who blinked his long black eyelashes.

"I can't jeopardize the plan again," Kief muttered.

Natch didn't resist when Kief retied him to the rail.

"I'll get you back Natch, just six more days," he patted his neck.

Giving Natch one last squeeze, he picked up the lanterns and walked away. Natch kept quiet. Kief turned back giving Natch a reassuring nod before going inside.

Stepping behind the board, he placed the lanterns on the shelf and went about his morning tasks. He looked out the window at Natch to see if the soldier who had taken him had returned. He wanted to remember who he was. A sudden movement from behind the powder house caught his attention. To his horror he saw the two guards that had harassed him brutally attacking Jimbs. They had shoved him to the ground and were screaming at him. One of the soldiers lifted up the powder box and started kicking him. Jimbs had been discovered.

Kief's stomach tied up in knots. He felt like he was going to vomit. If he got involved, their whole plan would be jeopardized. He knew Jimbs wouldn't want that.

But when the soldiers pulled out their clubs and began beating Jimbs more severely. Kief snapped. Grabbing his satchel off the hook he fumbled around for his father's small double slinger. The soldiers didn't notice him approaching from behind. About five paces away, Kief raised his slinger and fired the first slug. It hit one of the soldiers between the shoulder blades, instantly knocking him to the ground. The other soldier spun around dropping his club and reached for his slinger. Before he could raise it, Kief fired the second slug at near point blank range, hitting the soldier in the chest knocking him backwards in a splatter of blood.

Kief rushed to Jimbs' side. Blood oozed from the gashes on his face and head.

With a crimson smile Jimbs mumbled, "Did you get em?"

"I got'em Jimbs," Kief replied, his heart breaking.

"Get the rest of them for me would ya?" Jimbs struggled to breathe.

"I will Jimbs, I will," Kief replied begging him to hang on.

But Jimbs just smiled, closed his eyes and went limp. Kief could hear the soldiers coming. He darted into the trees. Clarin had been hiding there to retrieve the powder boxes.

"I heard the slugs and stayed put. I'm so glad it wasn't you."

"It was me; we have to get out of here."

Clarin flashed him a look of horror, "This way," she pulled him into the forest toward her horse.

"Natch," Kief spun around.

"NO!" she cried, but Kief was already heading back.

He ran to the edge of the forest and whistled. Natch spotted him through the trees and started pulling on the end of his lead rope with his teeth. Kief had trained Natch well. And at that moment he was glad he'd taught him to pull on the end of a quick tie knot to release it. A jerk and Natch was free, trotting toward Kief.

"That-a-boy Natch," Kief grabbed the rope and swung up on him. It's a good thing I retied that idiot commander's quick tie, Kief thought.

"C'mon!" Clarin said as he met up with her.

At the bottom of the canyon, near the road, Kief could see soldiers gathering around the main mine house preparing for a search.

"Clarin, they caught Jimbs with the powder boxes. When they started beating him with their clubs I couldn't stand and watch

anymore. I tried to save him but I was too late."

"How horrible! So you fired the slugs?" Clarin asked.

"I did."

"Did you... ?"

"Yes," Kief replied as he prepared to break out into the open. "Tell the others to meet me at the cave."

"Don't let them find you," Clarin pleaded, desperation in her voice.

"I won't," Kief cut out across Dunton Road and up the other side of the canyon.

The mountain was steep and Natch slipped several times as he tried to find footing. Kief looked back to make sure Clarin had returned to the cover of the forest. She was gone. Gray clouds gathered above as thunder heads began to rumble.

Friends

Kief clicked Natch to pick up the pace. He wanted to get above the ridgeline before he was spotted by the soldiers. Drops of rain began to fall. Natch twitched his ears flicking the water from them, as the slow drizzle softly pelted the leaves of the surrounding trees.

Kief stroked Natch's mane, "Sorry to leave you so long. We have to hurry now, boy."

Soon the rain came down in drenches. The pebbly soil turned to mud and a myriad of tiny streams trickled over the ground. In the distance, Kief could hear soldiers searching the mountainside for him. Natch sensed the danger and moved swiftly up the mountain. It wasn't long before Kief was soaked all the way through. The rain was making it easier for the soldiers to follow the deep footprints Natch was leaving in the mud.

"We have to do something about the trail we're giving them, Natch. Let's get above the tree line and head out across that rocky glen. We'll lose them there."

Kief looked back straining his eyes and ears as Natch climbed for the summit. There was no sign of the soldiers.

They had been so close. Kief squeezed Natch's wet leather reins. And now Jimbs is dead. He wanted to cry out. The Gars had taken everything from him. Kief felt utterly hopeless. If he showed his face at the mine or in town again, they'd capture and kill him on the spot for sure. By now, Kir-Trad was probably putting pieces together. Kief cursed, I should have killed Kir-Trad when I had the chance. Crossing over the stony peak, they came down the other side to a stream. Lightning shot across the sky and thunder shook the forest. It brought back a flash of memories when he'd sit in his bedroom gazing out his window at the storms, rain rattling on the roof. He remembered the waterfalls of rain pouring off the high pine branches out his window. The streams washing the stone streets clean, carrying away leaves, twigs, and horse dung. The rain was so thick he couldn't see the houses across the way. And then his mom would call him down for hot apple cake and milk.

A wet branch whipped him in the face bringing him back to his terrible reality. He directed Natch into the stream and they turned down the mountain wading in the middle of it. Kief was certain he'd lost the soldiers but he didn't want to leave any chances. He rode in the stream for some distance, being careful that Natch didn't step out and leave a print. Eventually, he spotted a rocky bank and he led Natch up and out of the stream. Ducking under the low branches, they weaved their way through the thick woods. He couldn't tell exactly where he was but he knew if he continued south, he'd eventually come out above Lake Shandon. Images of Jimbs' brutal beating blazed across his mind, his helpless bloody face looking up at him. Kief couldn't grasp the barbarity of it. It was hard for him to accept, but Jimbs' death had saved his life. That was the second old man to die at the hands of the Gars, not to mention his father. Kief swore he'd make them pay... all of them.

Lake Shandon lapped up on the shore under a thin layer of mist. Kief passed the favorite spot where he'd come to fish many times with his dad and brothers. When Balt caught his first fish, he'd screamed and thrown the fish in the air when it squiggled in his hand. He'd jumped around the flopping fish on his tip-toes, while Kief and Curchin watched, laughing. And Balt was the tough guy. Then the memory of his father's laughter echoed in his mind and his emotions poured out like the rain around him. He sobbed and sobbed as Natch carried him to the other side of the lake. Why did my father go with the soldiers? Why didn't he hear them coming? He should have run.

He clicked Natch into a gallop to clear his head and rode hard the rest of the way to the cave.

"Jimbs now too?" Tarc asked, stepping out into the rain to meet him.

The cave was cold and they had only lit one lantern. They hadn't even bothered to light a fire.

"They know our whole plan now," Patin accused Kief without hesitation.

"Not necessarily," Clarin rebutted.

"They know Kief's up to something; he announced it when he slugged the soldiers," Patin exclaimed throwing his hands in the air.

"I'm with Patin on this one," Luften joined in, "Discovering Jimbs with the powder is one thing, but now they know you're involved. That jeopardizes the whole plan and all of us."

A renewed surge of anger filled Kief from his feet to his head. He felt his ears getting hot. That was the last thing he was expecting from his friends.

Tarc joined them, "You've gotta keep your cool, we are all going to pay if you don't watch it."

"It's too late for that," Patin snapped.

Kief couldn't believe what he was hearing. Fuming, he bolted out of the cave. He jumped on Natch and galloped into the forest. It wasn't until he reached Lake Shandon that he slowed down.

"None of you were there," he cried out angrily in the silence.

The rain had stopped.

"None of you have lost what I have lost," he shouted out as he passed the fishing spot.

He'd lost everything, so what did it matter? Kief decided to go at it alone. The plan hadn't been completely ruined. The soldiers at the mine knew he was involved in something but they didn't know what. Twilight was fading and soon he'd be riding under a canopy of stars. Only thirty more boxes. Kief knew he could move them—it was just a matter of finding that many by sunrise. Suddenly he remembered the mining accident at tunnel 84. The tunnel collapsed on two miners. The miners were rescued, but the tunnel had to be closed because there was an explosive's storage area near the collapse. Too risky to dig for fear that a spark would set off the powder, the tunnel had been left dead. Kief decided to check it out.

The black flag, indicating the tunnel's closure, flapped in the light of the moons that stubbornly shown through the lingering storm clouds. Kief removed one of the lanterns hanging at the entrance and carried it into the mine before lighting it. In the narrow tunnel, he could hear his own breathing. It resonated back to him, heavy and hot and hurt. He would need tools to uncover the powder but he wanted to take a look to see what he was up against. Kief followed the small set of cart tracks about a hundred paces into the mine where he came upon the collapse. He could see the corner of the storage shed sticking out of the rubble. "Shouldn't be too hard to get to it," he said propping his lantern on a rock and digging into the crumbled pile with his hands. He hurled a rock at the wall, blasting it to powder, muttering curses under his breath. He would need a shovel, a pick ax, and some time to get through it.

"What's going on here?" a terribly familiar voice shot a chill straight through Kief. Whirling around he faced the same soldier that had arrested him before. He held a heavy slinger in his hand and a dim lantern in the other. Light from the spitting glow flashed off the big barrel of his slinger and shone up on his face transforming him into a fiery demon in the blackness. "Ah, it's you," he shook his head with a sinister snarl. "If there wasn't information I needed about some missing powder boxes, I'd blow you to bits right now! Turn around and drop to your knees."

Kief didn't move.

"Now!" the guard barked preparing to fire his slinger.

Kief forced his knees to kneel. He was still carrying his father's small double slinger in his satchel, but he knew he wouldn't have time to draw it before the soldier's slugs would rip through his heart.

The guard set down his lantern and jammed the barrel of his

slinger into Kief's back, searching him for weapons.

"Drop your satchel," he ordered.

Kief slowly pulled off his satchel and the soldier ripped it out of his hands. Jamming Kief again with his barrel, the soldier ordered him to pick up his lantern and get moving up the tunnel. Kief slogged up the path, his feet scrapping on the gravely ground. Once he left the mine, the soldier would call his cohorts and there would be no escape. He looked down at the light he was carrying. The soldier had left his on the ground back at the powder shed. Desperate and angry and hopeless... Kief twisted the knob... blackness enveloped them. He dropped just as a deafening crack blasted in his ears and two slugs whizzed over his head ricocheting off the rock walls. Tiny sparks flashed in the dark. Lunging, Kief snagged the soldier's ankle. Burying his fingertips into his boot he yanked the soldier to the ground, the barrel of his flailing slinger connecting with Kief's cheek, splitting it open. He crawled up the burly body, his hand connecting with the soldier's, feeling for his knife. Kief grabbed his thick wrist prying back his hand. Sharp rocks dug into his skin as they thrashed back and forth in the obscurity of the tunnel, smashing against the walls. He could feel the soldier's sticky breath on his skin as he tried to bite Kief's hand. The soldier was definitely stronger, but thanks to Tarc—and Flinch, Kief knew how to handle a man. He locked onto him from behind. The rock in the soldier's grip glanced off Kief's temple, sending him into a rage. He circled his adversary's throat with his arm and clamped down. The soldier kicked and squirmed. Kief squeezed with all his force, the soldier pounding his arm with his fist and clawing at his face, but Kief was locked down like a vice. When the flailing stopped, Kief lay in the silence with the motionless soldier.

He pushed him aside and sat for a long moment catching his

breath before feeling around for the lantern.   Disoriented in the blackness, he couldn't find it, nor could he tell which way led out. As he tried to determine the slope of the corridor, he was startled by a glow on the ground a few paces behind him.   Crawling toward it, he could make out the outline of his satchel. Lifting the flap, he saw light emitting from the small pouch holding his stone. He pulled it out; it was hot, as it had been the day he'd taken his family to High Valley. It shone brighter than any light he'd ever seen, like he was holding a small sun in his hand, only it didn't hurt his eyes to look at it. As he held the stone, it became almost translucent as though he were looking through the opening of a small window into a sea of blue. And then clear as a white cloud against the turquoise sky the number four appeared and then disappeared in its expanse. Kief marveled at the stone. Turning it over in his hand, he could see through it the same no matter which way he held it. For a moment he was mystified by it and wondered how his grandfathers had come upon such a thing.

Using the light from the stone he searched for his lantern. It was behind him. He'd been searching in the wrong direction. As he lit the lantern, the light from the stone faded. He returned the stone to its pouch and dragged the soldier's lifeless body back to the buried powder shed.

"Don't move," he heard a chilling voice behind him.

Wheeling about he faced another soldier, his slinger fixed on Kief. A slug fired. Kief gasped for air and grabbed at his chest but felt nothing. The soldier fell forward onto his face. Tarc emerged from the shadows brandishing his double-barrel crescent slinger. He motioned for Kief to keep quiet. Picking up the slinger loaded with two slugs that had been meant for him, and handing a new crescent to Tarc, Kief grabbed the lantern and closed the shade flaps. The faint glow was just enough to light the way. They crept to the entrance. Two soldiers' horses stood alone outside the tunnel. Removing the saddles and bridles they slapped their rears and sent them running into the forest.

"How did you know?" Kief asked as they lugged the horses' tack back into the mine to hide it.

"Someone has to watch after you," Tarc replied harshly.

"What's that supposed to mean?" Kief shot back as he dropped the saddle on the rubble next to the dead soldiers.

"You never think, Kief," Tarc threw up his arms exasperated. "You just explode with no regard for the consequences."

"At least I do something," Kief shouted.

"Dying doesn't count as something," Tarc shouted back. "You act like a cornered animal; attacking in frenzy without using your head to figure a way out."

"This head," Kief stepped toward Tarc pointing forcefully at his forehead. "This head is what came up with this great plan of ours."

"And not using that head is what has been getting all of us in a lot of trouble lately! Has it even occurred to you how much danger all of our families are in right now—all of us are in right now? I'm as willing as you are to put it all on the line if it means getting rid of the Gars, but I'm not stupid about it!" Tarc turned away in disgust.

"Well they didn't take your father did they?" Kief lashed out.

Tarc cleared his throat and lowered his voice, "You don't even know what this is all about do you? This is bigger than you, bigger than avenging your father, bigger than all of us."

"It's about making them pay for what they've done," Kief lifted a clenched fist in front of his face.

"No! No it's not," Tarc shoved a finger into Kief's chest. "It's about freedom! That's what our oath is, to restore freedom! If you see The Dark Eagles as a way for you to get back at the Gars for killing your father then you are missing everything!"

Kief stepped back and dropped to the ground under the weight of his sudden self-awareness. Rubbing his face with his hands, he leaned back against the wall. He felt small.

He sat quietly for a moment and then confessed, "I tried to kill Kir-Trad." Tarc let him talk. "The evening I went spying, I really went there to kill him. They found my shoulder slinger. When I was arrested and set free, Kir-Trad had it in his hands. He knew it was mine."

Tarc paused, "Why'd he let you go?"

"Show of power, he was trying to win me over. I think he wants the stone and suspects I have it," Kief replied.

"What would he know about the stone?"

"I dunno, I just had the feeling he knew about it."

"Well, he certainly knows about you taking the powder."

"Yeah," Kief replied feeling low.

"Do you think that head of yours can come up with any great ideas to get us out of this mess?" Tarc grinned, and then extended his hand for Kief's, "That's a nasty gash on your cheek, I'll bet Clarin will be more than happy to take a look at it."

"What do you… "

"I might not be smart enough to go to the Merchant Academy, but I'm not dumb, either. I've seen what's going on there."

A smile broke on Kief's troubled face, "How'd you find me?"

"After you ran off, we divided up to search for you. I took the upper mine area. When I heard the slug fire from the tunnel I came running. That soldier," he pointed, "was running into the mine just as I got here and I followed him. Good thing Luften pulled out the slingers. He knew you'd be getting into more trouble."

"Guess he knows me by now." Kief looked down at the two dead bodies, "What do we do with those guys?"

"Let's drag them deeper into the mine where no one will find them."

They left the lantern at the collapse and dragged the soldiers further into the tunnel. When the light was a faint glimmer, they stopped and dropped the corpses. They hurried away from the eerie darkness back to the light and the buried powder shed.

"I guess this is your new plan?" Tarc nodded at the pile of rocks and dirt. "How much powder do you think is under there?"

"At least thirty boxes," Kief smiled. "They keep things well stocked up here."

"So, should I leave you to dig or would you like some help?" he joked.

"I was planning on letting you do all the digging," Kief slugged Tarc's shoulder.

"It'd be faster with a few tools."

"Yeah, I'm sure the upper tool house isn't guarded."

"Good, you get the tools and I'll round us up some more workers," Tarc said.

As they reached the mine entrance, a piercing screech made Tarc jump. He raised his slinger and ducked for cover.

"Relax," Kief said. "It's just a dark eagle," he tried to spot where it was. "I've gotten so used to seeing them flying around and screeching at me, it doesn't even faze me anymore. I still can't figure out why they're showing up all the time, though."

Tarc turned to him, "Are you an idiot?"

Kief stared back with a blank look.

"They're protecting us!"

"You think they're here for us?" Kief asked. "You believe those old legends?"

"Yeah I think they're true," Tarc thought he spotted the eagle, "is that it?" he pointed. A dark shadow launched off the tree and flew away. "Remember what Patin said about the Saans' charge to protect the world from evil?"

Kief stayed fixed on the trees.

"Maybe there's some connection between you and the black raptors?"

"Could be, I love to fly," Kief replied. "So, we meet back here in twenty strokes?"

"Make it fifteen."

Tarc ran to the rendezvous point, where the others had already gone after hearing echoes of shots being fired.

"It won't be long until they figure out that they've got two more soldiers missing," Luften warned. "By morning they'll be mad as bulls and on the search again."

Hurrying to the mine, they met Kief with a stack of tools inside the entrance.

"Grab a few lanterns there," Kief pointed, "where'd you come from, Flinch?"

"Clarin came and got me after you lost it," he said, "I guess some things don't change do they?"

Kief didn't say anything. He'd walked that tunnel several times now, but in the cold silence, it seemed to take forever to get to the shed. He knew they wanted an apology, but he didn't offer them one.

"This is going to take forever," Patin complained.

"If you can get your arms to move as fast as your mouth, we'll be done in no time," Tarc said.

Flinch and Kief swung the picks. The others shoveled. And nobody said much of anything.

When they'd finally uncovered the top half, Patin collapsed on the ground, "This is impossible," he mopped his dripping face with his sleeve.

"We're half way," Clarin replied.

"You gonna let a girl out work you, Patin?" Flinch taunted.

"I don't have a problem with that," Patin came back, "besides it's just my sister and there's no one here I need to impress."

"So the dead soldiers are back there?" Sefrana looked down the black tunnel, changing the subject.

"I hope they haven't wandered off," Tarc replied heaving a shovel full of rocks.

Sefrana gave him a forced smile, "Real funny!"

Kief and Flinch stepped aside with their picks to let them clear away the loosened rubble.

"I'd have done the same thing," Flinch said quietly to Kief, "in fact, I'd have slugged them even if they hadn't killed Jimbs."

"You okay?" Clarin nudged Kief. "I'll take a look at that cut on your cheek when we've finished."

"Yeah, I'm alright."

"It's going to work out, you'll see," she assured him. "You just need to have a little more trust in the plan—and your friends," she smiled, her bright eyes flashing through him, even in the dimly-lit tunnel.

They were as bright as his stone, he thought; only his stone sure didn't make him feel like those eyes of hers did.

Late in the evening they finished uncovering the shed. Patin had loosened up but Luften was still mad at Kief. Kief just ignored him. There were thirty-four boxes of powder—just enough. They stacked them into the mine carts, and pushed them to the entrance. They loaded two boxes in each of their saddlebags and held one in their laps, carrying them down to the old loading station.

"Me and Tarc will climb through the broken window in the

back," Kief whispered, "and you can bring us the boxes."

They slipped through the window, a few boxes in hand and stacked them in the car. They had all thirty-four stacked in no time.

"A hundred and four boxes, that should do it," Kief smiled.

The storm clouds had dispersed and the setting moons looming large on the horizon shone brightly through the slits in the shed.

"I believe it will," Tarc said patting his back, "I believe it will."

Messengers

Sunlight flooded the entrance of the cave. Kief lay on his back tracing the detailed patterns of grays and browns on the rock wall with his eyes. Luften was still sleeping. Outside, birds chirped in the tall pines and the wind whistled through the needles. The events of the day before seemed like a distant nightmare, and now in the light of a new day, Kief was happy it was over. They had decided it was best for everyone if he disappeared from town entirely. Luften had let Kief have it on their ride back to the cave. They had arrived just as the horizon began to show the color of a rising sun.

Now that the car was filled, Kief felt a huge relief, though he knew that was really only the beginning. He still had no idea how they were going to distract the soldiers so they could get the loaded car out of the old station. They didn't have much time to come up with something.

As he lay there considering what their next plan of action should be, Tarc and Flinch came tromping into the cave followed by everyone else.

"Hey Kief," Tarc said, "How was your sleep on the rocks?"

"I slept great! How'd you sleep on that old lumpy bed of yours?"

"I'm pretty sure lumpy is still better than rocky," he smiled and plopped down on the rocks next to him.

Luften winced as he sat up on the opposite wall of the cave, "How are things looking? Any movement with the soldiers?"

"Well if you mean by movement, troops going house to house looking for the missing soldiers; yep, they're moving," Tarc replied.

"And worse," Sefrana added, "We just heard they moved the celebration to the 21st."

"What? That's two days from now," Kief was shocked, his momentary sense of comfort dissipating completely. They weren't ready.

Luften smoothed out his hair and situated his hat on his head, "Well, what do we have left to plan?"

"We have to figure out how to distract the soldiers... " Kief said.

"Flinch is pretty fast," Tarc said slapping his back.

Flinch grinned, "I'd just need to outrun you, Tarc."

Luften laughed, "That's just it, it's too risky to send any of us. We'd be captured and tortured until we gave up the plan."

"What about the fire pipes?" Clarin spoke up excitedly, "They make a lot of noise."

"That's perfect!" Tarc said.

"Yes, perfect," Kief pointed at Clarin.

"What are the fire pipes?" Luften asked.

"See," Tarc said, "if you haven't lived in Shaflann, you have no idea."

While the watchtowers provided a look-out, wide fire paths running between each of the towers were cut along the outer edges of town. A line of steel pipes, with spray nozzles placed in the pipe every twenty paces, ran down the center of the paths allowing for the town to be isolated from any threatening fire. The pipeline was fed by water from Lake Shandon. When the gate was opened, lake water would rush into the pipes and down the hill. The intense pressure in the lines forced the trapped air out at the spray nozzles with a loud hissing noise. During the calm of Sun Rhythm evenings, when they would test the lines, the hissing could be heard all the way up to the mine.

Clarin, can you release the water at the fire shed?"

"Of course," she replied confidently, "that's easy."

Sefrana didn't look nearly as confident, "What about the people in High Valley," she asked. "They'll be in the square along with the soldiers."

"That's the other problem I can't figure out," Kief replied.

"Yeah, it's not like we can announce it," Patin replied.

"We need something only people from High Valley could understand," Clarin said.

"It's a flaming car right?" Sefrana spoke up.

"It will be," Tarc grinned.

"Remember the last flaming car that flew into High Valley?" she tucked her hair behind her ear.

"The Winzert family," Flinch replied.

"Yep," Sefrana straightened up on the log she was using for a seat. "If we can send out some sort of warning that hints to the flaming car just a few strokes before the train car comes into town, it may be enough time to get them running."

"That may work," Kief rubbed his forehead, the remaining specks of dirt from his sleep on the rocks prickling his skin. "I'm thinking the main portion of the square will probably be covered with Gar troops anyway, like Luften and I saw when they were practicing. The townspeople will mostly be on the perimeter."

"So how do we get a message out that everyone can see?" Patin asked, "We can't just unfurl a banner."

Grabbing a stick, Luften drew a circle in the dirt, "I saw something last year at the academy. It was a globe made of thin paper filled with pure oxygen."

"We could use the festive paper globes we put on the lampposts during the New Year Commemoration," Sefrana piped up. "My dad has some left over in storage."

"I'm sure we could get some oxygen vessels from the mine," Luften finished.

"Okay, let's give it a try," Kief shrugged. "Tarc, see if you can get an oxygen vessel from Bonds and, Sefrana, you get the paper globes."

"And I'll get my paints too," she smiled.

Tarc and Luften rode for the mine early the next morning. Tarc had a hard time concealing his excitement, but then, most of the miners had their heads down as they plodded slowly up the road.

At the mine house, they found Bonds talking with some of the miners. When he saw them, he quickly finished his conversation and walked over, "Hello boys," he said, and then, lowering his voice he asked, "how's Kief?"

"He's good," Tarc waved him off, "but we need an oxygen vessel."

Bonds looked around for soldiers and then back at Tarc, "An oxygen vessel huh? Come with me."

"And we need some igniters too—five stroke," Luften added.

"I have some here," Bonds said walking over to a shelf. He handed Tarc an old canvas bag, "there should be some fives in there."

Tarc rummaged through the bag finding some fives as they followed Bonds out behind the smelter to a holding facility. There were several vessels about the size and shape of a large pumpkin with the word 'oxygen' written on them. Bonds picked one up and handed it to Tarc, "Take this out the back door and up the hill. You can get your horses to carry it when we're done here."

"Thanks Bonds," Tarc said.

"No problem, I'm always here."

Bonds went back inside the smelting house and Tarc and Luften carried the vessel up the hill. Luften slipped a couple of times.

When Luften had lost his footing for the fourth time, Tarc smirked, "You need me to get someone to help you on that end?"

"Shut up and keep moving," Luften barked.

"Wow, Luften, I didn't know you could get mad," Tarc mocked.

Luften laughed, "You missed my ride back to the cave with Kief—I gave him a piece of my mind!"

"Yeah, me too, in the mine tunnel. I think that whole thing

scared him sufficiently."

They found a suitable spot behind a tree to hide the tank and returned with their horses. The vessel was awkward and it took them a bit to find a way to strap it on the back of Luften's horse.

Shuffling through the old inventory, Sefrana found eight globes that were blank. The rest were globes she'd already painted for her father to sell for the New Year Commemoration. The first day of New Rhythm every year they had a big celebration with food and music and dancing and competitions of all kinds; baking, log cutting, horse racing. The paper globes were placed on the lampposts throughout the village. Hot air rising from the lamps filled the globes and the light illuminated the lamps in a glowing spectacle of colors. She paused to admire her favorite one, yellow-bellied sparrows with orange circles representing the sun. She wanted to look forward to the next New Year Commemoration, maybe she'd find the nerve to try to bake something to enter in the contest.

Folding the blank ones, she came out of the back room. Her father was dusting his shelves.

He stopped and turned, looking over his glasses resting on the end of his nose, "I don't think it is safe to be seen with Kief anymore," he said matter-of-factly.

She walked up to her father and kissed his cheek and hugged him. "Kief is deep in the forest, they won't find us. I have to help, father."

He sighed and hung his head, "I know you do. Please, please, be careful. I couldn't bear to lose you."

"I will father. I love you. You be careful while I'm gone."

She could see his sad face through the thick glass as he watched her load the folded globes into her saddle bags. But before she could change her mind, she kicked her horse into a gallop.

"Where are you going?" A soldier shouted at her just before she reached the cover of the forest.

She jumped, a wave of dizziness sweeping over her. The first words she spoke didn't come out so she repeated them, "I... I'm going to see mmmy... friend."

"And who is that friend?" the soldier demanded with a snarl as he rode toward her.

"Clarin," she replied hoarsely, swallowing the lump in her throat.

"Open your saddlebags," another shouted as he dismounted and yanked her off her horse.

Sefrana opened her saddlebag fearing the worst and then she heard Luften's voice inside her head, 'they don't know what you're up to, just stay calm,' but her hands still trembled.

The soldier ripped the contents from the bag, tearing a few of the paper globes. "And what are these?" he barked.

She blurted out the first thing that came to mind, "They're for the upcoming Gar celebration in the square; we're going to decorate them."

"Huh, maybe some of them are worth keeping alive," the soldier looked her up and down. He reached up and stroked her hair with his filthy hand. Her chin quivered.

"Not so fast, you'll get your chance," his companion said deviously.

The soldier dropped the wad of paper globes on the ground and mounted up. Shaking, Sefrana smoothed and refolded the globes placing them back in her saddlebags.

By the time she reached the cave, Sefrana and her horse were in a panic. Luften took the reins. As she dismounted, she burst into tears. Clarin took her hand. Sefrana could hardly relate her encounter.

"And one of them looked at me in that way," she stuttered, "And the other one said he'd get his opportunity soon."

Luften growled through clenched teeth, "If one those grimy fools touch you... "

She burst into tears again.

Patin looked around, "Where's Flinch?"

"He's fine," Tarc assured. "He's Flinch, he'll be here."

Sefrana pulled the globes from her saddlebags. "They ripped two of them," she said wiping the tears from her cheeks.

"I'm sorry," Luften said softly. "You were impressively calm."

"You call this calm?" she replied.

"In the moment you were, and that's all that counts," he smiled at her.

Finding a clear spot on the ground, Sefrana spread the paper globes out. She situated herself on the ground in front of her strange canvases.

"What should we write?" she stopped, realizing she didn't know what she needed to paint.

"How about *Remember line#2 and the Winzerts, death is coming, run now!*" Patin said.

"That's a little obvious don't you think?" Luften replied. "Might as well tell them a train car full of explosives is coming."

"They won't know it has anything to do with the train," Kief liked it. "And when they do see the car flying down the track, hopefully they'll think it's full of armed men and that they can handle it easily with their battalion of soldiers. They won't run— have they yet?"

"I hope you're right," Luften wasn't convinced.

"It's true, we have to give the citizens as clear a warning as possible," Sefrana insisted.

Luften decided to let this one go and agreed.

Sefrana painted the six paper globes while everyone else talked the details of the plan. When she finished, Patin was excited to test one with the oxygen. It was like he'd forgotten what they were for and he was back in science class doing an experiment. Grabbing the first globe Sefrana had painted, which was now dry, he walked over to the tank. Luften ripped it out of his hands.

"Easy there," Sefrana said. "We don't need any more torn."

Patin looked at him with an accusing stare but Luften ignored him placing the globe inlet over the vessel nozzle and slowly opening the valve. As oxygen hissed into the globe, Patin's eyes widened. It didn't take long before the oblong globe, as tall as Luften, was full and hovering above them.

Luften tied the end closed with a string, "How's that?"

"Looks great!" Sefrana cheered admiring Luften's ingenuity and her fine calligraphy.

"It's Flinch!" Tarc called out.

"Where have you been?" Sefrana demanded walking toward him, "We got worried that something had happened to you. And what's up with the pack horse?"

"After we broke our meeting yesterday, I got thinking," Flinch said as he swung to the ground, "How are we going to get the floating globes above the crowd? We can't just walk out in the middle of the square and let them go. So I had an idea. We could tie the globes to the feet of birds and then release them a distance from the square. And then I had the idea to use red winged gulls, the ones that live among the eves of the government buildings and time tower in Town Center. When they're released, they'll fly home across the square."

"That's brilliant!" Patin was amazed that Flinch had come up with such an idea.

"I went down to the square this morning and trapped eight of them."

"So that's what you have in the cages?" Sefrana said laughing at his cleverness. As tough as Flinch could be with people, he had a way with animals.

"Well, with that, I think our plan is complete," Luften declared.

"Yes, but we'll need to make some changes in assignments," Kief said as they sat down at their camp. "Patin, why don't you go with Flinch to release the globes near the square? I'll get Bonds to help me and Tarc push the car out of the loading station."

"Yep," Patin agreed, looking forward to the experiment as much as watching the attack.

"So that means Luften, you'll need to go with Sefrana to take out any guards at the maintenance platform."

"And Clarin, you're still our lone noise-making distracter."

"I'm good with my job."

As they settled in for some sleep, Kief played through each step of the plan in his mind. It was sound.

the Dark Eagles

Luften woke first the next morning. He nudged Kief, "It's time."

Kief rolled over and lay there a moment. The plan is easy enough, he said to himself. The most difficult part would be the timing; he hoped they got it right.

A somber quiet hung over the morning as they each contemplated their individual roles. It was one thing to make plans to blow up an army; it was quite another to carry them out. Up to that point, Kief hadn't felt nervous; but as time for the mission had arrived, he had a hard time keeping his nerves calm.

Flinch and Patin were the first to load up. They had the longest journey ahead of them. Flinch wrapped the oxygen tank in a cloth to disguise it the best he could and strapped it on the back of his pack horse along with the birds that were cooing pleasantly in their cages. Patin carefully folded the painted paper globes and placed them in his saddlebags. As they made preparations, Sefrana packed lunches and handed sandwiches wrapped in paper to them. Patin stuffed them in his satchel.

"Well, this is it," Kief said extending his hand in the eagle grip to his companions.

Tarc slapped Flinch and Patin on the back as he walked with them to their horses, "We'll see everyone back here at dark."

They mounted up and reined their horses into the forest. Patin had already started into Flinch with questions, who had no interest in providing much in the way of information, which added more to Patin's anxiety. Flinch seemed to enjoy it.

Luften and Sefrana loaded their crescent side slingers and placed them in their saddlebags with food and water flasks; they would have to stop at the stream and fill them up on their way.

Kief brought out one of his father's shoulder slingers from the cave and handed it to Luften, "Use this to fire long range, it's more accurate."

Luften hefted up the long-barreled shoulder slinger and looked down the eyepiece, aiming it at a tree, "This should do," he said.

"There shouldn't be more than three or four guards on the maintenance platform," Kief said.

"I hope there aren't any," Luften responded as he strapped the shoulder slinger to his horse. Swinging up in the saddle Luften turned to Sefrana who was still standing beside her horse nervously fingering the tangles out of her hair, "You ready?"

"I'm ready," she sighed climbing onto her horse.

Luften reined Odin into the forest toward the steam line tracks.

Sefrana turned back to wave three times, "Don't forget the lunches I packed for you!" she called after them.

Kief had a pang in his heart. It was his plan. If they didn't all make it back, he would be responsible for their deaths. By Dark he would know.

"Everything will go fine," he called out trying to reassure himself. Theirs was the only mission that was certain to involve a direct conflict. He watched as two more of his friends disappeared into the trees.

Clarin turned to Kief, "I guess I should leave for the fire shed."

"Yeah, it's a good idea to get up there now so you can scope out the place and find a safe spot to wait," Tarc said.

"I don't think there will be soldiers, but keep your eyes open just in case," Kief said as he hid a side slinger in her saddlebag.

"Are you going to be okay Clarin?" Tarc asked.

"I'll be fine," she responded, "I'm okay alone, if that's what you mean. Your big muscles are needed elsewhere," she punched his burly arm.

Tarc turned red.

Clarin loaded her lunch into her saddlebag and meticulously fastened the buckles. Then she smoothed her horses' mane and checked the saddle and reins, adjusting and readjusting the clasps.

"Remember, open the water gate at a cadence past Dusk," Tarc said.

"And don't forget, 'righty-tighty, lefty-loosy' when you turn the wheel," Kief held her horse as she finally climbed up in the saddle.

She laughed and took his hand, "Okay, I won't forget that important piece of advice."

He squeezed it and looked long into her big brown eyes, "You be careful Clarin, there's no one there to watch your back."

"I'll be fine," she smiled at him sweetly, "I'll be watching from high above Lake Shandon on Pryes Peak." She rode off looking back only once to wave before disappearing into the forest.

Kief sat down heavily next to Tarc.

"She'll be alright," Tarc assured him.

"What if we aren't alright? I worry about them losing us as much as us losing them. We can take care of ourselves in this craziness, but could they? Sefrana and Clarin, and my mom, and yours? We can do this... right?" he looked at Tarc.

"Of course," Tarc shook Kief's shoulder.

He was always straight with Kief and the fact that he'd never doubted the plan gave him confidence, "My heart's racing a hundred times faster than any urt bout, I can tell you that."

"It'll all go away once the pipe blows," Tarc smiled. He had told Kief the same thing before his very first bout.

"You mean pipes," he grinned. "I'm glad you're with me Tarc. I'm not sure I could have done any of this without you."

"Nope, you couldn't," he elbowed him.

They sat quietly watching the woods for some time.

"They'll probably have guards posted all over the silver mine and they may not all leave when the pipes begin to whistle," Tarc said.

"Yeah, I've been thinking about that," Kief said soberly, "We'll just have to see what it looks like when we get there."

When it was time, they loaded their things onto Natch and Sarjen. Natch twitched his ears and flicked his tail.

Avoiding Dunton Canyon all together, they climbed the ridge and came down above it. The mine grounds were covered with soldiers. They could only spot a few miners, and Bonds was not among them.

"He must be in the mine house," Kief whispered.

"I hope so. I'll go—I'm not a wanted man," Tarc replied.

"Just get in quickly, and if he's not there, get out fast."

"I will," Tarc handed Kief his reins and rushed to the door, disappearing inside.

Kief had a clear view of the door from his hiding place in the trees. Four guards came around the side of the building and disappeared inside.

Tarc! Kief wanted to scream, but it was too late to warn him. He quickly tied up the horses and pulled his slinger from his saddlebags along with some extra crescents. Moving in closer behind the cover of a thick pine, he raised his slinger preparing to fire at the first soldier that came through the door. His hand was shaking; he held it against the tree to keep it steady. Sweat trickled down his cheek. He took a deep breath to calm himself. He'd have to hit his target with each shot; he wouldn't have time to reload more than once. The door opened and the first guard came into his sights, just as a dark eagle swooped in low and then perched on the pine next to him. By the time he was able to set his sights again, the four guards had come out and disappeared around the house as quickly as they'd appeared. He'd missed his shot!

"Now those eagles are starting to annoy me," he muttered. "I should have fired!"

When Tarc didn't return right away, Kief's mind started to panic. There had been no shots fired, but there were other ways to take care of someone. His mind flashed to the lifeless soldier that lay under him in the dark of the mine. He cringed at the thought. He began to run through his mind what he would have to do if he had to go it alone. But to Kief's relief, after what seemed an eternity, the door opened again and out came Tarc followed by Bonds. They moved quickly to the forest where Kief was waiting.

"I thought you were a goner Tarc, what happened?" Kief asked.

"So, one moment I was talking with Bonds, and the next he was stuffing me into a closet."

"The soldiers have been making regular rounds. When the door opened, I knew it was them and shoved him in," Bonds replied.

"Way to think fast Bonds," Kief said.

"Yeah, I can't wait till all this sneaking around by you boys is over," Bonds said. "So today's the big day, huh?"

"Yep, and then it'll all be over. We need your help, though. There's a car in the old loading station that we're pushing down the tracks; we need you to help us get it started on its way."

"No problem," he smiled, "the only problem I see is all these putrid soldiers wandering around," Bonds replied loathingly.

"Yeah, we have a plan for diverting them. But they may not all follow the distraction, that's our worry," Tarc said.

"Me and my miners will be glad to take out any stragglers," Bonds grinned.

"You have slingers?" Kief asked surprised.

"Oh yeah, all these men hid them throughout the tunnels before the Gars arrived. They've been waiting for a day like today."

Tarc was grinning from ear to ear. Kief was excited to hear that so many men were ready to fight.

"We need you at a cadence past Dusk at the old station," he said. "Tell your men that's when the excitement begins and to be ready."

"We'll be ready," Bonds replied, as he turned to go. "I better get back before somebody starts missing me."

Kief and Tarc stayed hidden in the forest talking about nothing and biding their time. A little before Dusk a faint rumbling and clanking came from the direction of the mine. To their horror, soldiers swarmed into the canyon and lined both sides. At their commander's shout, they all turned and charged into the forest.

"We've gotta get out of here," Tarc said frantically.

They swung up onto their horses, but it was too late. One of the guards had already spotted them. He blasted his horn and every soldier turned in the direction of the alarm. They flew through the forest, branches lashing their faces and underbrush tugging at their boots; behind them, a pack of hostile soldiers in close pursuit. They climbed higher and higher until they reached the rushing waters of the upper Tubin River.

"It's too deep, we'll be swept away," Tarc shouted above the roaring rapids.

"I'm taking my chances with the river," Kief yelled back as the soldiers closed in on them.

They plunged into the raging water, the chaotic rapids engulfing them. They were swept quickly downstream by the powerful current. Kief held tightly to Natch in the icy cold, swirling water gasping for breath. By the time the Gars reached the edge of the water, Tarc and Kief had disappeared around a bend.

Carried at the mercy of the river, Kief was heading straight for a massive boulder jutting up in the middle, the water exploding on its face. He could feel Natch swimming with his might as they swirled around the boulder nearly getting caught in its powerful eddy. Natch continued to struggle, pulling them out and making for calmer waters. Kief looked back up the river. There was no sign of the soldiers. He reined Natch the best he could to swim for the bank. Sarjen and Tarc reached the edge about fifty paces below them. Exhausted and shivering, they stopped in a clearing to catch their breaths.

"What was that?" Tarc was more angry than scared.

"They had to have known we were coming," Kief replied.

"But how, no one knows about our plan," Tarc said.

"Well, maybe they were just doing a sweep of the forest around the mine then, as a precaution and we happened to be there at the wrong time," Kief said, dumping the water out of his boots.

"Could be," Tarc had taken his shirt off and was wringing it out, "because there's no way they could have called a patrol together that quickly, even if they had seen us with Bonds." He had finished with his shirt and moved on to wringing his pants, "Do you think they found the train car in the old loading station?"

"Not yet anyway. Bonds would have known."

Tarc pulled his soaked time piece from the pocket of his pants, "Oh! It's almost Dusk, time is short!"

"Yeah, I know. Get your clothes back on and let's get down to the loading station," Kief pulled himself back up on Natch.

Tarc was struggling to pull his pants back on, "I'm hurrying,"

he snapped, "at least I'll be dry in no time." He stopped, "But won't the soldiers be waiting for us?"

"They're looking for us in the forest, they won't expect us to return to the mine," Kief laughed at Tarc who was hopping on one foot fighting to get on his second boot.

Patin and Flinch rode into High Valley without seeing a single soldier. The streets were so full of people, that they were able to easily blend in with the crowd. After stopping in to warn Kief's family, they rode for Town Center. They searched for a secluded place, which was proving to be difficult, where they could launch the gull globes. A couple of soldiers walked by and Patin slunk into his saddle.

"Relax!" Flinch had had enough. Since they had ridden into town, Patin couldn't stop getting all wide-eyed and twitchy every time they passed a soldier. "If you look like you're up to something, they'll think you're up to something."

"Right," Patin replied sitting up tall in his saddle.

"Don't overdo it, just be natural."

Patin slouched some and Flinch just shook his head. He stopped his horse and glanced around the square again.

Patin was looking at the line of stores running along the street just south of Town Center opposite the stage and time tower, "Flinch, let's check out the alley behind those stores. I'll bet a few of them have stairways up to the roof."

Making their way through the crowded square, they were happy to find the alleyway empty.

"There's some stairs!" Patin blurted out.

"Quietly!" Flinch hushed and wrinkled his brow at him. "Wait here," Flinch motioned as he dismounted and ran to check it out. "It's good," he smiled as he returned, "let's unload everything quickly, those soldiers are always showing up out of nowhere."

At that, Patin jumped into frantic mode again. Flinch gave up trying to calm him and unloaded the oxygen tank. They lugged their gear up the stairs and returned for the bird cages.

"We need to move the horses," Patin said. "If soldiers see them in the alley, they'll suspect something's up. Get it? ... Up!" he joked and let out a nervous laugh.

Flinch chuckled, "Yeah, Patin, I get it, but that still doesn't make it funny."

"You laughed," Patin replied.

Flinch laughed again, "We'll take the horses out front and hitch them at the bakery post. Then we can cut through the bakery and out the back door."

"I like that," Patin pointed a finger at Flinch.

They worked their way through the crowd to the front of the bakery and hitched up their horses. In the middle of the plaza, a procession of soldiers marched in rhythm. On the opposite end, near the governor's house and time tower, was the newly constructed stage and podium, the huge Gar banner waving in the breeze.

Patin mumbled under his breath, "Too bad they spent so much time on such a nice stage!"

"Yeah, I'm heartbroken," Flinch replied.

Soldiers stood along the streets surrounding the entire square, though it was hardly necessary. There seemed to be much more celebration than hostility. Flinch pushed his way through the packed bakery grumbling in disgust.

Patin whispered, "Well, at least we're less noticeable in such a lively bunch." Flinch grunted and stepped up to the counter to buy some bread. "What are you doing Flinch?" Patin whispered nervously.

"Blending in. Besides, it smells good."

After paying for the bread, they slipped through the kitchen and out the back door into the alleyway. A group of soldiers was coming down the street.

Flinch pushed Patin back inside, "Soldiers!"

"Did they see us?"

"I don't think so."

They waited and listened at the door.

"What are you boys doing back here?" a booming voice came from behind them. Spinning around they faced a fat baker in an apron, waving a stubby finger at them, his greasy dark hair pulled up behind his head.

"Oh, we're sorry," Patin replied, "we took a wrong turn."

"Are you thieves?" He barked, "What do you have there?"

Flinch could hear the soldiers stomping by on the other side of the door behind them.

He lowered his voice, "No, we're not thieves. It's bread that we bought from your store," he held out the paper bag for the baker to see.

"Get out," he shouted angrily.

Flinch tried to stall, retelling him how they were new and that they must have gotten turned around. When the baker looked as though he would literally pick them up and throw them out the door himself, Flinch pulled on Patin and they shuffled out into the alley. The baker kept shouting at them through the closed door. Fortunately the soldiers had turned up another alley and the baker's voice was lost in the noise of the celebration.

"Hurry," Flinch prodded Patin as they ran up the stairs to the rooftop.

They sat down next to the birds. Flinch tore off a piece of bread and handed it to Patin.

"Boy you were right—those soldiers are always just magically appearing," Patin breathed heavily, his eyes darting at the stairs between each bite.

"They didn't see us," Flinch reassured Patin. "If they had, they'd be here by now."

"Grumpy baker... but he sure makes good bread," Patin wiped the crumbs off his shirt.

Kief and Tarc looked across the Dunton Canyon trail from the cover of the trees. To their disappointment, there was still a large group of soldiers along the path and surrounding the main mine house.

"They must have known you were still around and up to something," Tarc muttered.

As they watched, about thirty miners finishing their shift dropped their gear off and left the building. One by one they rode out of the stables and down the canyon toward Shaflann.

Tarc turned to Kief, "Where are they going?"

"Wait," he replied.

When the miners reached the mouth of the canyon, out of sight of the guards, they broke off and scattered into the forest.

"Alright," Tarc said excitedly, "now what?"

"We wait for Clarin," Kief smiled.

The peacefulness of Lake Shandon enthralled Clarin. A fish

jumped, sending ripples across the deep blue water. She watched them until they spread apart and disappeared. A few birds called to each other through the clear evening air. In the calm, Clarin said a prayer for her friends.

Her time piece read nearly a cadence past Dusk. Stepping out of her wooded concealment above the fire shed she crept cautiously down the hill. A dead tree leaning against another creaked in the wind, unsettling her just a little. She lifted the rusty latch to the fire shed. It popped and screeched. She scanned the edge of the forest and then stepped inside the small hut, which was really nothing more than a covered shelter to protect the valve mechanism from the weather. Removing her time piece from her satchel, she waited for a cadence past Dusk.

Luften and Sefrana followed the same path that he and Patin had taken when they went to the maintenance platform the first time.

"How many guards do you think there will be?" Sefrana asked nervously.

"Last time there were three, I'll bet the same this time around."

"Three is too many," she said hoping for no more than two.

"One is too many," Luften answered.

"So how are we going to do it?" Sefrana asked, hoping she wouldn't have to slug anyone.

"Just gonna pull the trigger," Luften replied insensitively.

"This is easy for you, isn't it? Just slugging someone," she challenged him.

"Yes, it's easy for me to slug someone who takes my home and

my family and kills the father of my friend," Luften defended. "To me it seems unfeeling to not want to kill them."

"But what if these soldiers wish they weren't here invading our country. Maybe they were forced to come," Sefrana said.

"They're here, that makes them part of it. We show them mercy and your father could be next."

Sefrana recoiled at the thought of losing her father. Luften's words were convincing though her heart still raced with fear.

"Don't think I like this, any of this. I'd give anything to be back at the academy showing Kief and Patin around. Well, maybe Kief..." Sefrana laughed with Luften.

They stopped a good distance from the platform and tied their horses to a tree. Quietly they pulled their side slingers from their saddlebags, and Luften unstrapped the shoulder slinger and extended the stock. Sefrana's hand trembled as she gripped the handle of her slinger. Crouching low, they crawled through the underbrush until they had a clear view of the maintenance platform. Three guards were posted just as Luften had expected. Two of them were talking, the other sat in a chair resting his head on the rail. A few maintenance carts sat on the switch tracks behind them.

"Three just like you thought," Sefrana whispered.

Luften raised his shoulder slinger for a look, he had a clear shot.

* * *

Clarin watched as the dial on her time piece moved to a cadence past Dusk. It was time. Her signal would set the whole plan in motion. A particular Star Rhythm ran through her mind of when she was a little girl out sledding in the snow. The weather

had turned unseasonably warm that year and the snow was wet and packed well. She had made a big snowball and then pushed it down the hill. She remembered how it grew with each turn, bigger and bigger until it was as tall as she was by the time it reached the bottom. Now she was sending another snow ball down a hill, she smiled to herself, it would grow and grow until it reached the bottom ending with a blast that would start an uprising everywhere.

Placing the time piece in her satchel, she grabbed the valve with both hands and without hesitation she turned it.

"Lefty-loosy, for you Kief," she whispered to herself.

It was hard to move at first but the rushing water caught hold and pushed it open the rest of the way. The tremendous volume of water gushing through the pipes rumbled so loudly Clarin thought it might burst. She stepped out of the fire shed and backed away a few paces holding her hands to her ears. In the distance she began to hear the hissing air escaping the spray nozzles like a sky full of screeching owls. She did it! She hopped on her horse and climbed Pryes Peak to wait and watch.

First Flight

"That's it Kief, here it comes," Tarc said excitedly as the faint hissing noise grew louder and louder. Kief's heart leapt in his chest.

The soldiers around the mine began to panic at the sound. The captain screamed orders. Those on foot mounted up and with others they galloped down the canyon toward Shaflann leaving behind a few to guard the mine.

Tarc finished counting them, "Twenty is more than I'd hoped."

"Just wait," Kief said confidently.

He'd worked with those miners over three Sun Rhythms. He had no doubts in their abilities to take on the soldiers. Mining is dangerous. The camaraderie between miners is unbreakable, as he'd observed during the collapse in tunnel 84. Not a single miner left the entrance until the two who were trapped inside were brought out of the darkness. Taking on the army was no different; they'd fight united until the last Gar dropped. Above the hissing they heard a bang—then another and another. Heavy slinger fire came from the woods on both sides of the canyon. The few remaining guards began to scramble in all directions. One fell, followed by another. The soldiers returned fire back into the woods, but it was futile; they were shooting blind.

"Go, go, go!" Tarc shouted out cheering them on.

The soldiers that were still standing rapidly reloaded in military fashion and fired again. But a barrage of slugs continued to shower them until only two were left standing. They ran for their lives down the canyon, but only got a short distance until they were slugged down too. The miners emerged from their hiding places hooting and cheering.

"Come on out Kief, it's all clear," Bonds shouted waving his arms at him.

Kief and Tarc rushed down the ridge, to shouts from the miners cheering them. Kief and Tarc joined in, only they were cheering for the miners. They jumped off their horses and ran to the entrance of the old loading station. They heaved open the heavy door and removed the chalks from the wheels.

"Get the fuses," Kief called to Tarc.

Tarc rushed back to his horse to retrieve the fuses from his saddlebag. To his shock, he found them completely soaked.

"Oh no, Kief," he shouted, "the river, it ruined them all!"

Kief rechalked the car wheels.

"What's the problem?" Bonds asked

"The fuses, they got wet when we rode through the river running from the soldiers. We need fuses, now!" Tarc demanded in a panic, looking around the station as if he'd find them there.

Bonds rubbed his chin and groaned, "The Gars took everything and locked it up."

"Who has the key?" Tarc asked desperately.

"Who else?" replied Bonds, "The captain! But there's got to be some strays around somewhere," he said as he started for the mine house. He shouted out to the miners, "We need some fuses, search everywhere!"

"A five stroke," Tarc hollered after them.

Eventually, one of the miners came sprinting down from the main house, "We found these four igniters in Sim's trunk," he said, puffing as he handed them to Kief.

"A four, a four, a seven, and a three," Kief muttered in disbelief, "None of these will do."

"These will have to do, your window of opportunity is closing," Bonds insisted.

"Yeah Kief, we don't have time," Tarc urged, "the soldiers will be back here soon when they discover the fire lines are a decoy.

Just pick one and we'll have to hope for the best."

Kief stared desperately at the fuses in his hand hoping that somehow a five would appear. Four would go off too early, three would be way too early, and seven would give the soldiers time to extinguish the fuse before it went off. Going off late was their only option. He reached for the seven and hoped the soldiers wouldn't extinguish it in time. The number four flashed through his mind recalling his stone that had shone in the tunnel of the mine. When they'd been working through the details of their plan, he'd had a thought: the four would work if he increased the speed of the car, but the only way that would be possible is if he didn't stop it on Krem Hill to climb off. He'd have to jump off the train car while it was moving. But at that speed, he'd be seriously hurt—or killed if he hit a tree.

He grabbed the four stroke igniter and turned to Tarc, "Ride as fast as you can to my house. In my trunk, get my scoop sail and meet me at the line bend just beyond Stivens Street. I'll slow the car enough for you to throw it to me."

"What? Are you crazy?" Tarc asked as he constructed in his mind what Kief was planning on doing.

"You know I have to. The four stroke will only work if the car is moving fast enough. And the only way that can happen is if I jump off over Dondor Bridge."

"But it'll be dark; you won't be able to see anything. You'll kill yourself!" Tarc protested, "Just use the seven."

"The soldiers will have that out in no time—you know it. It's the only way," Kief insisted.

Tarc knew he was right.

He sprinted back to Sarjen and pulled a soaked banner from his saddlebag. "Clarin made it," he said as he unfurled an orange cloth. In the center was painted the large shape of a black eagle.

He tied it to the front pole of the train car, "Now you're ready to fly," he smiled.

"Alright," Kief replied enthusiastically.

"Don't get lost between here and Stivens Street," Tarc shook Kief's hand in the eagle grip and rode off.

"Let's get this car moving then," Kief shouted unchalking the wheels and jumping on board.

Bonds and a few of the miners heaved the train car forward.

"If anyone was meant to fly, it was you Kief. Soar like an eagle!" Bonds saluted him as the car picked up speed.

"I will Bonds. Take care of Natch for me," he saluted back.

Kief could hear the miners cheering as he rolled down Dunton Canyon toward town. And he could hear Bonds above them all.

As Luften peered down the barrel of his shoulder slinger, he heard the faint hissing of the fire lines off in the distance.

"Clarin released the water," Sefrana whispered excitedly from behind him.

The guard that was sitting was the first to notice the sound. He picked his head up off the rail and leaned forward, pausing before standing up and saying something to the other two. They stopped their conversation and looked up the mountain toward Shaflann. The hissing grew louder and louder as the pressure built in the pipes. The guard that was sitting barked at one of the others while pointing in the direction of the sound. The soldier, obeying orders, stumbled down the steps, mounted his horse and rode swiftly up the trail. The other two soldiers lifted their heavy slingers and scanned the area.

Without giving notice to Sefrana, Luften fired a slug. He hit one of the soldiers square in the chest, knocking him over backward. He writhed in pain on the platform for just a moment and then lay motionless. Sefrana turned her head away unable to watch. The remaining soldier slipped inside one of the maintenance carts for protection and fired a slug in their direction. It made a loud cracking noise as it struck the tree just above their heads. Luften sighted in on the soldier and fired a second slug hitting him in the arm. His slinger dropped to the floor of the platform and he ducked out of view. Luften quickly reloaded his shoulder slinger and aimed for another shot.

"Sefrana, you have to keep an eye out behind us in case that other guard returns," he said calmly.

She mustered enough courage to watch the road, and kept her focus set there.

A clanking noise alerted Luften and the maintenance cart creaked slowly forward.

"He's making a break for it!" Luften lowered his slinger and rushed to his horse.

Sefrana turned to watch Luften ride after him.

"He's already got the gate open, you're going to have to close it for Kief to get by," Luften ordered bolting after the soldier.

Sefrana jumped on her horse and rode to the platform. Running up the steps she encountered the dead soldier, his frozen eyes seemed to see everything. She stepped cautiously as if not to stir him. At the sight of the pool of blood next to him, she wretched; struggling to get past him to the platform levers. Sefrana nervously fiddled with the mechanism until at last she figured out how it opened.

The pipes were still whistling loudly in the distance as she rode after Luften and the fleeing soldier. The cart had picked up speed by the time Luften caught up with it. The soldier raised his heavy slinger over the edge of the rusty cart wall, Luften raised his in response. They both fired and missed. The soldier fired two more slugs but the cart rattled so much he couldn't get a clear shot at Luften. As the tracks rounded a bend and went down the steep embankment, the soldier grabbed at the brakes to slow it down. Luften took advantage of the opportunity and reined his horse to a stop. Raising his shoulder slinger, he fired a second slug. This time he struck his target. The cart picked up speed without the soldier pulling on the brake.

Luften galloped desperately after the runaway cart, slowly gaining on it. Dondor Canyon was coming up fast. If the cart reached the bridge, all hope would be lost. It would roll all the way to High Valley with the dead soldier inside. Throwing his shoulder slinger to the ground he kicked Odin into a sprint. Dondor Bridge came into view. Riding his horse up alongside the clattering cart he prepared to jump. To his shock, the wounded soldier pulled himself up and pointed a shaking slinger at Luften, his feeble fingers trying to find the trigger. Before he could find it, Luften drew his side slinger and fired a slug striking him in the head.

He was now out of time. Luften leapt with his might and caught hold of the side of the cart, the vibrating steel determined to shake him loose. Odin continued to chase behind. The bridge was just a hundred paces away. Luften lifted himself with his might and climbed over the wall and into the cart. The rushing wind blew his hat off. It flapped behind his head from the chinstrap. Cranking down on the brake, it screeched loudly throwing Luften forward against the front wall, knocking his cheek on the edge and splitting it open. Warm blood trickled down his face as he held tight to the brake lever. The maintenance cart finally came to a screeching halt a few short paces from the bridge.

The fallen enemy's blood began to pool at the lower end of the cart, surrounding Luften's boots. He didn't like it and jumped out as soon as the cart was secured. Odin had stopped next to the cart breathing heavily.

"Oh my!" Sefrana shouted pulling her horse to a stop. She was at a loss for words.

"I'm fine," he replied.

"No you're not, look at your cheek," she said.

"It's not bad," Luften wiped the blood with his arm, "but this is." He pointed to the cart sitting smack in the way of Kief's course.

"Oh no," Sefrana cried suddenly realizing that Kief would be rounding the corner any moment and collide with the maintenance cart. She flipped open her saddlebag and pulled out a rope. "Come on, the cart is light enough, let's yank it off the tracks," she said handing one end to Luften.

Luften, surprised at Sefrana's pluck, took the rope and helped her thread it through the highest spots on each end of the cart for leverage. Sefrana tied the rope to her saddle and Luften did the same. Pulling the knot tight, he noticed he'd cut his hand as well though he couldn't remember when. Sefrana jumped up in her saddle. Luften winced, moving a little slower. A gust of wind blew up from the gorge bringing a swirl of fluttering leaves like dancing birds.

"On three," Sefrana said as they gingerly moved forward until the ropes were taut, "one, two, three!"

*

*

"Look at all those soldiers," Patin muttered, his chin resting on the edge of the short wall around the roof of the bakery. The aroma of fresh baked bread wafted up from the brick chimney. "How many do you think?" Patin asked his indifferent companion as he ducked back down behind the cover of the wall.

"What does it matter, we're going to kill them all anyway. But if you have to know, I'd say close to two thousand," Flinch replied, concentrating on the oxygen vessel valve he was connecting.

"This is insane. If the plan doesn't work, we have to get out of here, fast," Patin said taking another glance at the assembly.

"It'll work; now give me one of those globes."

Taking care not to tear it, Patin unfolded one and handed it to Flinch.

"Do you have the string?" Flinch asked.

"It's right here, but you don't need it yet do you?" Patin was getting tired of being ordered around.

"Just have it handy when I do," Flinch responded curtly. He placed the opening of the paper globe around the vessel valve, the words of the message illegible in their wrinkled state. He turned the valve. Oxygen rushed into the globe making a hollow hissing noise.

"Do you think they hear it?"

"I guess if they do, we're in trouble then aren't we," Flinch grumbled.

The globe slowly inflated to about the diameter of a horse's belly. It was twice as long as it was thick, looking somewhat like an elongated egg. It hovered ever so slightly above the roof.

Patin was caught up in the physics of the floating globe when Flinch demanded, "String!"

He smacked the string in Flinch's extended hand. Flinch tied off the opening and tied a second string to the other end, "Here, connect these to the bird cages so they don't drift away."

Patin guided the weightless globe and tied it in place. They worked filling the remaining globes, the commotion from the crowd growing louder and louder. Flinch was offended at the display. People were coming out in droves, happy to celebrate the new occupation. The Gars had flooded High Valley with messages about how much better life would be under the Gars, and apparently many believed the lies.

Flinch shook his head, "Maybe we shouldn't send the globes out at all."

"What do you mean?" Patin asked, he wasn't about to have come down there and put his life on the line for nothing.

"From the looks of it, half of these people are already Gars!"

"Maybe they're just scared," Patin replied.

"Maybe," Flinch said incredulously.

A breeze blew across the roof top. The birds cooed to one another in their cages. As they watched the soldiers in formation, one of the globes came untied and floated out toward the plaza. Flinch restrained himself from extending out to grab it as it was clearly too far out of reach. They both dropped down below the cover of the wall and waited, but nothing changed immediately.

"What do we do?" Patin asked in a panic.

"Shhh," Flinch responded sharply, "teach you how to tie a decent knot for one thing." Peering back over the edge, they saw a few people had noticed the globe and were watching and pointing at it. Some of the guards on watch became aware but paid it little attention.

"Most of them can't read it, they don't even speak Jarmondon," Patin muttered with a grain of hope.

At the stage, people parted as a group of soldiers gathered under the globe. Raising their heavy side slingers they fired piercing it with holes. The oxygen in the globe slowly leaked out until the globe floated lightly down toward the ground. A soldier

caught it before it hit the ground and handed it to his superior. The commander ripped it out of his hand infuriated. He held it up and appeared to be reading the words.

"We're done for," Patin said frantically.

"Don't move Patin, I don't think anyone noticed the globe until it was long past the street here," Flinch grabbed Patin's arm.

The soldiers carried the globe to the stage. The commander climbed the steps and approached the leaders. He showed them the message and they laughed it off.

"It's just a show of power. They're concerned, you can be certain of it," Flinch said.

"Look there, the soldiers are making their way back through the crowd," Patin started to point but Flinch smacked his hand.

"I see them."

The squad of soldiers walked the entire perimeter of the square, stopping at each guard post. "Now they're putting all the soldiers on alert," Patin said, "they know something's up."

"Yeah, but they don't know what."

"Not yet," Patin turned to Flinch, "but if they get talking to people, they might figure it out."

"*Might* is a long way from *will.*"

That seemed to calm Patin for the moment. They watched as the soldiers performed a military demonstration for the officers, marching in different directions and stepping in unison.

"They're pretty good," Patin admired.

"Sorry we're going to take away your entertainment," Flinch apologized sarcastically.

"I never said I was enjoying it, they're just good," Patin defended.

They snapped and clicked and halted to attention. The noise of the crowd quieted down as one of the officers moved to the podium.

He shouted something in Saandonese and then introduced the general in Jarmondon to the citizens of High Valley and Shaflann Bucken.

Patin fumbled in his satchel to find his spectascope. He focused in on the stage.

Patin pshawed loudly, "That looks like Kir-Trad getting up on the stage!"

"No way," Flinch grabbed the spectascope from Patin. He growled, "That betrayer! I hope he goes down with the rest of them."

Patin snatched it back and looked through it again, "Oh, now they're dismissing him off the stage."

"They must have seen him for the conspirator he is, they don't even want him around," Flinch said, amused. "No one wants a traitor."

Patin pulled out his time piece, "Kief's car should be on its way now."

Flinch turned and looked up at the track coming over the ridgeline above High Valley. "Let me see the scope again," he looked through—nothing yet.

Tarc jumped off Sarjen at Kief's house and flew through the backdoor and up the steps. In his room, he flung open the lid of Kief's trunk and grabbed the scoop sail. The sail was neatly folded, the lines and harness ready for the next flight. Under the sail Tarc found the black mask. He decided Kief needed that too, and stuffed it in his pocket.

By the time Tarc leapt back on his horse the sun had set behind the mountains. He galloped swiftly toward Stivens Street. The

hissing water pipes had stopped and the guards around town were reassembling. Two of them started after Tarc through the forest. He saw the blur of the train car streaking through the trees and kicked Sarjen to catch up.

Kief spotted Tarc and applied the brake to slow the car.

"Go Tarc," Kief cheered. "They're right behind you!" A slug whizzed past Tarc's head and hit the train car.

"Yeah, I know," Tarc shouted above the rumbling of the car. "Here take the sail; I'll lose them in the forest. It's not the first time I've done that—kind of getting used to it by now!"

Kief leaned out the car and was immediately met with a small branch that smacked him in the face and nearly knocked him out of the car. When he found his balance again, Tarc raised the scoop sail for the handoff. Another slug ricocheted off the side of the car.

"Got it," Kief grasped the sail.

"Good luck Kief. Meet you at the cave," Tarc raised his fist in the air. "To the Eagles!"

"To the Eagles," Kief replied waving to his friend. He watched as Tarc dashed into a thicket like a rabbit, foxes close behind.

The train car rumbled along quickly picking up speed as soon as he released the brake. Kief was outside of Shaflann within moments, and racing down the mountainside. Approaching the maintenance platform, he spotted the downed guard but found no sign of Luften or Sefrana. He flew through the open gate. The powder boxes rattled together and knocked against the sidewalls as the car shot along the track. He applied the brake slightly and locked it in place to keep the car from running away as he prepared the fuses. Steadying his hand the best he could, he positioned the igniter that would set off the explosives. His father had taught him how to do it and he'd even set off a few explosions in the mine. Once they were set, he strapped on his scoop sail harness. The vibrations of the car combined with his shaky nerves made it extra hard to buckle the clasps. The bridge was approaching fast! When he finally got them all connected, he noticed his mask tucked inside the sail. "Tarc", he smiled. He quickly tied it around his face and released the brake letting gravity increase to maximum speed, pushing the train car to its limit. Wind rushed against his face, his heart pounded like a big basin drum. The trees of the forest rushed past him in a blur. He touched the brake lightly as he rounded the last corner and then released it in the straight-of-way. Then he saw the familiar rock outcropping just before Dondor Canyon. He was almost there.

"Go!" Sefrana shouted. Luften and Sefrana kicked their horses. At first, they didn't move as the ropes pulled taut and the horses sought for traction, almost dancing in place, their muscles bulging and trembling. Then it tipped, slightly, the far wheels lifting off the track and then slammed back down. They dug their heels into their horse's sides again and tugged even harder. It tilted and rocked until its shifting momentum brought it crashing to the ground. The soldier tumbled out, his clothes and armor soaked in blood. Sefrana clapped her hands over her mouth, and sickened turned away.

Immediately behind them they heard the rattling and clanking of a train car.

"It's Kief," she shouted.

Kief waved as he soared past his friends, the banner Clarin had made fluttering in the wind.

"He's going awfully fast," Luften said as he raced by.

Sefrana's cheering faded into a frown when she could tell Kief wasn't slowing the car to stop it on Krem Hill.

"He has to stop the car before he jumps off, right?"

"That was the plan, I hope the brakes aren't out."

Kief stooped down next to the box with the igniters and started the fuses. The clattering of the speeding car echoed off the canyon walls. Straightening up, a rush of wind came through the open door engulfing his face like a wave. I think the car's moving plenty fast, he said to himself. Scrambling over the stacks of powder boxes, he stepped out the back door onto the rear platform. He could see the rails of the tracks flashing past through the cracks in the floor. Squeezing his scoop sail tight to his chest he climbed the short ladder to the roof. The gusts of wind pulled at his entire body, trying to blow him off like a dried leaf. He clung to the metal ridges of the roof, pushing his way toward the center. The other side of the canyon was coming up too fast. Otoo hung low over the horizon like an ember in the sky; the first stars of dark flickering, lighting up the canyon below him. Kief didn't look down into the deep gorge, keeping his eyes fixed on his footing. He clung to his scoop sail, his palms perspiring, rehearsing in his mind how he planned to jump. Placing one foot against the edge, he took a deep breath and leapt... out into the dark and emptiness.

"Oh!" Sefrana exclaimed as she watched a dark silhouette climb atop the train car and then soar out into the great expanse of the canyon.

Once clear of the bridge, Kief tossed the sail above his head. Like always, it flapped violently above him before opening with a pop as it filled with air.

Luften stood in awe, "I guess that's Kief's scoop sail?" he asked keeping his eye on Kief.

"Yes, and that was not in the plans," Sefrana said. "He's never jumped from that high before."

Untying the ropes that connected them to the toppled maintenance cart, Luften and Sefrana rushed down the canyon path. They lost sight of Kief as they entered a grove of trees and then spotted him again when they emerged.

"There he is!" Sefrana hollered.

Luften grinned at her excitement, "Best keep it down Sefrana; we don't know who may be out," he cautioned.

"Oops," Sefrana replied putting her hand to her mouth, her eyes getting big.

As soon as Kief's sail was open and flying smoothly he turned his attention upward and watched the car race across the last hundred paces of the bridge; Clarin's banner of the dark eagle floating boldly behind it. The car had grown small and Kief realized how high he'd really been. Cool air rushed up his pant legs and sleeves, his mask fluttered in the wind. He extended his arms and flew. The view was spectacular. The silver moonlight danced on the flowing river, he hoped he wasn't going in—that would make it twice in one day, and it was cold. The evening breeze carried him back under the bridge and down the canyon. Drifting, he found himself calling upon the dark eagles, "Help us do this... if you really are the protectors of freedom...please help us... and please protect my friends."

Happily for Kief, the wind pushed him away from the river toward the canyon wall. He prepared for a rough landing in the tree covered cliffy wall. As he drew closer to the ground, he spotted a patrol of soldiers riding on horseback along the river road. He hoped they wouldn't spot him but that was like hoping someone hadn't noticed a merchant ship coming down the river. Pointing and shouting at the white sail hovering above them, they sprinted in Kief's direction. A tree branch struck Kief's foot and his attention was quickly brought back to the problem of landing. He braced himself as he was thrust into a tangle of pine needles and branches knocking and banging about until at last he crashed to the ground; his sail ensnared in the limbs above. Unlatching his harness, he abandoned his scoop sail and scrambled up the mountainside. He could hear the soldiers tramping through the thick brush on foot. They stopped when they reached his scoop sail to investigate. Kief hoped they wouldn't take it. They didn't. And they were gaining on him. Now he wished they had taken the time to retrieve it. He gritted his teeth in pain and tried to increase his pace, but realized he wouldn't be able to outrun them once they were on the trail to Shaflann. He looked for a place to hide. They didn't have dogs; if he found a dark enough place they wouldn't be able to find him. Kief was so intent on listening for the soldiers, he was taken off guard when Luften and Sefrana come around the switchback in front of him. He motioned them to keep quiet.

"Soldiers, they're right behind me," he whispered and pointed to the grove of trees below them.

"Get up here now," Sefrana ordered as she extended her hand and helped him up onto her horse. "You could have told us about that part of the plan, Kief," she scolded as they turned about.

"It wasn't part of the plan," Kief defended, "but I wish I'd thought of it—that was great! The fuses got wet and we had no other choice."

"Wet, how'd that happen?" Luften asked.

Kief told them about their earlier encounter with the soldiers as they galloped up the mountain.

Flinch and Patin stared down at the crowd. Everyone stood quietly listening to the general praise the good people of Holpe's Island. When he told them High Valley was to become the world's capital from which all power would flow, they joined the soldiers in cheers. He made promises of future prosperity and advancements in technology and comfort under the new rule of the Gars. Flinch was beyond loathing and couldn't wait to blow up the whole lot of them.

"New greatness," he grumbled. "Kief, get that car down here, I can't listen to another word," he looked up at the mountain.

Street lamps began to flicker on like fire beetles coming out of their holes. A large mirrored lamp cast a bright glow on the stage illuminating the general and his officers. Two assault transports sat along West Street with soldiers manning the cannons, attentively scanning the crowd.

Patin looked at his time piece again, "It's time Flinch, let's release the gulls."

Flinch nodded in agreement. Patin opened the first gull cage and tied a globe to its leg. Returning it to the cage he grabbed another. They tied the rest of the globes to the gulls until they were all tethered.

"Let's send them home," Flinch gave the word.

They opened the cages and released the gulls. The birds launched toward the tower but then panicked at the sight of the globes trailing behind them. Scattering, they turned back and flew the opposite direction, away from the square.

"Oh no," Patin cried, "they're going the wrong way!"

Flinch stared up at them helplessly. There was nothing they could do. They were out of reach and there was no way to bring them back. The crowd had noticed them and, thinking it was part of the celebration, watched in awe as they flew away into the evening sky.

Patin panicked, "We have to stop Kief!" he shouted, jumping up from his hiding place.

Flinch jerked him back down, "There's no way at this point."

"Then we have to warn them," he insisted.

Flinch peered over the wall and studied the crowd for a moment and then slumped back down, "It will hit mostly soldiers. There aren't too many townspeople next to the tracks."

"Next to the tracks," Patin became hysterical. "There are one hundred boxes of powder on that train car! People as far as fifty paces away will die!"

"I can't bring the gulls back," Flinch barked at Patin.

Then they both heard a loud screeching in the sky.

Patin hunched lower, his eyes darting around.

Then they heard it again.

"Look," Patin pointed. The gulls were flying back toward the square and the screeches grew louder and more frequent as the gulls pulling the globes approached. "Gulls don't sound like that," he said.

"It's the dark eagles," Flinch replied in wonder, staring up at the miracle.

The gulls, chased by the raptors, dropped low over the crowd, the dark eagles' screeching drawing everyone's attention to the globes. Flinch caught a glimpse of the majestic black birds before they banked away into the starry sky.

"Where are they? I can't see them," Patin said.

"They're gone," Flinch replied looking off into the darkness.

The crowd was now fixed on the globes. The general stuttered and paused. An officer directed a soldier to shine the mirrored light on the globes. As the crowd read the words on the globes they cautiously began to move away from the square.

The general quickly called on his troops to bring order. Squads of soldiers wove in and out of people and buildings searching for the offenders. A group of them ran into the alleyway behind them.

"They're coming Flinch, what do we do?"

Before Flinch could respond, they heard the clatter of men coming up the back steps. He sprang up on the wall and looked for a place to jump. The ground was too far. Then he noticed the thick wood beam extending from the front of the bakery that held its sign.

"Jump," Flinch shouted at Patin as he leapt onto the beam and then down to the ground.

Patin followed climbing up on the wall. But, before he could jump, the soldiers grabbed him and jerked him down. He landed hard on his back, letting out a loud groan. One hit him powerfully in the face, nearly knocking him out cold. Patin lay there motionless while they searched for Flinch but he was lost in the sea of people. Turning back to Patin, the same soldier that had hit him grabbed him by the throat and began to choke him.

He barked a few words in Saandonese before screaming at Patin in broken Jarmondon, "Where he go... what you doing? Your birds?"

Patin, getting a hold of himself, quickly thought up an alibi. "It was just a prank, we were playing a joke."

The soldier slapped him again and yelled something to the others. They dragged Patin to his feet and down the stairs. Blood flowed from his nose and onto his shirt. They wouldn't stop

jabbing him with their slingers.

"Run Flinch, run," Patin mumbled with a smile.

Escaping into the crowd, Flinch moved slowly, keeping his eyes on the cracks between the buildings for Patin and the soldiers. He stared in helpless shock as they passed the bakery and headed toward the square. He followed them through the crowd and scolded Patin under his breath, "He should have jumped." He glanced up at the mountain, if that car didn't come right away, he and Patin would be caught in the explosion. A flicker in the moonlight caught his eye. That's it, that has to be it, Flinch thought. Then he heard it, a faint clanking in the distance, growing louder and louder.

As the lone train car approached the square in Town Center, panic ensued and people began running in every direction away from the tracks. Soldiers shouted and fired slugs into the air in an attempt to reassemble order, but stopped when they saw the runaway car.

Flinch stood with the joy of a lost sailor watching his rescue ship approach. When he caught sight of the banner of the dark eagle fluttering in the wind, his heart swelled and he raised his fist in a silent cheer. The car whizzed by him, and he looked intently, just to ensure Kief wasn't on it. It continued down the track alongside the plaza full of soldiers and came to a stop about twenty paces from where the general stood on the stage. Soldiers jumped in front of the general and quickly surrounded the mysterious train car with heavy side slingers aimed at the intruders. Shouting in Jarmondon one of the soldiers demanded for the people in the car to come out. No response was heard.

"No explosion!" Flinch uttered in astonishment. "What happened?"

They heard it, a thunderous boom echoing up from High Valley. Spinning around they saw the fiery flash from the blast reflecting off the cloud cover over the city. An ominous stream of black smoke rose up into the moon light.

"You did it my friend, you did it," Luften congratulated Kief.

Sefrana turned and hugged him.

He smiled over a grimace of pain, the gash in his leg burning, "I just hope it was going fast enough."

"You shot by us like a jezer cat, you were definitely going fast enough," Luften said confidently.

They had done it, at least it seemed that way. They wouldn't know for sure until Flinch and Patin made it back.

"I hope the globes worked," Sefrana said softly as she stared at the smoke rising in the sky.

"Yeah, me too," Kief replied.

They stood watching the smoke cloud in the sky grow bigger and bigger. Kief felt a chill. The physical stress and mental anxiety was beginning to take its toll. He needed to get to the cave.

Flinch was blown to his knees in the deafening blast as if Dot itself had fallen out of the sky and landed on High Valley. A massive, blinding ball of fire shot high in the air like a spewing volcano above where the train car once stood. Flinch put his arm in front of his face protecting it from the heat. He blinked, his eyes trying to recover his sight. The stage was completely gone, including everyone on it. The corpses of charred soldiers extended out from the blast point a good hundred paces. Soldiers beyond that perimeter were bloodied and burning; some running for cover while others lay squirming in the square dying. The few unwounded soldiers scattered in every direction into the throngs of terrified townspeople, like mice in a snake pit.

Flinch marveled at the horrific yet triumphant scene. The bodies of dead soldiers stretched all the way to the streets. From what he could tell, most of the soldiers had been killed in the explosion along with the general and his leaders. Dodging through the mangled, smoldering corpses, Flinch ran to rescue Patin, when he stumbled upon the remains of the banner that was tied to the car. He picked it up, still steaming from the blast. To his amazement; most of the banner was still intact. The edges had been singed but the eagle was nearly perfect. He stuffed it in his satchel.

The streets were in utter chaos, people scrambling in every direction. Flinch pushed his way through the crowd. In front of him he saw his horse Sind, spooked and wandering. He grabbed the reins and tried to calm him as he made his way toward the alley behind the bakery hoping that Patin and the soldiers who took him were still there.

In Shaflann, soldiers were running around in disarray and people were flocking to the streets in wonder of the plume of smoke in the moonlight. With so much confusion, Kief, Luften, and Sefrana probably had no reason to worry, but they decided not to take any chances of running into trigger-anxious soldiers and slipped around town unnoticed. Climbing the mountainside to the cave they could see fires burning in the town square.

As they approached, light from the cave entrance shone through the trees.

"That's Clarin's horse!" Sefrana exclaimed excitedly.

Kief's heart skipped a beat.

Luften jumped off his horse and helped Kief down. Clarin rushed out of the cave.

"I saw the explosion from the top of Pryes Peak; you did it Kief, you did it," she hugged him.

Kief couldn't conceal his groan.

"What happened to you now?" Clarin asked.

She helped Luften get him to the log by the fire and knelt down to take a look.

"I slammed into a tree," Kief gritted his teeth as she peeled back his blood-soaked pant leg.

"That wasn't too smart now was it," Clarin teased. She retrieved a clean bandage, water, and a bottle of alcohol from her stash.

"Sssss," Kief hissed, "that burns."

"That'll teach you," Clarin smiled replacing the cork on the alcohol bottle.

Clarin took a closer look. She grabbed his foot and moved it about, "Does that hurt?" she asked, "How about this?"

"It all hurts," Kief laughed through his groaning.

"You big baby. I don't think it's broken," Clarin said, "just a good cut and bruise." She wrapped the bandage around it and rolled down his pant leg, "So how'd you slam into a tree?"

"He jumped off Dondor Bridge with his scoop sail," Sefrana answered for him, "and landed in a grove of pines, that's how he did it," she said, as if he deserved it.

"You crazy boy," Clarin shook her head. "I think I would have liked to have seen that."

"I guess I am a little."

As they cozied up around the fire they chattered and laughed recounting the stories of their missions. Sefrana couldn't stop telling them about Luften's daring race down the mountain after the soldier in the cart. And Luften didn't mind hearing her tell it over and over again.

"I guess things went smoothly at the lake," Kief turned to Clarin.

"Just the way I planned it," she winked.

"Oh, that was our problem, we didn't plan things right," Kief nodded at Luften. "I'll remember that next time."

Kief gave all the details of his mission from the mine, the chase, the wet fuses, the train car ride, and finally, his jump off the bridge.

"Anyone for some hot chocolate?" Sefrana stood to get the kettle.

"That'd be nice; too bad we don't have milk or chocolate." Luften replied.

"I brought some up this morning hoping to celebrate," Sefrana pulled it from their food stash in the cave.

"This morning," Luften sighed, "that seems like forever ago."

"Tarc sure will be excited… if he ever gets here," Kief said, and looked into the trees. He'd expected Tarc to be at the cave with Clarin when they'd arrived.

Sefrana heated the milk on the fire and mixed in the chocolate. After more talking and a few rounds of hot cocoa, Kief started shivering.

"Are you okay?" Sefrana asked.

"I think he's in shock," Clarin set her cup on a log. "Come on, let's get you taken care of," she helped him over to his bedroll.

She wrapped his blanket around him tightly and grabbed a second one from the cave. Kief gave her a barely audible 'thank you' from under the covers and was out. Clarin stayed awake with him for a while until his shivering stopped and then she lay down to sleep. When neither Sefrana nor Luften could keep their eyes open any longer, they laid down as well, hoping that the other three would show up shortly.

Around Dark's 1st Cadence, Tarc came into camp. He shook Kief awake, his energy as vibrant as if it were midday.

"Good to see you in one piece," Kief mumbled to his best friend, and then closed his eyes again.

"Hey, I'm not the one that was in danger of being broken into pieces" he chuckled.

"Did you bring Natch?" Kief asked adjusting the bag he was using for a pillow.

"Who do you think is making all of that noise?" Tarc looked at the horses.

"Hey boy," Kief called out in the darkness, too stiff and too tired to walk over.

"You could see the explosion from town, it was amazing!" Tarc said, showing no signs of exhaustion. "The rest of the soldiers are cowering back down to High Valley. I've been watching them all evening, they don't dare stay around." Tarc looked around at the others who were sleeping, "Guess no word from Patin or Flinch huh?"

"No, I figured they probably won't be here until closer to dawn," Kief replied.

"I guess all we can do is wait then," Tarc said.

"You should probably get some sleep in the mean time," Kief said anxious to be in that sound slumber again where he didn't feel any pain.

"But I'm not that tired."

"You're tired, lie down and see."

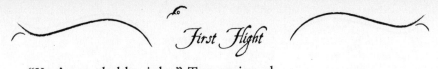
"You're probably right," Tarc resigned.

He opened out his bedroll and lay down next to Kief. He was out immediately. And so was Kief.

New Adventures

Flinch caught sight of the soldiers and Patin who were now retreating further into the dark alleyway behind the bakery. Tying Sind snug to a rail, he pulled his slinger from his saddlebag and slipped into the alley after them. He thought he could make out about seven soldiers in the shadows but he wasn't sure, and he couldn't see where Patin was in the midst of them. Flinch stayed close to the walls of the buildings, hiding behind crates and discarded items from the stores that cluttered the alleyway. As he drew closer, three of the soldiers trailed behind the others arguing and yelling at each other, exchanging a string, of what

Flinch was certain, was every Saandonese curse word in the book. Their argument became so heated; they stopped altogether, their comrades disappearing up an adjoining alley. Blast, Flinch uttered under his breath, he was sure Patin was with them that disappeared, and now he would have to get through these three idiots to get to him. He didn't have enough ammunition as it was, and he certainly didn't want to have to waste it. He quickly crept closer, he had to take care of them swiftly, or he would lose Patin and the other soldiers in the dark frenzied confusion of the streets and alleyways. His advantage was that they were so involved in their argument, they wouldn't notice him approaching in the shadows and he could easily jump them—it would be like any old urt match. His disadvantage was that they were trained soldiers, and they had really big slingers.

One of the soldiers shoved the short one not involved in the scuffle, who stumbled forward nearly falling to the ground. Lamplight from the window of a building they were next to shone on his face. It was Patin!

Flinch's heart started to pound. He stayed concealed trying to come up with a strategy. He clenched the wooden grip of his slinger, his fingers touching the triggers. He would wait until they continued up the alleyway and then slug them from behind. The soldier that had pushed Patin shoved his comrade and raised his slinger. This should be good, Flinch thought to himself as he waited for the soldier to kill the other. One less for him. Instead the soldier touched the barrel of his slinger to Patin's temple and pulled the trigger—too late. He was already dead and on his way to the ground, his slug just grazing the top of Patin's head. Flinch had fired first hitting the soldier square in the face.

The second soldier spun around firing off two slugs at Flinch who had ducked behind a crate. The slugs missed him, ricocheting off the bricks of the building. Flinch could hear the soldier fumbling for a fresh crescent on his shoulder strap. Bursting out of his hiding spot, he charged. Firing his last slug, Flinch hit him in the leg. The soldier stood like an iron statue, the slug hardly affecting him as he clicked in a new crescent and raised his slinger at Flinch. Diving, Flinch tackled the soldier just as he fired. The slug whizzed past him, the powder discharge scorching his skin. Using one of his perfected urt moves, Flinch hurled the soldier to the ground. They rolled smashing into a crate and breaking it to pieces. The soldier slammed his slinger into Flinch's skull, knocking him dizzy, followed by a knee to his face. Flinch lost his hold on his foe and was staring down the barrel of his slinger when a powder blast came from behind them. Patin had picked up the other soldier's weapon and fired; a wild slug hitting the soldier in the arm. He dropped his slinger. Flinch grabbed it and backed away wiping the blood from his flowing nose.

Hands trembling, Patin clicked in a new crescent and aimed his slinger at the soldier's head.

"Slug him Patin," Flinch said callously.

Patin hesitated, tightening and loosening his grip on the slinger.

"Here, I'll do it," Flinch raised his.

"No," Patin demanded staring at the wounded soldier lying on the ground, slanted squares of light shining on him from the window.

"He was going to kill you and given another chance, he will, I can promise you that."

Patin continued to stare at the twisted and villainous face. He had a gnarly scar on his cheek near his left ear and the bottom of his lobe was missing. Patin imagined he'd been in a brawl and taken a blow to the head with a knife or sword.

The soldier spat on the ground defiantly as he prepared to die.

Patin lowered his slinger. "No, you won't make me be like you," he said and slowly backed away.

A devious grin covered the soldiers face. Though wounded and weaponless, Patin was scared stiff by the man and wanted to get out of there as fast as possible.

Flinch kicked the soldier in the mouth knocking him back, "Get that smile off your face," he growled.

The soldier shook his head with a defiant bloody smile as Flinch and Patin walked backwards up the alleyway leaving the soldier alone.

As they made their way through Town Center, smoke and the smell of burnt flesh sat unpleasantly in the air. Hundreds of smoldering bodies covered the square. A pile of melted steal that was once the train wheels and frame lay in a blackened crater. Patin was speechless riding behind Flinch on Sind. But it didn't last long. Flinch suddenly turned and rode in the opposite direction of Shaflann.

"Where are you going?" Patin tugged on his shirt.

Flinch didn't reply. A spooked horse was rambling in the street. Dismounting, Flinch calmed the horse and handed his reins to Patin.

"I'm not riding him, he'll throw me for sure," Patin objected. "Let me ride your horse and you take him," he scooted onto the saddle.

"Get off my horse Patin, you're riding this one."

Patin reluctantly climbed down and stroked the horse's mane. He'd already almost lost his life once this evening—he didn't want to take his chances with Flinch.

"Easy boy," he said and gingerly pulled himself up into the

saddle.

"See, that wasn't hard now was it."

The horse pranced nervously and Patin kept a tight rein on him. Sind was still jumpy too but the two horses helped calm one another. Riding down a quiet street they saw a man descending the steps of a luxurious home carrying a trunk to the carriage waiting for him. As they drew closer to the fancy horse carriage, Flinch read the name 'Kir-Trad' inscribed in gold lettering. It was the traitor himself! Flinch glanced around for accompanying soldiers, but saw no one. A single driver sat in the front of the carriage. Kir-Trad climbed into the passengers' cabin.

"Wait here," Flinch ordered Patin and he rode up alongside the carriage and peered inside.

Kir-Trad jumped when he saw him, "What are you still doing out Flinch, it's dangerous, you need to get back inside immediately."

Without uttering a word, Flinch drew his side slinger, pointed it at Kir-Trad's chest, and fired two slugs. The powder discharge echoed up the empty streets. Kir-Trad groaned and slumped over dead. Patin stared in unbelief. The carriage master jumped out of his seat, and ran back inside the house. Flinch didn't look at Kir-Trad after he slugged him; he just turned and motioned to Patin. They wasted no time in getting out of there. Galloping down the street they rode off into the moonlit countryside toward Shaflann.

Kief and Tarc rode for High Valley. He was anxious to see his family again and bring them home. They talked excitedly about the success of their plan and the miracle of it. Kief couldn't believe that Flinch had come across the banner and that it had

survived the blast.

"That hasn't been the only miracle," Tarc shook his head.

"Yeah, I guess there've been a few," Kief smiled.

"What about the first time you saw that dark eagle and it took your map, you'd have killed it with that stick if you'd had a chance."

Kief grinned sheepishly, "I've done a few stupid things in my life, that sure wouldn't have been the first." Kief hung his head looking down at the ground as they winded down Dondor Road.

"Hey, what's up with my buddy," Tarc drew close enough to throw a punch at Kief's arm.

"I guess..." Kief tried to get it out. "I guess I'd expected somehow that this would all make up for them killing my father, but it hasn't. I don't really feel much different, and I still miss him."

"You'll always miss him, Kief. It's because you love him and he loves you."

"I suppose I'd hoped that the map and the stone were somehow going to help fix things, especially after seeing the stone's power."

"What powers?" Tarc turned to Kief with a confused look.

Kief told him about the stone heating up and distracting him when he was about to do something rash and about his experience in the cave.

"There really was a number written in it?" Tarc was amazed.

"That stone knew, somehow, it knew," he said, still incredulous himself, "and the map, with all the strange writings. They mean something. I think they tell the future."

"The future?" Tarc laughed.

"I know, it's crazy, but I had a professor at the academy translate

some of the writings. She mentioned whales spewing venom. And after the Gars attacked, I heard someone describing their ships like whales rising up out of the sea. And they attacked with their cannons."

"No way," Tarc's mouth dropped wide open.

"Yes, and she also said something about drinking from a tree. I think it has to do with the fuel from the chatra trees that Patin discovered."

Tarc sat up in his saddle excited, "So maybe the writings will tell us other things, do you think?"

"I do," Kief replied, "but we need to find someone who can translate the rest because I can't do it."

"Maybe the eagles know someone?" Tarc suggested with a grin.

"Right," Kief chuckled. "I'm sure they do."

At High Valley, they rode for Town Center. As they neared the square, Kief and Tarc had to cover their mouths and noses with their sleeves; the stench of smoldering bodies was so horrible. Men were piling the corpses in stacks preparing to burn whatever remained.

"Look at this place," Tarc muttered.

It wasn't as joyous as they'd expected, it was ghastly.

"They did this to themselves," Kief said.

"That's for sure," Tarc replied clearing his throat.

Kief studied the bodies as they rode across the square; trying to find any that weren't wearing a Gar uniform. He breathed a sigh of relief when they'd reached the other side and hadn't spotted a single one.

Riding toward Kief's grandmother's home they came to the jail.

Kief stopped in front, "I think this is where they kept my father

before he died."

An elderly man stood solemnly near the front door. Kief watched him curiously. The man stood motionless staring straight ahead as if he was looking beyond the building.

After a moment Kief asked, "Are you okay sir?" With no reply, he asked a second time a little louder, "Sir, are you okay?"

The man turned and looked at him, "I'm fine. They didn't want me. It's the others that trouble me."

"What do you mean the others, were you in prison here?" Kief asked as he jumped off Natch and approached the man.

He looked at Kief with sunken dark eyes, "Yes I was in there, but I was left to escape free when that train car blew."

"My father was in here! Did you know him?" Kief asked desperately.

"What's your name boy?" he asked in a commanding tone.

"Kief Stadd, my father is Klar Stadd."

"Stadd, Stadd," the man mumbled, "yes I do remember a Stadd. Strong man, very determined. He kept quiet though, didn't cause much trouble like some of the others."

Kief smiled at his dad's fortitude "Did you see him before he died?"

"I didn't know he died, did they kill him in transport?" the man frowned, "I'm sorry to hear that."

"What do you mean in transport?" Kief asked confused.

"On their journey... to Gar."

"What, what do you mean on their journey to Gar?" he stammered as he drew closer to the old man.

"The prisoners, they were all shipped to Gar," he replied matter-of-factly, "as slaves to work the Wells in Desolation."

"There were seventeen prisoners that were executed; my father was one of them," Kief said stubbornly.

"No," he said agitated at Kief, "no one was executed, the Gars don't believe in wasting a good slave. They were all sent to Gar. If your father survived the journey, I can safely assume he's still alive."

"Are...are you certain?" Kief stuttered grabbing the man's shoulders, intently examining his face for the truth in his eyes.

"Absolutely, I saw it through my cell window," he shrugged Kief's hands off and pointed up to a barred window on the second floor. "They were all escorted onto the transport in chains. They shipped them out after Dark, I suppose to keep it a secret."

Kief turned to Tarc who was now at his side, "I don't believe it, my father's alive. He's alive!"

The elderly man pulled back when Kief reached out again, this time to hug him. And then Kief's legs gave way, the old man catching and holding him, lowered him to the ground. He had unusual strength for his age.

Tears of joy streamed down Kief's cheeks.

Tarc asked the man, firmly, a third time, "Are you sure?"

"Yes, I'm sure," he replied becoming upset at their repeated questions, "I may be old but I'm not blind!"

Kief wiped his eyes and face and looked up at the sky. The morning sunbeams cascaded over the buildings, spilling onto the streets.

Tarc extended his hand to Kief, "Come on, let's go get your father!"

Fundautum
Facts

Fundautum

Mass $3.6 \times 10^{24} kg$

Radius $5.4 \times 10^{3} km$

Earth

Mass $6.0 \times 10^{24} kg$

Radius $6.4 \times 10^{3} km$

Fundautum has 15% less gravity than Earth

Earth	Fundautum
100 lbs	85 lbs
125 lbs	106 lbs
150 lbs	128 lbs
175 lbs	149 lbs
200 lbs	170 lbs

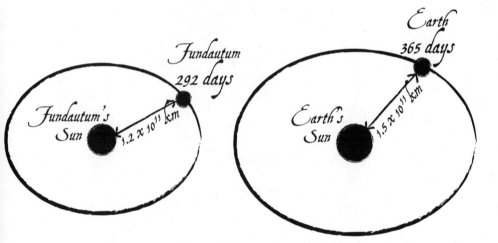

Fundautum
292 days

Fundautum's Sun

$1.2 \times 10^{11} km$

Earth
365 days

Earth's Sun

$1.5 \times 10^{11} km$

Fundautum has fewer days in a year than Earth

age on Earth	age on Fundautum
10	12 1/2
12	15
15	19
17	21 1/2
20	25
25	31 1/2
50	62 1/2

Fundautum's Moons

Earth's Moon

Mass 7.3×10^{22} kg

Radius 1.7×10^3 km

Dot

Mass 10.0×10^{22} kg

Radius 1.8×10^3 km

Otoo

Mass 2.5×10^{22} kg

Radius 1.1×10^3 km

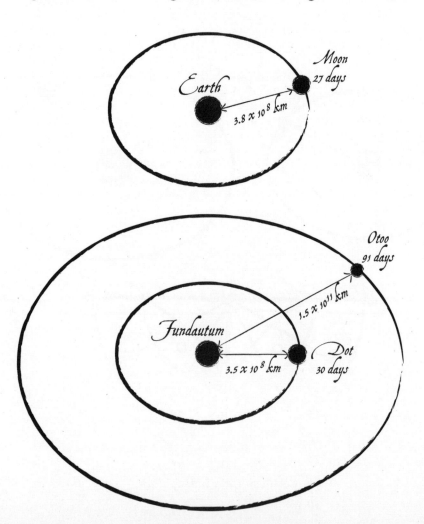

Earth

Moon
27 days

3.8×10^8 km

Fundautum

Otoo
91 days

1.5×10^{11} km

Dot
30 days

3.5×10^8 km

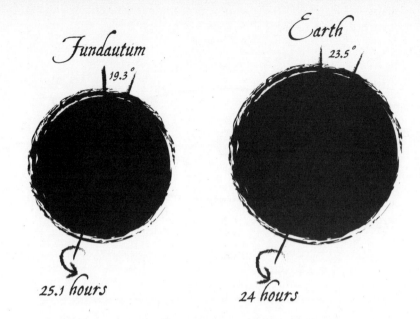

Fundautum

19.3°

Earth

23.5°

25.1 hours

24 hours

Fundautum Time

Day

2nd Cadence

1st Cadence

1st Cadence

2nd Cadence

Dawn

Dusk

2nd Cadence

1st Cadence

1st Cadence

2nd Cadence

Dark

1 cadence equals 2.1 hours
1 stroke equals 1.26 minutes

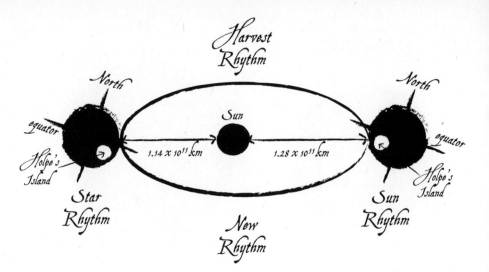

Fundautum has a more eccentric orbit than Earth. Its seasons are determined by both the angle of its axial rotation and its distance from the sun. The northern climates are extremely harsh while the southern climates are more mild.

Rhythm Chart

Air Composition on Fundautum

| | Earth | | Fundautum | |
	Density (kg/m³)	% in air	Density (kg/m³) ×	% in air
Air	1.293	100.00%	1.775	100.00%
Nitrogen	1.251	78.08%	1.301	69.78%
Oxygen	1.429	20.95%	1.486	20.36%
Argon	1.784	0.93%	1.855	0.78%
Carbon Dioxide	1.977	0.04%	2.056	0.03%
Xenon	5.850	0.00%	6.084	9.04%
% more flight lift on Fundautum over Earth				37.3%

× Fundautum's atmosphere is thicker so the air pressure is 4% higher

Fundautum's air is 37% more dense so there is more flight lift on Fundautum.

Earth Scoop Sail

Fundautum Scoop Sail

Fundautum scoop sail is 27% smaller than one on Earth

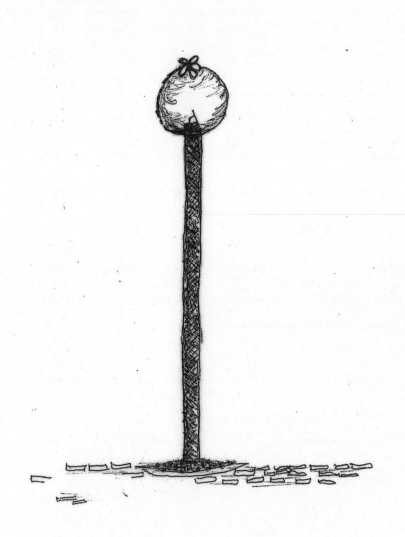